9/10

The Road To Nowhere

Books by Elisabeth Ogilvie

The Road to Nowhere
The Silent Ones
The Devil in Tartan
A Dancer in Yellow
An Answer in the Tide
The Dreaming Swimmer
Where the Lost Aprils Are
Image of a Lover
Strawberries in the Sea
Weep and Know Why
A Theme for Reason
The Face of Innocence
Bellwood

Waters on a Starry Night
The Seasons Hereafter
There May Be Heaven
Call Home the Heart
The Witch Door
High Tide at Noon
Storm Tide
The Ebbing Tide
Rowan Head
My World Is an Island
The Dawning of the Day
No Evil Angel

Books for Young People

The Pigeon Pair
Masquerade at Sea House
Ceiling of Amber
Turn Around Twice
Becky's Island
The Young Islanders

How Wide the Heart
Blueberry Summer
Whistle for a Wind
The Fabulous Year
Come Aboard and Bring
    Your Dory!

The Road To Nowhere

Elisabeth Ogilvie

McGRAW-HILL BOOK COMPANY
New York   St. Louis   San Francisco
Toronto   Hamburg   Mexico

1 2 3 4 5 6 7 8 9 F G R F G R 8 7 6 5 4 3

ISBN 0-07-047700-0

LIBRARY OF CONGRESS CATALOGING IN PUBLICATION DATA

Ogilvie, Elisabeth, 1917-
   The road to nowhere.
   I. Title.
PS3529.G39R6 1983   813'.52   82-21670
ISBN 0-07-047700-0

The Road To Nowhere

1

JULE AWAKENED IN THE NIGHT with Roz's voice so ringingly clear that she dropped back four years in time and thought she was sleeping on the sofa in the island house and Roz had just shouted to her.

"Is Mummie dead?" Jule cried to the darkness, fighting out of the cocoon of deep sleep, one hand scrabbling desperately for her flashlight. It was the cat who soothed her with his protest at being disturbed on the foot of the bed. In a slow nauseating slide back to the present she fumbled for her bedside lamp, put it on and stared around her room, breathing hard and sweating. She put her elbows on her knees and her head in her hands, whimpering, "Oh God, oh God," lids squeezed tight against tears. The cat padded around her, purring, making throaty little sounds and touching her ear with a delicate paw.

She was alone, except for the cat, in her own place. She lifted her head and her blurred vision moved over her books, her records, her guitar, her dishes. The cat was warm and living in her arms, ecstatically nuzzling her neck, bunting her jaw.

She tried frantically to hold onto Roz's voice and the sense of her presence, but it was all going away too fast. She cried. She had cried like this before, but she could always be hardheaded in the daytime. The fury and the anguish couldn't stand the light.

Sometimes she didn't have these dreams for weeks at a time, and thought they were finished. When they returned it was a self-betrayal. She called herself a weakling, a masochist. Who wept for *her*?

Now, sitting up in bed cuddling the cat, she thought, Howl now and get it over with! Hodge didn't wish to be wept onto, and besides the wetness made his loose hairs stick to her nose and lips. They separated by mutual consent. After her heartbeat slowed down and she steadied herself with the familiar small sounds of the flat and the noise of a big plane going over, she fell asleep again, the cat pressed heavily against her legs, gently vibrating until he too fell asleep.

She overslept and couldn't take time for breakfast, only to fill the cat's dish. He cried these mornings, with spring outside the windows and seeping into the flat. But the street was too busy and the dogs too many. "I'll do something," she promised him. It was a distracted promise. How could a voice have been so fresh and resonant in her brain, as if she had just heard it yesterday and had been hearing it all along in daily life?

Wearing jeans and a white fisherman-knit sweater, she rode her bicycle downtown through the blustery April morning. It was warm one moment and chilly the next as the clouds billowed past the sun. Gulls flew against the clouds; behind the refurbished old blocks on the far side of Main Street the unseen harbor would be alternately gunmetal and turquoise.

Clean Sweep's office had once been a dress shop on Linden, just off Main. The lindens were long gone but their spectres were inherent in the name, which even in winter had an ambience of summer shadows.

She unlocked and opened the front door to the jingle of sleigh bells, and wheeled her bicycle inside. It was her day to stay by the telephone. The van had already gone, and by noon Clean Sweep would have a big house on Talbot Avenue ready for the owners' return from Florida.

She made coffee in the back room, took one of the fresh doughnuts Dan's mother had sent in, and a clean paper towel to put under everything on the desk by the telephone. She was twenty-two and looked younger. Her black hair was cut short and blown feathery in the wind, her eyes a very dark blue. They were cautious, they gave away nothing. Her nose was thin and distinguished, and the fullness of her lower lip was disguised from a lifetime of keeping back words and cries. It was always on guard, like her eyes, and this constant wariness gave strength to the narrow oval of her face.

Her mug had a name on it; Lib had given them each a special one at Christmas. Juliet, Lib had insisted, because it was such a pretty name. She hardly saw herself as Juliet. Sometimes, knowing herself as tough and cynical, she even laughed at it.

Before she could pour the coffee the telephone rang, and she answered, "Clean Sweep! May I help you?" She discussed a date, what the job would entail, and entered it in the diary. There was an adolescent look to the back of her neck and her shoulder blades when she leaned over the desk, writing.

Now she lifted the mug, and with the first sip she was back where she didn't want to be. It was the damned dream, of course. None of the others had done this to her, and she wondered resignedly if coffee would do it to her all her life. She had better shift to tea.

The doughnut was ignored, and so was the library book waiting in the drawer. She folded her hands on the desk and gazed out at the street beyond the window, through the words "Clean Sweep" read backward, and Dan's poster-painted coat of arms, which featured crossed brooms, a bottle of furniture polish, and a vacuum cleaner, *rampant*.

Early shoppers came purposefully from the parking lot be-

tween the colonial red brick bank and the back of the Steb-
bins block on Main Street. Passing the window they were in-
substantial to her, nebulous shapes forever shifting like
shadows on water. Sometimes when she sat like this she
thought, What if I'm only dreaming, and I'm really back on
the island?

But what a peculiar dream of freedom, when one had all
the world from which to choose.

The glass in the door darkened, sleighbells jangled, and
someone came in. She was jolted back again, gazing without a
blink at the newcomer while she tried to steady everything,
saying automatically, "Good morning."

"*Good* morning!" It accomplished for her what the cat had
done earlier. She pushed back the chair and ran to the embrace of long arms and old tweed.

"What are *you* doing here?"

"It's almost Easter or don't you read the calendar? I've
brought some friends down to the island. Why don't you
come for the weekend?"

She backed off from him. "Have some hot coffee and a
fresh doughnut?"

He helped himself and took the client's chair. She answered the telephone again, and set down the name of a boy
who wanted to get on the list of summer workers, doing
lawns and other yard work. "We'll give you a try," she promised, and he thanked her profusely, his voice cracking.

Billy B. slouched in the client's chair with his legs
stretched out. He seemed to grow longer every year, if that
were possible. He wore jeans and topsiders, and the jacket,
leather-patched because of its old age and not for style, was
Harris tweed. She'd known it for as long as she'd known Billy
B. Though he wore his hair short it was always slightly
shaggy, and it was what she and Roz called hair-colored, with
a cowlick standing up at the crown. His face was sharply an-

gled as to nose, cheekbones and jaw. Any thicker, they'd have been knobby. He always looked at home wherever he was.

She put her elbows on the desk, propped her chin on her hands, and said, "Well."

"You haven't answered me yet about the island. Do you have something else especially thrilling to do?"

Under his bright gray eyes it was impossible to lie. "No. I've had invitations to Easter dinner, but I'm not going. If it's a nice day I'll take a lunch and ride somewhere on my bike."

"Come to the island," he repeated. She shook her head.

"It's time you went. It's time you exorcised some ghosts."

"I don't have any ghosts."

"Then why are you afraid of Osprey Island?"

"Why should I love it?"

"Because I'll be there." He grinned. "Now tell me, doesn't knowing me make up for a lot of things?"

She said somberly, "You were the lifeline."

"But no longer, eh? Now that you're a self-sufficient businesswoman." He tilted back in the chair, fingertips meeting.

"I don't know how self-sufficient I am," she said. "I want to make a deposit on a house and I can't afford it. My savings from this job won't do it, what with my rent and food, and I can't afford a bank loan."

He sat up rapidly, and she shook her head. "I'll always want you for my friend as long as you'll be one, but no loans."

"What's this about a house?"

"It's a place I can lease, right on the edge of Limerock Harbor. It was the gardener's cottage on one of the old estates. The people are willing to have me and the cat too, but they want a deposit. I don't blame them. I might have weird friends who'd break up the place."

"Do you have any like that?"

"No, but how do they know?" The telephone interrupted

her. She set down a new client's name and date, and Billy B. watched her over his coffee mug. "The last couple," she continued, "looked mild as milk and made a big thing out of going to church every Sunday. He went crazy on speed one night and half-killed his wife along with nearly destroying the cottage."

"What's the matter with the place you have now?" He had been her first dinner guest there, in a ceremony of celebration.

"She's been very nice about the cat, but it's against her rules. She's given me a month. Besides, I want a place where he can get out, and I'll have more leg room too. I found out about the new place because we do the maintenance over there."

"Are you going to eat that doughnut?" he asked. She handed it over to him on the paper towel. "So if you won't go to the bank, and you won't accept a helping paw from Old Dog Tray ever faithful, what do you intend to do?"

"I know where to get it," she said quietly. "Roz owes me eight hundred dollars, and she's lucky if I don't charge her interest."

He was half-laughing, incredulous. "You've never been near her! Never wanted to!"

"I've also never forgotten the money. I didn't want to go after her at first, because I was too stunned and then I was too furious. I said to hell with the money—you heard me often enough. Then I was busy trying to get caught up with high school, and then I got into *this*." Her grin ridiculed herself. "I swore that whatever I did when I got off the island, it would never be housework. Well, at least I support myself with it, and I've been able to afford the night courses. The time's gone fast. It really has, Billy," she appealed to him, as if making excuses for herself. Well, that's what she was doing.

"I thought the estate would be settled before this. But I'm getting ready to say the hell with that too. I need a place of my own where I can have my cat, and damn it, that eight hundred dollars is burning a hole in my mind."

"Tell me something, Jule," he said. "Is that all you want in the world, a little house? Young, healthy, very intelligent, and that's all you want?"

"I'm not going to give up my cat." She was as near belligerent as she ever sounded. "He came to me. He picked me out because he needed me." An image of a pail of water on a back doorstep. Sea smell, gulls calling in a morning sky, and drowned kittens in a bucket.

"I didn't say," she went on with dignity, "that I was going to devote my life to being his handmaiden."

The man laughed. "I grant you your cat. Personally I like him. I'll grant you two cats, if you like. But where are you going, Jule? You're making an honest living, yes, but you've been studying, you must have quite a batch of college credits by now. And you've got a damned good brain. So where are you going from here?"

She lowered her eyelids and spoke to the desk. "I live one week at a time."

"You're too young to be that cautious. Have you just exchanged one prison for another? You're keeping yourself in limbo. Jule, I want to understand, that's why I keep needling. Don't clam up on me. This is old Billy B., remember?"

She longed to tell him what he wanted to know, but she was inarticulate on the subject. The years had gone by, and sometimes she dreamed and woke up able to imagine the insane horror of someone sealed into a plastic bag. But she knew that she was sane, if immobilized.

I never want to see her again! she had cried once, but the wish had never been granted because she saw Roz or heard her in those dreams, and this was far worse than the visits of those two long ago lost in the sea or become ashes dispersed on the wind over St. George Bay.

"A live ghost is worse than a dead one any time," she said suddenly. "And to understand all is not to forgive all. I don't care what somebody or other said. He wasn't the last word on the subject. I am."

It was intended to make Billy B. laugh, and he did. "Jule, you don't need to be haunted by anything or anyone. If you weren't such a stiff-necked, self-righteous little piece of granite you'd have taken my offer, and by this summer you'd be graduated with a degree, knowing exactly what you are and what you hope to become. It was a loan. I made that clear; you wouldn't have been beholden."

"But if I had taken it, who'd be here now to give you coffee and doughnuts whenever you come to Limerock?"

"I'd have had you going to school where I could keep a hard eye on you. Nurtured you. All the Benedicts would have been in on it." He unfolded and walked around the office, carrying his cup, talking to the calendars, the posters, the bulletin board, the duty roster, the window. "I respect you, Jule. Whatever you do is all right with me. Okay, you need a new place to live. Accept my loan now, for whatever the deposit is, and you can pay it back any way you want to. Get Roz off your back forever. She went without a word or a look. Why do you give her the importance of one instant of your attention?"

He finished up at the desk, towering over her. She tipped back her head to look up at him, thinking, Because I can't help my dreams. Something isn't finished.

"I know that look," he said. "The protective shield. On certain faces it would be vapid. Witless. On you it's mysterious. Remember what Tony said? 'Her eyes were deeper than the depths of waters stilled at even.' Tony and his wife are at the island. The swallows are there, and the ospreys are back."

She shook her head, smiling. "But I will take your loan to hold my house. And then I'm going to get it from Roz, and pay you."

When she actually put it into words, there was a contraction in her midriff as if someone had just yanked a thin rope excruciatingly tight around her. Her smile flickered into a wince, steadied again.

He put his hands on the desk and leaned forward. "Then come and tell me about it afterward. I'll be on the island for the rest of the month, the others go back next week. I've got a commission for an educational complex and it's the biggest thing I've ever done. It's been turned completely over to me to come up with something new and magnificent." His bony face was illumined; she wanted to reach up and take it between her hands, but she kept them quiet.

"You will. We—I always said Billy B. can do anything."

"Can he stop you from calling him Billy B.? It makes me sound like a friend of Winnie the Pooh." He straightened up, and she left her chair then, went to him and put her arms around him and laid her head against his chest.

"I'm glad you're in Maine for a while," she said to the old Harris tweed.

"But you won't come near me. I have to come to you."

"I'm a disappointment to you."

"You couldn't ever be. You're Jule. Unique and precious. If I try to shake you up it's for your own good. But how do I know I'd like you as a free spirit? You might fly away." They kissed, and he added, "Then I wouldn't have anyone to bully."

He wrote a check for her, then they walked to the door, his arm around her shoulders, hers around his waist.

"It's just that I don't think you should go alone to see

Roz," he said. "You're bound to be on her conscience, if she has any vestige of one, so you'll be about as welcome as Banquo's ghost."

"I'll be all right," she said. "I'll come back with my shield or on it, and either way there'll be eight hundred dollars tucked in my pocket."

2

LIB WAS OVERJOYED to swap vacation time with Jule and thus have two weeks in July. The deposit was made on the lease, the cat was taken to board with the vet for two days, and Jule had a reservation at the Fernwood Motel, which she had found in a guidebook telling what to see and where to stay in Maine. The item mentioned Birnam Marsh, but added that the Jean Deverell Memorial Preserve was open only to serious ecology students.

Jule told the team she was going down east to see a relative. At the time the Roz story appeared, there'd been an article in the *Limerock Patriot* about it, but Jule, hidden among the Peabodys, could be brought in only as a dim background figure. The Landfall and Port George people had been very reticent after the first shock. The Deverells had allowed no publicity either, and then a local herring seiner went down with all hands and this erased the other matter from the regional consciousness. Calling herself Juliet Moreton, Jule had yet to meet anyone who connected her with a four-years-past sensation. Those who remained of the original Clean Sweep team knew, of course, but apparently never gave it a thought.

On the Thursday before Easter, she rode to Bangor on the bus: a short, demure girl in pleated tartan skirt, white blouse, and dark blue blazer. She kept a composed face turned toward the tinted windows. Outside in mid-April sunshine the state moved hesitantly into spring. Later it would rush, bursting out in explosions of emerald and pearl. If anything called for a pagan festival it was the return of spring to Maine.

The swallows are there. The ospreys are back.

Her hands lay in frozen stillness on her bag. I don't have to do this, she thought wildly, and at the concept of giving up, taking the next bus out of Bangor back to Limerock, the havoc lessened in her chest and she was able to take a long breath. Yes, she could do that. It was so beautifully simple. *Yes.*

Except that she'd still be tied. The dreams were restraints as authentic as handcuffs and leg irons. Whether this was the right thing or not—but at least she'd made a move. Dared to take a step.

She could be very sorry about it. But I can always walk away before it's too late, she thought. She clung to that, because she was frightened.

She took a taxi to Tremaine. The Fernwood Motel lay outside the town, on a secondary road in farming, fishing, and deer-hunting country. It was not so far from the coast that a strong east wind wouldn't fetch at least a whiff of the ocean and sometimes a sea fog.

"I always thought Juliet was such a pretty name," the woman said when Jule registered. Her room was at the end of the unit and there were only a few other cars there. The instant she was alone she walked across to the big mirror and ran her hands through her black hair, to loosen her tight scalp. The ancient question came, even though she knew the technical answer. *Who are you?*

For the first time her mouth lost its apparent serenity and she tucked her lower lip under her teeth and turned away from the reflection—as she had turned her head away from Mummie before the woman could see the shattering of the impassivity she hated, Jule's one weapon against her.

She took out the telephone book and was annoyingly conscious that her clever self-assured hands were now clammy and fumbling.

"I'm hungry, that's all," she muttered in excuse. She'd been awake since three, had put in a morning at the office, taken the cat to the vet's, and hadn't been able to manage to get down anything more than a few cups of tea and some toast, her stomach had been in such a state.

You'll make a great showing if you faint at their feet, she thought. Dramatic if nothing else.

She washed up and walked across to the restaurant in a gusty, blazing sunset. Homemade chicken pot pie was a specialty, and she ate a good supper after all. She'd forgotten to bring something to read, so she went back to the registration desk where there was a rack of paperbacks, and used up some time studying them. She knew she was putting off the moment for which she had made the journey.

Finally she took the only two possible choices besides espionage, the Third Reich, and the genre described as the sexy steamy exposé of what really went on in the worlds of theatre, movies, advertising, politics, medicine, and big business.

Ngaio Marsh and James Herriot looked like refugees lost in a brothel.

When she went back into the room she allowed herself no time to consider. She looked up the number and printed it on the nearby pad in large, clear letters, and before she could lose her impetus she dialed very deliberately, saying each digit in a firm voice.

The distant telephone rang only once before a woman's voice answered. "Deverell residence." It wasn't Roz, she knew with a weakening rush of relief.

"May I speak with Miss Jean Deverell, please?" It came out sounding young and annoyingly short of breath; she was angry with her body for humiliating her like this.

The low voice, brisk without being curt, said, "Who is calling, please?"

"Will you just tell her that Jule's at the Fernwood Motel, room fourteen." It was as if she'd been running for a long time and couldn't slow down. "Please. Just that much."

"*Jule?*" the voice questioned.

"Yes. Thank you." She hung up and backed to a bed and sat down, chafing her cold hands, staring at the telephone as if it had turned into a cobra in her hands, weaving hood and all.

At this very moment Roz could be hearing her name. In the next moment Roz would know for a fact that Jule was near. She remembered Roz in a rage as clearly as she remembered Roz laughing. She could get out now. She could be *gone*. Maybe the very act of coming here, even without seeing Roz, was all she needed to release her from limbo.

Still she didn't move. She forced herself to take long slow breaths, and reason began to replace panic. Roz might not even be there. She could be in Europe or the Caribbean or New York, so Jule would escape after all. Then she realized the answering woman would have told her at once that Roz wasn't there.

Roz might be married now. Certainly there would be men, and what if one of those called? *I am Jean's husband.* Or her father, rigid, autocratic. Or fiancé, if they used that word outside of books. *My wife does not wish to speak with you. Miss Deverell does not talk to strangers. . . . Just what do you want of my daughter?*

Eight hundred dollars that belongs to me, and tell her to stop hiding behind her guilty conscience. If she can't look me in the eye she can send me a check.

Her mouth tucked up in a one-sided cynical grin. I can just hear myself. . . . It had never occured to her that Roz might refuse to be seen, but it had occurred to Billy B. Roz could have looked her up through the Peabodys at any time during the four years, if she had wanted to.

"Well," she said aloud, unlacing and spreading out her hands, gazing at them. "I could always write her a letter saying *You dirty rat*. There was a time when Roz would have appreciated that. She'd have come right back at me. Now she'd probably have me arrested."

After a time she took off her shoes and lay down on the bed with pillows piled behind her. There was very little traffic, and from the woods behind the motel grounds there came the voices of tree frogs, peepers in some hidden alder swamp. The April dusk welled into the room. Fatigue took over. She drifted, weightless, while she waited for the telephone to ring.

3

IN THE BEGINNING the word was Mummie, and there was no doubt that Mummie was flesh. She had looked like a giantess to the children when they were small, and she had put on weight with the years, and while the flesh built up solidly on flesh, Jondy grew smaller by contrast. By the time the twins were fourteen she was enormous in her rocker, and Jondy, obediently kicking off his rubber boots before coming into the presence, was like a wispy youth until you saw the gray in his yellow hair, and looked into his withering face.

In her rages she never screamed. But her voice could flay, and then slice the bloody pulp from the bones. It went on and on. One felt one would do anything to stop it. Give in, of course, but supposing one ever became strong enough to grip the great column of the throat until there was no more breath to keep the voice going? No more breath ever. *No more Mummie.*

It was Jule who had the visions and they'd begun with the first certainty that Mummie was a name and not a fact. She knew you couldn't feel this way about your own mother. If Roz had such visions she'd have told them to Jule, because she couldn't keep anything to herself.

For Jule these pictures were all the more ghastly because she was the one who went around rescuing bees and moths from the rainwater barrels, keeping improvised birdbaths full in hot weather, and losing sleep over new eider ducklings being gobbled down by blackback gulls. How could she ever actually want to *kill*? Even Mummie?

Well, Mummie was safe enough. If Jule had ever flung herself at that thick strong throat, she'd have ended up in a corner across the room. It had happened to Roz when she'd screamed once at Mummie. They'd been fishing for cunners off the wharf and two boys in a dory swung into the cove and began asking questions; it was the girls' first autumn on Osprey Island after moving from Landfall. They'd gotten as far as, "What's your name? Are you going to live here? Where are you going to school?" when Mummie sent Jondy for them.

"Sluts!" she'd hissed at them. "Trollops! Two bitches in heat is that what I've got here?"

"Beatrice," Jondy said shakily. Jule was getting sick, as usual, but Roz went up like a dry pine set afire.

"What are you trying to do to us?" she raged. "Keep us in prison all our lives? Did you pick us up cheap to make us into slaves? Or are you saving us from the world? You're saving *yourself*! What are you running away from?"

Mummie was standing at the table fitting pie crust into a pan. One sweep of her thick arm, and Roz's nose gushed blood and the girl went crashing backward across the kitchen, fell over a chair, and tried to sit up, dazed and bleeding.

Jondy's tan turned yellowish gray. He made little noises in his throat, his pale blue eyes swimming in impotent tears. Nobody went to Roz. Nobody dared. She sat there with the blood running over her lips and chin and dripping onto her white T-shirt with the map of Maine on it. Then Mummie turned back to her piecrust, saying to Jule, "Stop that nosebleed and clean up the mess."

Jule, who was the smaller twin, tried to haul Roz to her feet, but Roz threw her off and scrambled up and made for the door, dripping blood all the way.

Out behind the ell woodshed Roz lay on her back. Jondy brought them a pail of cold water, fresh from the well, and a handful of towels, whispered, "Never mind the kitchen floor, I'll mop that up." He scurried away again. Jule applied cold compresses and Roz sobbed with rage and the pain in her nose.

"I hope she broke it. They'll have to take me to a doctor then. Then I'll tell what she did to me." She sat up and spat out blood. "Just you wait! I'll get her some day!"

"Lie down," Jule implored her. "If you bleed to death you can't tell anything to anybody."

Roz obeyed, talking around a fresh compress. "What kind of father is *he*? It's bad enough having the Bitch of Buchenwald for a mother, but to have a damn little squirt who's a-fraid of his own shadow—if I ever get away from them, I'll never own them! I'll say I was a foundling. I'd rather be!" she shouted. "Ditch-delivered by a drab!"

They read Shakespeare up at the main house, looking for the dirty bits. *An old black ram is tupping your white ewe.*

"That one was birth-strangled," Jule reminded her. "You wouldn't want to be dead, would you?"

"No, I'm going to *live*, and it's going to be somewhere else besides this! Where the hell are the authorities? We're supposed to be in *school*."

"Keep still so the blood will clot," said Jule. "Maybe Mr. French will do something."

"You know damn well that she can take care of anything that comes up. If somebody came out to investigate, she'd be sweet enough to make you puke, and say we're getting over TB or something, and she'll have them so hypnotized they won't even ask for a doctor's certificate."

She popped up again. "Jule, don't just *stare* at me. Didn't you ever *think*? Aren't you ever scared when you realize we're her prisoners as long as she lives?"

"I think of it in the middle of the night." Along with other things she couldn't put words to. "It's like trying to imagine Space. That always scares me to death because it has no end."

"But *she's* not Space. She's got to end sometime." Roz spoke quietly now, as if she were thinking out loud, gazing up at the gulls gliding in their eternal lazy circles. "I wonder why Jondy hasn't arranged a handy little fall for her; she could trip over a rug in the kitchen and smash her skull against the stove. Or she could fall off the wharf at low tide and hit the rocks. But he's afraid to. He's like her dummy. He'd have no existence without her."

"Jondy tries," Jule defended him. It was all she could say for him.

4

ON LANDFALL, which was the only other place the girls could remember, they had no relatives, and the girls were never allowed to roam freely. If they were sent to the store, they could never linger to watch the harbor activity; Mummie timed them. They went to no one's house to play and no one was encouraged to come to theirs. They loved school because it was their only social life, and a few parents were kind enough to hold their children's birthday parties at school so that the Saunders twins could be there.

Mummie herself never set foot outside their dooryard except once, when she'd had to go to Limerock to see the doctor. Jondy had taken her in his own boat, so she wouldn't have to mix with the mailboat passengers. It was a Saturday.

"I shall know if you step off these premises," she told the twins, "and I shall know how to deal with you."

She was even more massive in her full coat; a silk scarf around her throat dimly veiled her extra chins. They saw this scarf only on rare occasions, like her hat, which was expensive and good. She'd always had it, as far as they knew. She wore gloves, and carried the leather handbag Jondy had given her one Christmas.

Her greenish-gold eyes were globular under thick white lids; the nose was impressively arched, in a large face where the accumulation of flesh had buried the elegant cheekbones, long jaw, and imperious chin they'd seen in the one photograph Jondy had secretly saved, and shown them to convince them that Mummie had once been handsome. (And slim.)

"Is that clear?" Her voice reverberated through the kitchen.

"Yes, Mummie," they said together.

She turned and Jondy sprang to open the door like a footman. As she moved out past him he grinned at the girls and mouthed a message. *I'll bring you something.*

Roz gave Jule a violent bear hug. "Maybe she'll find out today that she's got only three months to live! Wouldn't it be great to just have Jondy? We could manage him like anything. Besides, I bet he'd be a different man without her." She saw glorious visions, then slumped in defeat. "It's no good thinking about it. We'll just feel worse when we find out it isn't true."

Jule did the chores, while Roz went through Mummie's bureau drawers in the hopes of turning up some clue to the past.

"Nothing!" she said in disgust. "You'd think they were born full-grown and married with the dear little twinnies on the way." In Mummie's mirror they saw themselves; not identical, but both blue-eyed. Roz was bigger, and she had an almost square chin cleft in the middle, dimples in her cheeks; and when she laughed her eyes disappeared in a thicket of lashes which, like her brown hair, bleached out to blond at the tips with the summer sun so that the merry or furious eyes blue as chicory flowers seemed fringed with gold. Her hair was thick and wanted to curl, a nuisance because it was hot and Mummie liked long hair. Once she'd cut it all off, after reading about Maggie Tulliver, and had spent a week in her room for punishment.

Jule, smaller, had straight black hair. She had endured in agonized silence the daily tight braiding until she learned to braid it herself. Her eyes were a darker blue than Roz's, slightly oblique, black-lashed; her smile slower, her narrow face secretive. *Sly*, Mummie called it. She had one dimple, in her left cheek, to Roz's three. Roz's teeth were pretty and even; Jule's lower teeth were a little crooked. Roz was developing, proud one day and worried the next.

"I'll never get huge like her," she said grimly. "I'd starve myself to death first. *You* won't have to try to stay thin, you're like Jondy."

They set off at a gallop for the harbor, trusting that nobody would give them away. They saw the mailboat come in and watched the freight unloaded, and Mr. French, the schoolteacher, a young man "from away" who'd wanted the experience of teaching in a one-room school, treated them to chocolate-covered ice creams on sticks. He was feeling generous, he told them, because his girl was coming to visit him, next boat. He walked up from the harbor with them, telling them all about her.

"I'd like to bring her to call on your parents," he said at the end, and they couldn't think why but were delighted at the importance of it. They were both innocently in love with him, like most of the other girls in the school, and a word of advice or praise from him was to be cherished.

Mummie had nothing to say about her visit to the doctor. Jondy brought them each a T-shirt with the map of Maine on it, a small bottle of toilet water, a box of jellies and bonbons to share.

They hugged him extravagantly and were told by Mummie that their behavior was indecent.

On Tuesday Mr. French's girlfriend arrived, and in the afternoon he brought her to school, where she won everybody over by the way she played the guitar and got them all singing. At recess she captained a girls' soccer team against Mr. French and the boys. It was a tie, with threats on both sides of a battle to the death tomorrow.

In the evening they came to call on Mummie and Jondy. The meeting was short. When Mr. French began to talk about the scholarships available at Marilyn's old school and said that the twins were extremely eligible because of their high intelligence, Mummie cut him short. Just this day, she informed him majestically, she and her husband had made the arrangements for their daughters' continuing education. Jule happened to be looking at Jondy and saw the smile go off his face, the furtive slide of his gaze, and the quick dark rush of blood that sometimes suffused his small features at something Mummie said; she knew by this that Mummie was lying.

The callers left, and Roz stood in front of Mummie and said, "Tell *us* the arrangements."

She hadn't needed to see Jondy's face and blinking eyes.

"Go to bed," said Mummie.

The immediate arrangements were to move to Osprey Island the day school closed; there was no waiting for the girls to attend the eighth-grade graduation exercises that night. They got their rank cards, Mr. French wished them well, and said they'd probably be going to Williston High along with the Port George youngsters, and he would like to hear how they were getting on. "I'm sure you'll do well wherever you are," he said. "You have the brains for it. . . . Marilyn always asks for you when she writes."

They began to believe in Williston High. It wasn't Paradise but close to it, and at the end of it they'd be eighteen and free.

5

JONDY'S PARENTS had been caretakers on Osprey Island and he'd grown up there. They made the day-long trip on his boat from one bay to another, and it wasn't a bad summer. At least they had more freedom than they'd ever had on Landfall. When Mummie had her long silent spells she didn't seem to care what they did when they'd finished their work. She knew they couldn't get off the island and that there was no one else on it; it was too rocky for clammers. They could go rowing, and on hot days they went paddling in whatever cove happened to be in the lee; wearing old shorts and shirts, they taught themselves a rough and ready swimming by wearing some life belts they found up in the Benedict house.

The Benedict house was fascinating. Jondy gave its care to them, to keep it always ready in case any of the Benedicts should arrive, something which hadn't happened for a good many years. Mummie never climbed up the hill, she'd never seen the place, and was utterly indifferent. She hardly stirred from the caretaker's house except to go out to the toilet. So the girls felt free up there. It was a sprawling, shingled, turreted mansion, filled with the detritus of successive generations from the time it was new in 1870 until about ten years ago. In the attics, in the bedrooms, and the library, there was a great assortment of reading matter, from paperback adventures and mysteries to old copies of the classics, and stacks of magazines. The most recent ones introduced them to the movies, and television of the sixties and early seventies. They had never seen either medium.

It was powerful stuff. They realized more than ever that the world across that stretch of water was an Ali Baba's cave of treasure which they could only tremblingly contemplate.

They dressed up in the clothes left hanging in the closets, the things people keep in their summer places and nowhere else. They studied amateur watercolors and pencil sketches, mooned over old photographs. They ran through the house whooping wildly till they were half-convulsed as if they were pursued by demons. They tried to play the out-of-tune piano. They slid down the banisters. Sometimes they would read away a whole wet afternoon, wrapped up in blankets on the big leather sofa in the library. When they were satiated with magazines they began on the books, indiscriminately. If it had print, they read it.

July and half of August slid by, and in a sheltered orchard behind the Benedict house pears ripened on old trees, and Yellow Transparent apples dropped into the long grass. They ate while they read, indoors and out.

In the caretaker's house there was no mention of school clothes.

"I don't think we're going," Roz said. "Damn their souls. I'm going to find out."

But even Roz didn't have the courage to ask straight out. She was twitchy and overactive; she ran faster and yelled louder in the big house, crashed her hands on the piano keys.

Jule began to have a perpetual pain in her stomach from anxiety and also from stuffing herself at the table, because not eating was a crime. She wanted to find out about school once and for all, and yet she didn't want to know.

No one ever told them they weren't going. It just didn't happen. Jondy's grin was furtive, he sneaked candy bars to them but sang and chattered nervously all the time when they were alone with him, so they couldn't corner him.

Up at the main house Roz finally blew up in a terrible tantrum, raging through the echoing rooms, swearing, stamping, sobbing. Jule vomited in showers through mouth and nose, and wondered if Mummie could keep her from starving herself to death.

The incident with the boys and the bloody nose took place after that. Then the girls brooded in an imitation of freedom, when Mummie had a much longer silent spell than usual. It was as if she had crossed some equator in her private world when they moved from one bay to the other, and was now living an entirely different life from the rest, all inside her head.

But at Thanksgiving she roused herself; she roasted the turkey and made two pies, and the girls did the rest. It was a grim ritual. Mummie always insisted that they dress up for this charade of Happy Families, which made it even more grotesque.

"What do we have to be thankful for?" Roz asked at the table in a deceptively innocent voice. Mummie's expression didn't change as she neatly amputated a drumstick.

Jondy said quickly, "Why, honeybunch, we're all together, we've got our health and strength and this good place to live in. You girls did good to find so many cranberries," he added in a well-known ploy to change the subject.

"Ayuh," Roz drawled. "We did real good. They were some slim pickin's."

Mummie said with menacing tranquility, "Watch your language."

"If we're going to be islanders all our lives," Roz said, "why can't we talk like islanders? Who's going to be impressed if we never say ayuh or nope and all the rest of it? The gulls?"

"Be quiet." The green eyes were like sea ice.

It was a beautiful, warm day, and there was a big football game at Williston High; they'd heard about it on the radio. That bit had slipped by Mummie. The battery-operated radio was supposed to be used only for the weather reports, not to bring corruption in the form of news and decadent music. (She had no idea what they discovered in print at the Benedict house.)

Tormented and enraged with longing, they walked all around the island on that long golden afternoon.

"They can't hold us after we're eighteen," Roz said. "It's the law."

"What does she care about the law? She's her own law."

"I wonder what those pills are for? Her heart, maybe? What if she couldn't find them sometime when she needed them?" She grinned at Jule's expression. "No, I'm not that dumb. But when we *look* old enough, we could run away down east, and rake blueberries, and work in the potato fields. Or we could be waitresses or chambermaids. We're good housekeepers, we could always find jobs. We can just take the dory and row ourselves over to Port George and start hitchhiking."

She had to be forever making plans; they were Life to her, big transfusions of new blood. Jule admired her gallant persistence. She saw herself as a little mole, digging in somewhere and keeping still. But she had her own plans. They could read their way through everything in the Benedict house, even the hard stuff. That would count as some kind of education, wouldn't it? Better than nothing.

When they got back to the house that day they were hungry, because Roz always was, and Jule had thrown up her dinner as soon as they were out of sight of the house. If Mummie was in her room with the door closed, they could get something to eat and take it outside.

Incredibly, there was company. Even more incredibly, it was Mr. French and Marilyn. He'd been home on the mainland for the holiday, and he and Marilyn had driven to Port George and borrowed a boat to come out to the island. Jondy, flushed and nervously smiling, told the girls to make coffee and bring out some pie.

"I can't seem to discover where you twins are going to school," Mr. French said, as if amused at his own obtuseness.

"We're going nowhere," Roz said. She set a cup before Marilyn with an absolutely steady hand. Jule slopped coffee into Mr. French's saucer and rushed into the pantry for a clean one; she was stabbed by stomach cramps and hunched over her folded arms wondering if she'd make it to the toilet in time.

Out in the kitchen Jondy was saying, flustered, "Not *yet*, but—"

Then Mummie uncoiled and struck, devastating them without moving from her rocking chair. Her voice never deviated from its even tempo when she damned them for their interference. She accused Mr. French of having an unnatural interest in her two little girls. He had shown this along with most of the other males on Landfall, which was why she had removed her children. But he was the worst, because of his position of responsibility.

"Mrs. Saunders, you're a liar!" Marilyn cried.

"*You're* a fool. Either marry him and get him where he won't be running his hands under little girls' dresses, or give him up and get yourself a real man."

"Like *yours*, you mean?" the girl exclaimed, splendidly. She walked out. Mr. French, who after the first shock had gone perfectly white, turned to go after her.

"And if there's any more interference," Mummie's voice followed him, "by *anybody*, I'll know who started it, and you'll end up in court. I can make the muck stick so you'll never get it off."

"Oh no, you can't!" Roz shrieked. She tried to run after them but Jondy closed and locked the back door so she couldn't get out, saying abjectly, as she clawed at him, "Roz-zie—honeybunch—"

"I *hate* you!" she screamed. "You're as bad as she is! If I could get in that boat I'd never come back, never! When I got through talking nobody'd ever make me come back!"

In the pantry Jule was frantically wondering if she could get out the window in time to tell Mr. French they would not lie about him, but she became aware that she wouldn't even reach the toilet. She heard Mummie's chair creak in warning, and Jondy's whispered, *"Beatrice."* Roz stormed up the stairs and crashed the door shut. Stairs had gotten difficult for Mummie with all her weight, so even when she was in one of her iceberg rages she wouldn't attempt them.

She went into the big bedroom across the hall from the kitchen. Sighing, Jondy followed her. He opened and shut the bedroom door very stealthily, as if the sudden snap of a latch would cause her to blow up and they'd all disappear in the explosion.

Dead silence now except for the clock. Ashamed, but relieved to be alone, Jule took a basin of cold water, a towel, and soap out to the toilet and cleaned herself up, shivering. After that she dipped more water from the hogshead of rainwater and scrubbed the flannel lining of her jeans and washed out her briefs, then draped them and the towel over the bay bushes at the far side of the shed.

She went back in and crept up the stairs. Roz had been crying hard. Her face was red, her lids swollen, and her eyes bloodshot. There was a dangerous set to her mouth, and she looked far older than fourteen.

"I will do it," she said. "I will get off here. I'll say anything. I'll say they aren't my parents. I've already started making up my real family. Do you want to be in it or not?"

Jule, poor little mole, knew better than to say it won't work. Because wouldn't it be heavenly if it did? "Sure," she whispered.

6

THE NEXT SUMMER Jondy brought them two kittens from Port George, and Mummie said nothing at all. Two mornings later Jule, up early to see if they were awake in their box out in the shed, found them drowned in a bucket of rainwater on the back doorstep. Mute with shock, she had gone upstairs again. She hadn't been able to tell Roz, but she could lead the way.

This was when the visions of killing Mummie began. But it was Roz who shouted at the woman, "I'll kill *you!*" Then she ran too fast for anyone to catch her, and Jule snapped out of her trance and fled after her. For once Jondy had disobeyed and not chased them; perhaps he had been in shock too. He had seemed to love the kittens as much as the girls did.

Much later in the day he found them in the brush camp they'd built deep in the western woods. He hugged them, and wept with them, and that was when they knew Jondy would never be any good to them, ever. Roz finally moved away from him in contempt, but Jule had hugged him back, in shame and pity.

She is not my mother, she thought. My mother would never do what she did.

Nobody ever mentioned the kittens aloud. But they were always there, little and helpless and drowned, whenever certain things happened or were said; Jule never knew when they would surface in her dreams.

The day after the murders the girls did their chores without speaking to each other, and Mummie rocked gently, staring out the window. At what? She never even stirred when one of the girls dropped a pan with a heart-stopping clatter. They walked out boldly afterward, and Roz, who had always to try something extra, took doughnuts from the jar, her eyes fixed on that turned-away head with the untidily pinned-up mass of dark hair, while Jule palpitated in the doorway.

Once outside, they ran. Jondy had gone to haul very early; lucky Jondy, who could escape to his boat. Jule worried that some day when he landed his day's lobsters at Port George he'd just tie his boat up at Ned Peabody's wharf and walk out of sight forever. But he always came back. Not for us, she thought, but because he won't dare to leave her. He thinks she'd find him wherever he went.

The morning glistened, all blue silk and gold filigree, and musical with birds, but empty without the kittens, who had lived with them less than two days but had changed their lives. Jule swallowed hard and widened her eyes to hold back the tears. Roz charged on ahead. Grief filled her with energy.

They went straight to the other end of the island, to the southwest point. The steep beaches were made of rolling, rattling popple rocks, and wild strawberries grew in the short turf among bleached sea urchin shells and silver driftwood. At the edge of the woods the trees were stunted and twisted. The girls went deeper into the woods than they had ever gone before, and finally they were so far away from the shore the tree tops seemed hardly to move, and the rote had become so muted you had to hold your breath to listen for it. Thrushes sang in here, their voices ringing and echoing like thin, fine chimes through the ancient silence.

Moving as if entranced, the girls went deeper. They came to a grove of big white birches and oaks standing up to their knees in bracken like green fountains. The girls were briefly stopped by a thick barrier of brambles. "After we get through this we ought to find a castle at least," said Roz.

"With a sleeping beauty," said Jule. "Or a sleeping prince." They giggled, feebly, and they hadn't believed they'd ever be able even to smile again.

They waded cautiously into shoulder-high bracken, expecting to step into soggy swamp. Instead, the place seemed to be paved with granite blocks, some sharply tilted, some thickly cushioned with mosses, and the big oaks could have been the borders of an avenue.

They were excited; they'd grab at anything to keep yesterday's horror at bay. They went on and on, sometimes down on their hands and knees to feel out the shape of the blocks, wondering where they'd been quarried and who'd brought them here.

"It had to be the Benedicts, of course," Roz said authoritatively. "They've had it for years and years, since right after the Revolution. It was probably all cleared off here and they planted the oaks and laid out the avenue. Maybe the first house was here. So there has to be a cellar hole at the end of it."

But it ended in a swamp grown with alders, some old and rotting. Brown water seeped over the girls' sneakers. The cellar hole must have filled up over the years, and they couldn't find even a trace of an outside wall. They went off to one side and lay on a dry hummock among the bracken, looking up at the green lace overhead, and they told each other what the house must have been like. They each had favorites from their reading, but agreed that it must have been a real mansion, after someone had gone to all the work of building such a splendid approach to it.

There was a roomful of framed old maps at the Benedict house. One took in Osprey Island, in detail. Jule had studied that one over and over. It showed the cabin sites of the early settlers, but nothing at this end.

"Then it was built long after that map was made," Roz insisted, "or so long before that whoever drew the map hadn't any idea of it. How do we know, maybe somebody in the sixteen hundreds had himself a nice little estate here."

"Jondy always says there isn't a square inch of this place that he hasn't been on, so he should know about this avenue," Jule said.

"It's easy to imagine Jondy as a kid," Roz said. "But you can't ever imagine Mummie as a girl, or a child—or a baby!" She hooted.

"We saw that picture of her when she was young," Jule said unwillingly, not wanting to talk about her here.

"But can you see her having *us*? Let alone what she'd have to do *first*?"

It was true that after they found out how babies were conceived, carried, and born, it never seemed to have anything to do with them and her. They'd gathered this information in first crude form at recess in school, but had refined their knowledge later by means of a medical book in the Benedict house.

"No, we are really foundlings," Roz said emphatically. "Somebody left us with her, and paid for us, and then just disappeared. . . . Or maybe they're still paying. We were illegitimate, so we were boarded out of sight, and they may have been paying her a fortune to keep us, expecting that we'd be educated and everything." She groaned. "Oh God, if there was only some way to find out!"

"You know how Jondy's always saying one of us has his mother's eyes, or his big toe or something." Jule wouldn't voice her own deep-sea certainty, for the very fear that if they faced Jondy with it—or were driven to the madness of confronting Mummie—they'd be given irrefutable facts, and the fantasies that sweetened their days would be murdered like the kittens.

Going back to the alder swamp, they followed the pavement westward, coming out in a little cove high-walled with rock, a perfect miniature harbor. Here the mansion dwellers must have landed their freight and anchored their vessels. There was a scrap of gravelly beach where rowboats could be pulled up, or larger craft heeled over for repairs to the hull. The girls had known the cove before this, but now it took on an entirely new personality.

Richly and ravenously inventing the people of the mansion, the girls ate their lunch of doughnuts, and periwinkles boiled in an old coffee can over a little fire in the rocks. Roz always had matches, and Jule kept a safety pin in her bra strap to be straightened out for a pick.

But all the time the sun was westering, the boats were going home, the sailing yachts beat up the bay toward a port for the night, and the girls knew they had to go back. If they were lucky she'd still be in her silence. Instead she was lovingly smoothing fudge frosting over a tall chocolate cake on the counter. Her hair was combed and pinned up into a smooth thick coil, and she wore a clean dress and fresh apron.

"Get the table set, girls," she said without looking around. They gave each other a glance and then went swiftly to their work. Roz kept looking sidewise at the cake; the tip of her tongue slid greedily over her lips. Jule's stomach seemed to be surging around like a tethered skiff in a rough cove. She was always made queasy by this manifestation of Mummie, and Jondy's nods and grimaces.

When they were little they'd been innocent enough to believe each time that the change was permanent, until they realized that she was simply being expansive because she'd made sure that they knew her power.

Now she was celebrating the murder of the kittens. She

hadn't given permission for Jondy to bring them; so she had watched him and the girls laugh at and love the kittens for a day, let them think it was all right, and then she had shown them.

If the only way to get away from you is to die, Jule thought, I'll find a way to do it that you can't stop.

Of course she had to eat something, because Jondy kept sneaking her these worried little smiles and she knew he was afraid that Mummie might notice something; then her mood would shatter and she'd start one of her inquisitions. Almost nauseated by the rich cake, washing it down with milk, Jule damned Jondy behind her narrow, composed face. You do it to us too, in your own way, she told him. She wished she dared to ask calmly across the supper table, "Where did you bury them, Jondy? I want to put a stone on the grave."

The next day she woke up very early; she had dreamed of the little grave, and the buried pavement under the oaks. Roz was sleeping deeply. Outside was the heavy silence of the fog, even the rote was almost absent, and for the moment no birds sang. Jule dressed in jeans and sweater, took her sneakers in her hand, and went down the narrow steep staircase.

She would look for the grave, and then she might drown herself, if she had the courage to simply go overboard from the rocks at the southwestern end and start paddling out into the ocean. They'd never know what happened to her, if she could get into a current that would take her out to sea.

She wanted Mummie to think that she'd been picked up by someone who'd helped her to get away. Mummie would hate that worse than thinking she was drowned. Jondy would weep for her, but his easy tears were contemptible. Roz would be furious because Jule had managed it.

And there at the kitchen table sat Mummie, fully dressed. She had the big Montgomery Ward catalogue open before her, and a pen in her hand.

"Jule," she said amiably, without looking up. "What got you up so early in this fog?"

"I have to go out back," said Jule.

"Everything all right?"

"Yes." Jule was halfway out the door.

"When you come back I want you to pick out some material. I'm ordering some cloth for you girls to do some sewing for yourselves, and they've got some pretty stuff here."

Jule said, "Yes," and kept on going. But she didn't dare go any farther than the toilet.

She never did find the grave, or ask Jondy about it.

7

WEARING THEIR DECK BOOTS, with long oil-skin aprons tied over their clothes, they stuffed firm corned herring into the nylon twine baitbags. They hadn't been allowed to bait up or paint buoys on Landfall, but Jondy had somehow convinced Mummie it would be all right here. He could use the help. At these times, if he wasn't telling them yarns about his boyhood, he was singing, and they sang with him. He had a sweet high tenor and put a good deal of feeling into "If You Were the Only Girl in the World" or "Danny Boy."

On the foggy day after their discovery in the woods, they had just began baiting up when Roz said, "What about the pavement in the woods over at Sunset Cove? The avenue of oaks?"

"Oh that," said Jondy with delight, "is a *story*." They knew an instinctive reflex of pleasure, of happily settling down to listen while keeping their hands at work. No fear of Mummie ever setting foot in the bait shed.

"Just after the Revolution a Colonel Benedict bought the island from the Commonwealth of Massachusetts—that's before there was a Maine—"

"Before 1820," said Roz.

"Yep. He built a big house from the lumber he cleared, and brought granite from Dix's Island for the foundation and the avenue, and he planted the oaks. He began his marriage in that house. He had people fishing for him, and farming. On the island they spun their own wool and linen, raised everything they needed to eat. It was a little kingdom."

His eyes shone with a luminous blue innocence, like a very young child's.

"They say that during the War of 1812 the colonel's lady charmed a British landing party out of raiding the place by appealing to the officers as gentlemen." He loved that phrase, and repeated it several times.

"They lost some babies. People lost a lot in those days," he said. "But finally they had a healthy little girl, and one night the nurse stole the child out of the house and went away on a boat that had come for her. A ransom note was left, with instructions, and they obeyed them to the letter. The money disappeared, but the child was never returned. Nobody ever saw her or the nurse again around these parts, and a Port George man and his boat disappeared at the same time. The happy kingdom was destroyed." His voice trembled. "The family couldn't stand to stay there any longer. They went away. Little by little the island was deserted. The woods grew up. The fine house was open to the weather and anyone who wanted to land and steal. There were squatters in it finally, and then it burned down, and in a hundred and fifty years the cellar hole became an alder swamp."

It was infinitely depressing to Jule, but Roz greedily wanted details. "Where did they leave the money? On the island or somewhere around Port George? How much was it? What was the baby's name? Where did the colonel go from here?"

All that Jondy could answer was that the colonel and his wife had gone down east somewhere, far from the coast and the islands that he'd loved. "If he had any more young ones that lived to grow up, they probably turned out to be lumber barons or potato kings. Well, it was a long time ago, and every family's got tragedies if you dig hard enough."

"What's ours?" Jule asked. She was trembling inwardly, but she drove herself on. "Is it on your side or hers? Did we have a brother who died? What is it she never wanted us to know?"

He very nearly spluttered. She kept her eyes on him, willing him to break down and incriminate himself, while Roz watched in delighted suspense. He was very red, his eyes shiny. He fought his way out of a thicket of stammers and unfinished exclamations, and said angrily, "What put such foolish ideas into your head? No, no, you're all wrong! She had the change too young. It affects some women that way. Maybe you'll be lucky."

"What change?" Roz demanded.

He floundered again, blushing. "You know what happens to you every month now. Well, it stops after a while. It doesn't happen any more."

"Thank God for that!" Roz said. "I wish it would stop next month. How long do we have to wait?"

"Shouldn't be till you're fifty or so."

Roz groaned. It had happened to Roz first, before they left Landfall. They had known that something of the sort was going to occur—Roz was the one who could gather such information in the schoolyard.

It had something to do with being old enough to have babies, which seemed absolutely ridiculous at thirteen. "We'll be laying eggs," Roz explained, and it sent them into paroxysms of laughter.

Mummie, of course, had never explained anything, though she ordered their sanitary napkins in bulk by mail order. They must have missed something in the medical book at the Benedict house; the news that some day the messy process would stop was welcome, but at fifty they'd be too old to enjoy it. Another reason to be depressed.

"Some women don't have a bit of trouble," Jondy rambled on. "My mother, now, you'd never know the difference. But some have all kinds of complications, and they even go mental." He looked all around, as if Mummie could be silently surrounding the bait shed like the lava flow at Pompeii, and then whispered, "Well, that's what happened to your poor mother."

"What was she like before?" Roz asked.

"Get on with your work, girl," he said.

"Come on, Jondy, tell us," she wheedled.

He pondered, gazing at the ceiling while his hand tightened and knotted a drawstring. *"Stately,"* he said finally. "Even when she was young. She had Presence." He spelled it. "It's what actresses have, and presidents' wives. Royalty, too. She was a handsome woman. Still is," he added quickly. "Even with all that weight. She started putting that on after the change."

"But what was she *like?*" Roz insisted.

"She was always what you'd call a passionate woman. Passionate in everything she did. You see flashes of it now," he said with sentimental pride.

"Like when she drowns kittens?" Roz asked cruelly. That put an end to the conversation.

The story of the lost baby and the lost mansion occupied them a good deal. They went to the place now as often as they went to the Benedict house. In winter when the bracken lay in a tawny mat under the snow, so that the oaks and birches stood clear and alone, they could imagine the house standing serenely at the end of the avenue. They'd agreed on something like Montpelier, the Knox Mansion in Thomaston, of which there'd been a picture in the Landfall schoolroom. Deciding on floor plans and furniture took up hours of drawing and reading in the Benedict house, which was kept warmed through the winter with oil heaters to protect it from destruction by dampness.

The story of the people themselves was the best of all, saved for special occasions. The mansion family belonged to certain times and places, and was never discussed in the same house with Mummie, even at night in their beds with the door shut.

They thought up names for the mansion, discarded them, decided again. Finally they settled on Lindisfarne, from an island off the English coast discovered in an old travel book belonging to a Cecilia Benedict. It was lovely to say, and lovely in print. They named the colonel, his wife, the lost baby, even the babies who died; they tramped through the woods looking for a tiny cemetery. For Jule the dead babies were always inextricably paired with the dead kittens whose grave she never found.

Then there were the people who worked in the mansion, and, going by the old maps in the big house, they placed the other dwellings on the island and invented families for them. They worked up a biography of the false nurse.

"Maisie," Roz said excitedly. "It *has* to be that, because it came to my mind so fast!" She snapped her fingers. "Her father was a fisherman and he had a lot of kids. They were some healthy for those days. Well, it was really good luck when Maisie got a chance to go and work at Lindisfarne, and she knew how to make herself liked and trusted. I'm not saying she had it in her mind then to kidnap the baby, but she was going to get everything she could out of it, believe me. Maybe she even had her eye on the colonel."

"Oh, no!" Jule objected. "Her trouble was that she wasn't very bright and she could be manipulated. She had this lover. What'll his name be? How about Peregrine? Perry for short. He saw the possibilities, and he worked the whole thing. He promised her the baby wouldn't be hurt, they'd just borrow her for a night or two, and this way they'd earn enough money to give them a good start, somewhere else. They'd go a long distance away, down south somewhere. Don't forget there were boats going to the West Indies with shingles and salt fish, and he might've had a relative who'd smuggle them out for some of the ransom. Maybe he thought he could become a rich planter."

"But what about Jane Marie?" asked Roz. "Supposing the baby was sick when they took her that night, and she died. They ran away with the money, but God struck them down for their crime; their ship went down with all hands off Hatteras."

Jule didn't want to think of the baby dying. "Maybe Maisie was crazy about her, and wouldn't give her up. So she grew up in Havana or somewhere thinking she belonged to Maisie and Perry. She became a blond beauty, and married a rich young Spaniard and went to Spain to live, or—"

"My *gosh*!" Roz marvelled. "There's a whole new story! Somewhere in this world there are descendants of the colonel from Jane Marie, the real heirs to this island, but they don't know anything about it. Wouldn't it be something to let them know?"

"How could you? Advertise in every paper in the world?"

Even though the girls knew every corner of the present Benedict house, and could play Bing Crosby, Rosemary Clooney, Nat Cole, and Jo Stafford on the wind-up phonograph, use the croquet set, play backgammon on a very old board, and look at pictures through a stereoscope, the Benedicts who owned all these things were not as real to them as those who had lived in Lindisfarne, at the end of a granite road bordered with oaks. The presence of that double line of venerable trees proved the existence of the mansion people. They, and false Maisie and criminal Perry, the whole household down to the mastiff Bosun and the terrier Tyke, were breathed into life every time one of the girls mentioned a name.

Of the living Benedicts who did secret errands for the State Department, made important medical discoveries, wrote plays, knew the Pope (that was in the Catholic branch), played polo with the Duke of Edinburgh, and were arrested in civil rights demonstrations, they came to know only one.

William Penn Benedict, Jr. Billy B.

8

THE FACT THAT the Benedict family never used the house nowadays was one reason for the Saunders family coming to the island when the other caretaker wanted to quit. The girls often wondered what Mummie would have done if the Benedicts still filled up the house in summer and reappeared in separate visitations during the rest of the year.

They were sixteen and had passed their third Christmas on the island when they first met William Penn Benedict. Christmases were worse than Thanksgivings; worse than anything. At Landfall, there'd been a holiday atmosphere at school and at church. Even though they'd never been allowed to be in the pageant, Jondy had managed somehow to wheedle Mummie into letting them go to it; with him, of course. It had been magic and luminous and holy. Here there was nothing but themselves, with Jondy trying to make a festival out of their choosing the perfect fir tree and stringing cranberries and popcorn like happy kids in the old books at the main house. Money was slipped to them by Jondy with a great air of secrecy for their shopping. It was done by mail order, of course, so nothing was really secret.

"Why can't we go to town just once to see all the stores and the lights?" Roz demanded. "Why can't we go even as far as Port George?"

No answer. The gifts to the girls were always lavish. New clothes, for where? Lockets and bracelets, cologne, scented

soap. Initialed stationery with no one to write to. Even hand-
bags this year, and nowhere to carry them.

Jule found she was in danger of staring into space for too
long, like Mummie; Roz, usually ebullient, was on her way to
depression. In their sixteenth winter everything was going
downhill, until Billy B. came.

Jondy had found the boy at the wharf in Port George when
he sold his lobsters one day just after Christmas, and the letter from the parents had been in the mail. It should have gotten there several weeks before, but it had been lost. It asked if
they'd be so kind as to board Bill for a couple of weeks. He'd
fought his way through hard exams and a case of the flu, he
was worn out, and besides, the only Christmas present in the
world he wanted was some time on the island where he
hadn't been since he was small.

A very liberal check was included.

It was too late for Mummie to draft a letter apologizing
and saying they were all having the flu at this moment. He
was *here*, and they were manifestly healthy.

Caught, she sat in her rocker with the letter in her lap, in
the frigid stillness which now lost its terror for the others because Bill in his ignorance was not intimidated by it. Shedding his L. L. Bean jacket in their kitchen, he was like an exotic
bird suddenly arrived among the sea gulls, except that the
strange bird would probably have been nervous. Bill was
calm.

Used to Jondy's permanently weathered skin, the girls
thought he was pale. He wore glasses that had steamed up
when he came into the house, so he took them off to wipe
them and his eyes were a pure light gray, dark-lashed in a
gaunt, long-jawed face. His hair was neither fair nor very
dark, and quite short; many of the boys they watched through
Benedict binoculars had hair to their shoulders or at least below their ears.

Thin, tall, he stood in the kitchen with the ease and unconscious arrogance of a prince visiting one of his peasants' cottages, while Jondy fussed around him.

Jule suddenly realized that Mummie, who controlled them and their circumstances absolutely, had really been stunned by the arrival of this pale, lean, gently smiling boy.

It was thrilling. Meanwhile Roz was spinning about the place like a top, standing on a chair to get out one of the best cups, rummaging through a drawer for one of the real silver spoons that had been a wedding present to Jondy's mother.

William Penn Benedict might not be handsome like the men in the ads, whom the girls used as models for the colonel and the other mansion men. But he was a *boy*—an older one, maybe even twenty—and he was in their house.

Jule put fresh doughnuts on a plate. Mummie had fried them that morning and had been quite good-natured. Now that mood had been shattered like a pane of glass, and she sat immobile among the shards. Jondy was sweating, talking too much, as if to keep Bill from noticing how Mummie was.

Roz, with the smiling poise of a girl who'd been associating with young males all her life, said, "Do you take cream, Mr. Benedict? We have only evaporated milk, and cow's milk in a carton."

"Evaporated is fine," he said. Roz put some in a little cream pitcher. She walked differently today, and she sang to herself as she moved. Roz had always responded to males, even in the first grade; she changed in their presence, like a trained dancer unconsciously reacting to certain music.

When Jule set the doughnuts on the table, he tipped his long head back and looked directly into her face with his odd light gray eyes. "Thank you. What's your name?"

"Juliet. They call me Jule."

"Hi, Jule." He smiled.

"Hi." She turned away, blushing with embarrassment.

Roz's voice lilted. "How about a piece of cheese with your doughnuts, Mr. Benedict? And I'm Roz, for Rosalind."

"Hey, Shakespeare! Sure, I'd love a piece of cheese. And I'm Bill. My father's the Mister."

The rocking chair creaked, triggering reflexes. Roz froze for an instant. Jule felt a sharp little pain in her stomach. Jondy, putting the groceries away, went into slow motion.

"Your mother wishes us to provide board and room for you for two weeks," Mummie declaimed. "We have no room, Mr. Benedict. The board can be supplied, but you'll have to sleep up at the main house. We keep it heated. You'll be warm enough."

His smile transfused the gaunt face with charm. "To tell you the truth I'd rather be up at the big house," he said. "I always loved it, but I was there only a few times when I was a young kid, because my father's work kept us out of the country so much. I'm looking forward to really getting acquainted with it. I'm also looking forward to my meals. These doughnuts are super, Mrs. Saunders."

To hear Mummie addressed as Mrs. Saunders was a shock. It was incredible that other people saw her simply as that, not a Being who by shifting her weight in a rocking chair could bring a houseful of people to a standstill.

"I'll get my own breakfast there, too, if you'll supply me with the chow," he went on. "Then if I sleep late, or if I'm awake early, I can look out for myself and won't cause you any trouble."

She nodded regally, and ordered the girls to load a basket for him. Jondy filled two plastic jugs with fresh water, since the cisterns had been drained for the winter. He tied the supplies and Bill's bag onto the sled, and Bill hauled it up the hill. It was a brilliant day of no wind, the sky and sea intensely blue. Free of Mummie, Jondy was expansive and welcoming; he kept saying how good it was to have a Benedict on the place again and hoped there'd be more of this.

"Well, I'll be back for sure, Mr. Saunders," Bill said.

"Can we count on that?" Roz asked, and they laughed at each other as if they'd known each other always. Jule in her own way was also tremendously excited. Just having him here changed the very quality of the sunshine and the air they breathed, and she was almost overcome with love for Roz and Jondy.

A pleasant warmth suffused the house, between the sun coming in and the oil heaters dispersed through the rooms. There was plenty of wood for the library fireplace and the kitchen range, and Jondy turned on the bottled gas so Bill could use the gas stove. The bathroom wasn't in use because of the drained cisterns, but the family had never gotten rid of the toilet in the woodshed off the kitchen. It dated from the first days of the house, and had been papered by successive generations with magazine pictures, old postcards, calendar art, and posters.

"The art gallery will more than make up for the chill," Bill remarked.

He picked a sunny room at the front of the house, and the girls made up his bed. Jondy gave him a lesson in lighting kerosene lamps, and his long fingers were quick and clever. He took kindly to Jondy's concern about fire. "I got it from both the parents," he said. "And believe me, I don't want to burn the old homestead down around my ears. I love it too much. I'm madly in love at this moment."

"Dinner's right at noon," Jondy told him. "Supper, half-past five. Come on, ducklings." He herded the girls out.

They coasted home, Roz screaming like a gull as they took off. Jondy tramped down behind them, grinning at their exhilaration but worried by it, Jule knew. It was bad enough that

Mummie had been trapped, but to have Roz practically demented by the novelty of a male stranger on the island could create a hellish situation.

The girls went back up the hill and flew down again in the time it took Jondy to get to the house. While they brushed snow off each other before going in, Jule said, "For heaven's sake, calm down. She'll be sure you're going to rape him or the other way round before nightfall."

Roz giggled. "I could *never* feel romantic about William Penn Benedict. He's nice, but he's not even good-looking. But what a Christmas present, Jule! Somebody else besides *them*! Somebody young, from away! I've got about one million things to ask him. How about you?"

"I've got about seven hundred thousand," Jule admitted.

Roz was so demure when they went in that it was overdone, but Mummie was out of her rocker and in the pantry, making a deep-dish turkey pie.

"I want something understood," she called to them. "You're to have nothing to do with him, and I shall make it clear to him too."

"Beatrice," said Jondy timidly. "We don't want to offend the Benedicts. This is too good a place to lose."

It was a lot for him to say, but she was not a fool; she knew he told the truth and there was nowhere else for them to go.

9

SHE CHANGED THE ORDERS; they were not to go into the main house when he was there. Stimulated by the outrage of his presence and her inability to do anything about it, she became very energetic and thought up a good deal for the girls to do besides their regular work. They cleaned cupboards that had never been dirty, they washed windows, and the sitting room floor that was hardly ever walked on. She decided that they should make patchwork for quilts. But even Mummie couldn't keep them at it for twelve hours a day. She had her own limits; she was too used to solitude, for whatever it meant to her, pleasure or refuge. So they still had some freedom, and they did not stay away from Bill Benedict. Roz began calling him Billy B.

When the weather was fine they took him all over the island. He talked about himself and his architectural studies, he asked them questions about themselves, and Roz told him glibly that the high school was closed for four weeks instead of two this Christmas because of the flu epidemic. From the way he listened, politely, his bony face immobile, Jule guessed that he might have heard something in Port George while he'd been waiting for a chance to get to the island.

They didn't stay out of the house either. They told him how they loved it, and he listened with the same thoughtful calm, as if he were a hundred years old and had heard everything; as if he could never be surprised anymore. He said funny things with a straight face. He played the out-of-tune piano; he said he didn't play well, but they thought he was marvelous. They liked everything, whether it was a little melody by Mendelssohn or something noisy and jazzy. They worked through the songbooks and sheet music.

He taught them to dance from the old records. "I couldn't teach you any of the modern stuff, even if I were any good at it," he said. "We don't have the right music. But I can give you the basic steps." One twin tended the phonograph while the other learned in Billy's arms. He was at once serious and casual, as if teaching girls to dance was nothing new to him, and Jule admired his poise because Roz was so enthusiastic it could have been embarrassing. She might claim she couldn't be romantic about him, but she was certainly enjoying herself.

To be in another man's arms besides Jondy's turned Jule as rigid and heavy as a piece of firewood. "Relax," Billy said gently. "Go with the music. You've got timing; I've heard you singing."

Immediately she fell all over his feet and hers. He didn't lose patience. He was unfailingly and grandfatherly kind. But when her turn was over and Roz floated toward him with open arms, her lips parted in rapture, her eyes glistening behind the golden fringes, Jule thought he must secretly rejoice.

"Practice alone, Jule," he told her, taking Roz into his gentlemanly embrace; she melted into it as if she'd had a dozen lovers. "Then we'll try again. I know you can do it." By herself she was light and easy. With him she turned to wood again, but with a palpitating spirit imprisoned in it.

One silent day when the sun shone dull silver through furry clouds, they walked him from Sunset Cove up into the woods to the pavement and the oaks. There was thin snow on the dead bracken, chickadees and woodpeckers were busy among the trees, and the shouts of crows echoed in the preternatural stillness before a storm.

He listened without a word to the story. Roz left out nothing and Jule wished she wouldn't run on so; if Billy B. stayed another two weeks there would be no secrets left. It was going to be bad enough when he was gone.

"It's a fabulous yarn," he said. "I've never heard it before. I'll ask my father if he knows what happened to them all."

At meals he accommodated himself to Mummie's atmosphere as if there were nothing strange in sitting at the table twice a day with this silent monolith of a woman. He kept Jondy talking, and freely answered Jondy's questions about himself and various members of the family whom Jondy had known, or knew about. He always complimented Mummie on the meal, and paid no more attention to the girls at these times than ordinary manners called for. They went along with this, and while they were doing chores in Mummie's presence Roz would drop remarks about his being conceited, or stupid, and she did it so well that Mummie had no idea they rushed to him as soon as they got out of the house.

After he had gone, it was as bad as Jule had expected. The only good thing was that Mummie relaxed, if that was the word for it. If Jondy was going out to haul, a long day's work in winter because the men went so far to their traps, the girls could often take a lunch and stay away all day. Up in the main house they practiced their dance steps, and talked endlessly about Billy B., about the way he walked, or held his head, or smiled; they recalled every little detail of what he did and said.

A letter arrived from his mother, thanking Mummie and Jondy. A package arrived from him. There was some special Dutch tobacco and a meerschaum pipe for Jondy, who had once said he'd always wanted one; expensive cologne and powder for Mummie.

Mummie looked at her gift without any visible reaction, and later the package disappeared. Jondy was childishly pleased and touched by the pipe, but he never smoked it in the house and not outside either, as far as the girls could tell. They had rushed their gift-wrapped boxes up to their room before Mummie could confiscate them, which she was quite likely to do even if she couldn't drown them like kittens.

They tried on their sweaters. "Well, he noticed *something*," Roz said. "The sizes are perfect." Hers was the exact cerulean of her eyes, and made them almost too vivid to be believed. Jule's was a soft dull rose which reflected into her cheeks. "And he knew what was perfect for you!" Roz said, as if astonished that Bill would have looked so closely at Jule when Roz was around.

Once in a while they got postcards with pictures of MIT and Boston, which Jondy sneaked to them outside the house when they met him at the wharf to wheel up the groceries. Bill always wrote, "I'll be seeing you," and they clung to that.

They were seventeen early in April. One day in the late spring, when Jondy was hauling and Mummie was in profound silence, they took the dory and went out fishing. They rowed out of the cove to a spot where they had often had good luck last autumn with pollock and mackerel. They were in sight of the house, but fishing was an allowed occupation and it helped out on the menu. Now there were green and white buoys in the area, and two boys in a much bigger, heavier dory than theirs, with an outboard motor, arrived on the scene to haul. Jule glanced nervously toward the house; Roz, pretending to concentrate on lowering her hook to the correct depth, looked pleased with herself. One of the boys, much taller now, was clearly one of those for whom Roz had suffered the bloody nose that day.

"What if they start talking to us?" Jule whispered.

"Speech is free." Roz was clearly hoping.

Jule's stomach squirmed. She admired but feared Roz's recklessness. It had been quite a while since she'd had one of those terrifying visions of killing Mummie. Billy B.'s entrance from the outside world and the promise of his return had released a little pressure.

As she'd expected and feared, the dory glided slowly toward them over the calm water. The boy they recognized had thick curly yellow hair bursting out from under his cap; he looked like the Dutch doll in a Benedict girl's bedroom. The other had a wispy black beard and straggling hair, a thin dark face, and sunglasses.

"Hi!" he called.

Jule answered unwillingly and leaned over the side as if she had a bite. Roz looked around with spritely surprise. "Oh, hello!"

"You girls ever go to the dances?" the blond asked at once. "No, I guess not. Who's he saving you for? Himself?"

"That's rotten!" Roz snapped at him.

"Hey, keep your cool! I like Jondy all right. He's a nice little guy. He sells his lobsters to my old man. But what do they keep you two locked up for? *Strict* is one thing, but you don't even go to school."

Jule said at once, "We're being educated at home."

"They're trying to keep us virgins," said Roz solemnly. "Then they can make better marriages for us. What with the Benedict connections and all."

"Ayuh, we get the picture," said the bearded one. "They're scared you'll be corrupted. Get into drugs and liquor and whoring around. So they same as keep you in prison. Jesus, what century do they think this is, anyway?"

"Which one of you gets Bill Benedict?" asked the Dutch boy.

Roz laughed. "He's not for *me!*"

"Hey, is he gay?"

"He can be fun," said Jule.

"That isn't what I meant. Wow, you girls are really sheltered. You don't even have TV, do you? If you did, you'd know about the gays. The queers. Pansies. Fairies. Fruit-cakes."

The girls stared at him like intelligent dogs trying to com-prehend a new sound. He and the other boy exchanged in-credulous looks, then the bearded one said, with surprising delicacy, "Some guys like men better than women. I mean, they fall in love with them."

"Homosexuals, you mean," said Jule loftily. "I don't know if Bill is one. I don't care."

"Well, you don't have much to go by, do you?" asked the blond.

"Hey, I hate like hell to break this up," said his friend, "but I have to get ashore and clean up and go to the hospital this afternoon. My mother's just had her appendix out. They had to rush her uptown yesterday," he told the girls. "Sirens going and everything. More damn fun. She never felt so im-portant in her life."

"Hey, we'll see you two around, I hope," said the Dutch boy. "Why don't you just keep rowing across to Port George some day? If I see you I'll give you a tow in." He grinned. "Buy you an ice cream if you won't have a beer."

"We may take you up on that sooner than you think," said Roz. The bigger dory circled away from them in a roar of engine and rush of bubbling white water, and streaked off to-ward the mainland. The girls' dory rocked gently in the wake.

"I just might," Roz said thoughtfully, watching. "And once I stepped on the mainland I'd be gone so fast, and hide out so well, that all the police in Maine couldn't find me. If she dared to call the police, that is."

"Why wouldn't she?" Jule asked. "She'd dare anything. Besides, we're still under age."

10

THE GIRLS FISHED until they had a good batch of small pollock to fry, then Jule took the oars to row them back to the cove.

"I could fake appendicitis," Roz said suddenly. "They'd have to send me off, then."

"She'd probably dose you with Epsom salts first."

Roz looked shocked. "That could kill me if I really had appendicitis."

"So—if you survived—she'd know you were lying. It's like throwing those poor old women into the water. If they drowned it proved they weren't witches; if they didn't drown, they were burned to death. You'll spend the summer up in your room. And me with you most of the time," she added gloomily.

"Epsom salts nearly kill me anyway," said Roz. "Remember the last time? Maybe I'll take the chance and act out even more agony. Really scare them."

"Try a toothache," Jule suggested, enjoying her rowing. "We haven't had our teeth looked at since Landfall." They'd been checked regularly at the yearly dental clinic held aboard the Sea Coast Mission boat. "She can't give you salts for *that*. She wouldn't go with you; Jondy would have to get a taxi and take you to Limerock, and you could get away from him with no trouble at all."

"You'd come with me, wouldn't you? If we could work it?"

"Can you see her letting *me* go?"

"Oh, well," Roz said on a sigh, which could mean she'd given up the idea or was resigned to leaving Jule behind.

They tied up the dory and washed her down, put her on the haul-off, and went out onto a flat ledge to clean their fish. Stroked by the sun, the water glistening and restless at their feet, they were like young cats at rest, without premonitions. The hungry gulls hovered around them, sometimes swooping so close that their wings caused a rush of air on their faces.

Jule chanted, " 'All ye as a wind shall go by,
As a fire shall ye pass and be past;
Ye' are Gods, and behold, ye shall die,
and the waves be upon you at last' "

Roz lifted her head and stared at her. "Look at the gooseflesh." She held out her arm.

"Swinburne. I love him. Billy B. says I'll outgrow him but I don't think so."

The hopelessness she usually felt when Roz talked about eighteen and freedom was dimmed to invisibility. It almost seemed possible this day that on the morning of their eighteenth birthday they would walk downstairs with their packed suitcases, and announce that they were leaving. Either Jondy could take them or they would row; they would write when they were settled. How simple it all was, and how very sweet.

They came into the kitchen now to find Mummie kneading bread at the kitchen table. The yeasty smell was good. The stare she turned on them was not.

"I've been watching you," she said. There was a thickness in her voice, and an ugly purplish red blotched her usual pallor. "A pair of tramps. That dory comes ashore on the next high tide and stays there. *For good.*"

"We're not tramps!" Jule's outburst surprised herself. "We didn't say or do a wrong thing!"

"Shut up, Jule," Roz said roughly. "It takes one to know one—or so I hear."

"And what does *that* mean?" Mummie's fists stopped pummeling the resistant dough.

"Two years ago you called us sluts and harlots and bloodied my nose. Why did you think that of us then, and why now? What's in your mind that's so dirty it has to come out like that?"

The ugly color left; the fleshy cheekbones were fishbelly white. Her eyes, Jule saw as one sees details in such moments, were swollen and glassy, veined with red.

Roz turned and ran, and Jule dropped the bucket of fish and ran after her. Passing the shed she saw Roz ahead, running diagonally across the newly green field toward the strip of western woods. She found Roz sitting under one of the great old pines, with her knees hugged tight to her chest, her eyes wildly glittering. "Did you *see* her?" she gloated. "I struck a nerve, didn't I? Now I know what she was, a prostitute! *A whore!* How do you suppose she ever got Jondy? Can you imagine *him* ever visiting a house like that? Talk about a lamb being led to the slaughter!"

She rocked with laughter, and an unseen heron took off with a startled squawk.

Jule crouched, her fingers digging in pine needles. "We can't go back to the house again till Jondy comes. And even then—my God, Roz, that was a terrible thing to say! She'll half kill you for it."

"I'll be ready for her this time. I'm a lot bigger now."

But Mummie was still bigger, and she could be maddened enough to go too far. I'll have to help Roz, she thought, a hideous chill spreading from her stomach out into her limbs.

This is how death would come; you were all at once tossed into the breakers, and no escape.

"Jule, you're feather-white," Roz said calmly. "Who knows, she may have dropped dead by the time we get back. Oh, God, wouldn't it be pure bliss? Let's concentrate on it." She leaned back against the ancient trunk and shut her eyes with a sigh.

Jule lay limply on the warm needles. The sun came down through the interlaced boughs in a shower of gold.

> *Now lies the Earth all Danäe to the stars,*
> *And all thy heart lies open unto me . . .*

This was love. Not for her, but she would always know what it was. Not for her. She saw herself as an eccentric, solitary, old woman, with no one left to know the young girl who still lived inside her.

They heard Jondy's boat come, waited a while, and then went back, half drugged with the stupor of relaxation that had come upon them after all the fury and fear. "If she lifts a hand against me this time," Roz said, yawning, "she'll be sorry."

"We all will be," Jule said.

Jondy was splitting kindling outside the woodshed and he grinned at them like a happy boy.

"I've got a nice surprise for you," he said. Jule went open-mouthed with shock until she realized he wouldn't announce Mummie's death quite like that.

"What?" asked Roz. "More kittens? Maybe this time she'll wring their necks; more fun than drowning them."

"Oh, Roz, honey," he said reproachfully. He felt in his hip pocket and brought out a postcard. "It's from Bill Benedict. He's coming."

Roz ascended instantly to heights of glory. But Jule noticed that the dory was in again and pulled up high on the beach.

So he'd been given the Word, and he was glad to be able to tell them something they'd want to hear. "Does she know about him?" she asked.

"Not yet. She wasn't feeling too well. She's taken a couple of her nerve pills and she's sleeping." That was a relief. "She wants you girls to put the bread in the oven when it rises enough."

The bread was baked and the girls were frying the pollock for supper by the time Mummie came forth from her room. Jondy at once gave her the news about Bill, and this must have been blow enough to keep her from taking up the earlier scene with the girls.

There was absolutely nothing she could do about a Benedict coming to his own property.

11

HE CAME AT THE END OF JUNE, and would
be there for a month at least. He had changed in six months;
he was bigger than they'd remembered, he seemed years
more mature. He had also brought a friend with him. They
were going to do their own housekeeping, and to accomplish
some serious work.

"But we'll have plenty of time to talk," he told the girls,
who helped carry their dunnage up the hill. "I brought some
new records, and a radio you can keep up here, and a batch
of books we'll leave behind, too. God, you two have grown!
Grown *up*, really." He looked at Roz when he said that, and
she smiled with candid pride.

"Yep. They tried keeping us in barrels and feeding us
through the bungholes, but it just wouldn't work."

Tony was good-looking like the men in the ads. He had a
ravishing smile, and charming manners, but Jule suspected
that Billy B. had told him enough so that even Roz's best efforts, which were very good indeed, weren't going to get her
anywhere.

"Do you think they're gay?" Roz asked on the way down
the green hillside twinkling with daisies. "Tony doesn't react
to me."

"I hate using the word 'gay' like that. It ruins it. Why
don't you use the right one? Anyway, I don't care what Billy
B. is. If he had one of those operations and showed up here

with bosoms and false eyelashes and long hair like Alice in Wonderland, I wouldn't care. He'd still be our friend."

"That long face of his and the big ears!" Roz doubled up. "Our friend Bettina Benedict. Well, I'm glad he brought a boyfriend instead of a girl."

One day Billy B. asked if the girls could go along to Port George when Jondy took them to get more supplies, and Mummie, taken by surprise at his ignorance and impertinence, waited so long to answer that for an incredible moment Jule thought she was going to say yes. Then she said, rather grandly, "I think not, Mr. Benedict."

The dory was launched, and the girls were invited to go fishing. Again, it was not allowed.

But Jule and Roz managed, as they had before. Mummie still had to have a daily nap, and never knew that on rainy days Tony taught them the new dances or that they sat by the library fire with mugs of hot chocolate and talked or played cards; or that Billy B. taught Jule to play chess while Roz went avidly through a stack of magazines he brought them from Port George, and Tony typed two-fingered, smoking his pipe and looking intellectual as well as handsome. There was a cozy domesticity about those times which the girls had never known before in their lives.

Jondy knew where they were, but it was never openly mentioned. "The Benedicts were always gentlemen," he was fond of saying.

Going ostensibly to pick wild strawberries, the girls spent an afternoon at Sunset Cove swimming with the boys. They still didn't have suits, but had worn their old shorts and blouses out of the house, under jeans and shirts.

Jule still felt about fifteen in terms of growth, but knew she was definitely improving. After the first few minutes when she was the only self-conscious one she began to feel perfectly happy in the water. Billy told them they swam the way loons walked. "My aesthetic sensitivities are outraged," he said. "Come on, Jule, I'll start on you."

"What about *me*?" Roz said to Tony. In her brief, clinging clothes she preened in the sun as innocently as a bird.

"You'll do fine," said Tony drily. "You'll always do just fine. You're a natural."

"A natural what?" she pestered him.

"Oh, you have a number of options." He was interested in Indian artifacts and had found a shell-studded area at the head of the beach. He sat on his heels and began scraping at it with a trowel. When Billy B. and Jule came ashore, Roz was telling the mansion story to Tony's broad brown back.

"Where are my glasses?" Billy demanded. "Roz, if you've stepped on them I swear I'll put you on a leash for a seeing-eye dog."

"That would be fine if it meant I could go somewhere," said Roz. "Did you ask your father if the colonel had any other children, and what happened to them?"

He got beer from the styrofoam cooler, and offered cans of iced tea to the girls.

"There was always a landing here," he said. "The Indians camped here because of the good shelter and the nearby springs. Then it was the first harbor and anchorage for the men who drove the Indians away. And there was a Colonel Benedict, and an avenue of oaks, and a granite road up the middle. *But—*"

Roz said belligerently, "But what?"

Studying his can of beer he said, "I hate to wreck what has to be the biggest, most complicated, multidimensional saga since *The Lord of the Rings*, but even you two princesses in a tower have to face reality some of the time. There was no mansion. Colonel Marcus Aurelius Benedict never built a house, because he could neither drain nor fill up that swamp."

Roz opened her mouth, but she could not speak. Jule felt

shock where she always did, in her stomach. Cruel, cruel! she cried inside. We had so little, why did you have to take that?

He said quickly to her, as if he'd heard, "If I thought that all you'd ever have would be this life, I'd never have told you the truth."

She looked into his bright, light eyes. "What else?" she asked. It could have meant, What else will I have? or What else is the story? He answered the second.

"He never built a house on the island. He held onto it, and he had people farming it, and there was a prosperous fish business. But he lived out his life in Damariscotta. To make a long story short, it was a grandson who came here after the Civil War, when the family was getting rich in one way or another, some of them not too admirable, and built a summer place. It was small at first, but they kept adding to it until it became the big house, called with great lack of originality 'The Ledges.' At one time when there was more than the usual amount of nuttiness raging through the family my grandfather suggested calling it the Booby Hatch, but they wouldn't even dignify that with a vote."

Tony chuckled. Roz was peony-red. Her eyes when they were filled with tears were an even more intense blue. "But Jondy told us all about it! How this Port George man disappeared at the same time as the baby and the nurse, and—"

Billy B. said gently, "Jondy spun you a good yarn. He wanted to entertain you and he did."

"Hey!" Tony was holding something up. "What a little gem! It's a perfect crescent drill! My God, I was *meant* to find this. It was waiting here for me for a couple of hundred years, maybe more. The last hand that held this was an Indian hand. Can you imagine it?"

Roz held his hand and crouched over it, admiring the drill, breathing softly on his arm.

"I thought we knew all there was to know about this island," Jule said, "but part of what we knew wasn't true, and something important like this we missed altogether."

She was sad, angry, and ashamed of herself as a kind of freak. She felt suddenly exposed.

"Cheer up," Billy B. said. "Forget the fairy tales. Life is better."

"Even ours?" Roz demanded. Tony withdrew his hand, murmuring something about another beer.

"Even yours," Billy B. said kindly. "What it's going to be someday."

"I'll have a beer, please," Roz said defiantly.

"Even if debauching jail bait was my thing I still wouldn't send you home with beer on your breath."

"One taste of beer doesn't constitute a debauch, does it?" Roz asked. "It's not going to topple us into the deepest pits of iniquity."

"Listen to that," Tony said in amazement. "You two kids can sure talk up a storm. At least Roz does. Jule just sits there looking deep. 'Her eyes were deeper than the depths of waters stilled at even.'"

"The Blessed Damozel," said Roz, rather smugly. "That's you, Jule."

"Make no mistake about it, these kids are well-educated in a very weird way," Billy said. "They've never been to the movies or watched television, but they've read Ibsen and Shaw, and can give you Shakespeare and the Bible by the yard. As well as a lot of tripe."

Roz was enjoying herself but Jule had again that sense of exposure as a freak. "We've got to get some strawberries and go home."

"They're so thick in the house meadow we'll get a couple of quarts in no time," said Roz. But Jule gathered up her clothes, and Roz, sighing, prepared to follow her.

As they walked away over the rocks they heard Tony say, "I still can't believe they're real."

"You should meet their mother," said Billy B., and then went suddenly silent as he realized he might have been overheard.

12

TONY WAS ENGAGED to a classmate in medical school, and Billy received letters and cards from a number of females. Roz read the postcards. "They all sign 'Love,' " she said, annoyed. "It can't really mean that. If you took it seriously you'd think Billy B. was a real heartbreaker, and that can't be so."

"Why can't it?" asked Jule.

"He's nothing like any of the lovers we read about."

"I don't think anybody in the world *is*."

Mummie, as usual unpleasantly stimulated by the presence of aliens, was very much with them for the month the boys were there. She never realized how fast the girls picked their berry quota after spending a couple of hours trailing around behind the boys. Once she said, "It took you long enough to fill your pails," and Roz said, "We had to climb all over the place to get them. There weren't an awful lot in one place. Look at us, from crawling over blowdowns." They'd deliberately taken a hard route home, to collect scratches on their arms and pitch on their clothes.

The wild strawberries went by, and the raspberries began. The afternoons seemed to last forever, and still the month was no longer than a sigh. But while it lasted they breathed the air of hope, because Billy B. behaved as if some day soon this phase of their existence would come to an end as a matter of course.

"Now look, you two, when you're on your own you'll need high school diplomas just to give you a start. I'll find out what you'll need for the equivalency exams, and send you the books. You're to set yourselves regular study hours, and absorb those books the way you've absorbed some of the trash in this house." He looked sternly at Roz, who saluted.

"Yes, *sir!*"

Now tell us how we're supposed to manage this around Mummie, Jule thought, but she didn't say it aloud for fear of damaging the fragile and iridescent tissue of these days.

It was a kind of miracle, that Mummie never suspected what was going on. If Jondy did, he kept the secret.

Mummie and Jondy never talked together in the girls' presence as Jule imagined ordinary parents did. Jondy rambled on for the girls' benefit and his own about what he saw when he was hauling, and repeated his conversations with Ned Peabody when he sold his lobsters. Sometimes he simply chattered, as if he couldn't bear her great marmoreal silence.

Yet they spoke in their room, and Roz tried to listen at the door. "They must talk about themselves!" she said to Jule, bewildered and indignant. "They *must* talk about their life before us." But she caught only meaningless fragments.

Before us, Jule would repeat to herself as an incantation to produce enlightenment. Nothing ever came of it. She clung to the illogical but somehow life-saving statement, *She is not my mother. She can't be.*

These words made her a house in which she could dwell hidden like the chambered nautilus or the least of the periwinkles on the beach, those who were too small to be gathered and boiled in a can.

There was one phenomenon. Sometimes Mummie *hummed.* It had made them uneasy even when they were young, because she could break off in midmeasure to ask a dreadful question or deliver an ultimatum. But as they grew older they tried to find clues in the tunes. What music wreathed its way through the bosky mazes of her brain? Certainly none of the tunes that Jondy whistled, or the songs he taught them while they were baiting up.

Roz changed Mummie from a prostitute to a courtesan, a word she dearly loved; then to an actress, then to a minister's daughter, who had met Jondy when he was in the army.

"With someone like him, wanting so much to please her, she wouldn't have to worry about one of those domineering males like Petruchio or Elizabeth Barrett's father. Maybe her father the minister was one."

She was very satisfied with her theory. She felt it explained the absence of evidence. "They cast her off so she cast *them* off. She has no past; her life began when she took up with Jondy and then had us. If she lets us go, it's letting go of her life. How's that for a novel? She broods about the injustices done her. She's got that unforgiving nature. Thank God we didn't inherit that, we have Jondy's optimism instead—"

"His *what*?" Jule scoffed. "He's no optimist. He just goes on smiling because he doesn't know what to do. Besides, he escapes every day. He can stand to come back at night because he knows he'll be out there tomorrow as long as it's good weather."

Roz ignored that. "But we've got her passion and her willpower. She cast off her loved ones, and we'll cast *her* off when the time comes. She's afraid of it, and that's why we moved away from Landfall. She thinks she can hold us here by sheer magnetism. As it was in the beginning, is now and ever shall be. World without end. Amen."

"Don't!" said Jule with a shudder. "You're freezing me.

Because there's only one way she could hold us here, world without end, isn't there?"

Roz's triumphant grin disappeared. "She's not that crazy," she whispered.

"How do you know?" asked Jule.

13

THE TIME APPROACHED for the boys to leave the island for the scintillating planet Earth. "We're exiles on a lost star in outer space," Roz said mournfully.

"Well, now that the space shuttle's working I'll be back," Billy B. said. He gave them brotherly kisses on their foreheads. Roz threw her arms around him and they hugged, then he came to Jule and drew her into his embrace because she was too shy to make it on her own. This was their last meeting before their formal departure from the wharf with Jondy, and Mummie a white mask at the kitchen window.

He was going to take a year off before graduate school and go to India and Nepal, but he'd see about their high school equivalency exams before he left. They promised him they would work, Roz with tears twinkling beautifully on her lashes, Jule feeling a chill in her bones, a premonition that they would never meet again because he would die horribly in India, if not on the way there or back.

Since the Benedicts were always gentlemen, he went in to pay his respects to Mummie. How she reacted, the girls didn't know. They stayed at the wharf, Roz joking with Tony in despairing giddiness, Jule iced with loneliness in the hot August sun.

When the boys had gone, life died on the vine as if a killing frost had struck it overnight. The month had bristled with possibilities but within a week these were unrecognizable in death. Billy B. had believed in them all, but when you belonged to the outside, Jule thought, you were as free to believe anything as you were free to go anywhere.

Now the girls fought because Roz insisted on talking as if escape were a sure thing. "I am positive that the day we are eighteen I am going to have everything packed and walk out of this house forever."

"She can stand in the doorway, and you can't budge her, and you'll be picking yourself up with a bloody nose again. And maybe a fractured skull if you hit the stove hard enough."

"And what will *you* be doing? Sniveling in the corner? 'Dear Mummie, I'll do anything you want as long as you don't hit me!' "

Jule slapped her, and she flew back at Jule. They rolled over and over in the grass, trying to punch and pinch, gasping inarticulate threats. They gave up simultaneously and lay side by side panting, looking up at the sky and the gulls floating on the wind. "I'll never snivel for her. *Never!*" Jule said fiercely. "I know we've got to get away or die, but I just can't see it happening the way you said. And you don't see it that way either, if you're honest about it."

Two weeks went by with no word from Billy B. They came back late one afternoon with blueberries, walking slowly, chewing abstractedly on sweet grass. Jondy's boat was beside the wharf, a wonderfully reviving sight. He always left Billy B.'s cards and letters in the fish house, including little surprises from him, too, so they could pick them up without being seen from the house.

They ran down there now, fiery with hope. But there was nothing in the fish house, and they were more dejected than before. Neither would put words to the thought that Billy B. had really forgotten them, and they were lost in outer space for sure.

The kitchen was stifling because Mummie had decided to do some baking in late afternoon. There were books strewn on the kitchen table amid packing materials; there were also tablets of paper, notebooks, pens, and pencils. Jule saw the display first with the rapture of a small child beholding a lighted Christmas tree, but rapture changed instantly to nauseated dismay. Jondy said something from across the room but she didn't look at him. Mummie stood behind the table, holding one of the books open in floury hands.

"Disgusting," she said. "Filthy." She slammed the book shut. It was a biology textbook. She went to the stove, lifted a lid from the snapping flames and began ripping pages out and putting them in the fire.

Jule sprang forward and a big arm barred her way. She threw herself against it and would have wildly bitten it if Roz hadn't pulled her back.

"*Beatrice,*" Jondy whispered. The flames roared up. Everything went into them. Math, English, History. Then the work materials. Roz, sobbing with rage, headed for the door, dragging Jule with her, but Mummie's voice stopped her short, from years of conditioning. The roaring in Jule's ears was not all from the fire. She knew that she had the strength to fly at the woman's throat and drive hard fists into the solid flesh until she forced a grunt of pain from those close-set gray lips. She'd have forced the woman down by the relentless pressure of thumbs on the windpipe, and the gasps would be sweeter than any bird song she'd ever heard.

But Jondy and Roz wouldn't let her do it.

There was all at once silence. The lid was back on the stove, and the last two pies were baked by the fires of cremation.

Then Mummie brought out from her room a box of stationery, pale blue with a gold B (Jule's unimaginative choice of a Mother's Day gift) and sat down to write a letter. The girls were forbidden to sit, or to lean against anything. Pins and needles came into Jule's legs, the skin began itching. She had a powerful desire to go to the bathroom and was afraid anything now would jolt the water loose. Jondy sat huddled in his chair, looking very dried up. After her tears, Roz was a statue with fixed blue stones for eyes.

Mummie now read aloud without inflection what she had written. She had told Mr. William Benedict that she had destroyed what he had sent, that she would destroy anything that he sent in future, and he was not to communicate with her daughters in any way, shape, or manner; or she would be forced to notify his father about what had taken place with her daughters.

"Beatrice," Jondy pleaded, unnoticed.

"Do you think they'd believe anything you said about their son?" Roz asked contemptuously.

"The Benedicts are always gentlemen," Jondy said. The words trembled.

"I know all about *gentlemen*," Mummie said.

"What will happen," said Roz, "is that Jondy gets fired. Where will we move the prison then? Out onto the Seal Ledges? Nothing but seals and gulls to corrupt us there. It gets pretty wet at high tide, but Jondy will be so close to his traps he can save gas." She was backing toward the door, feeling behind her for the knob, and she was out through the entry before Mummie could get around the table. "I'll never come back!" Roz shouted, on the wing.

Mummie turned on Jule. "Wipe that insolence off your face before I do it for you. And get out. If your sister touches that boat I'll hold you responsible."

Jule ran down to the boat with the glorious sensation that nothing could keep her from taking off like a gull over the water when she reached the end of the wharf. Roz would be trying to start Jondy's engine, and all she knew was that she was going too. Nothing mattered, whatever they'd do when they touched the mainland, where they would go, how they would answer questions, just as long as they went *now*.

The cove, the wharf, and Jondy's boat lay caught in silence like a scene in a paperweight. A gull, undisturbed until now, lifted off from the bow of the boat.

Jule ran again, dashed into the toilet and out across to the trees. Inside their shade she stopped and tried to call, but her throat was so dry only a croak came. Sweating and queasy, she forced herself to walk on through the woods. At the top of the long rise she came out to the orchard where the apples on the ground gave off a cidery sweetness in the late afternoon heat. They were to have kept their schoolbooks in the big house, to do their studying at the big library table. Jondy would have known about it eventually, when he inspected the house to make it ready for winter, but he'd never have told on them.

But he *had*. He had brought the package to Mummie. Jule had known he was timid and a coward, but not that he was a traitor.

She walked through the rooms from back to front, hearing only the soft pad of her sneakers and the faint creaks and clicks of an old house. Sun lay peacefully on faded carpets and bare floors. It shouldn't have felt like a haunted house but it did. Billy B. would be out of their lives forever now. She didn't believe that Jondy would be fired, he was too responsible a caretaker, but they'd say his wife was crazy, and that if any of the family went to the island they must shun those girls as if they carried the plague. Even Billy B. could have decided already that they were a lost cause.

She went out onto the front veranda, leaving the door open behind her. The sea was delphinium blue in the late afternoon; there were a few sails on the horizon, a herring carrier going to the west, lobster boats heading in toward Port George. Nearer, a small fast red runabout with a big engine was streaking through the passage between the southwesterly end of the island and a spatter of ledges.

There were three people aboard. Jule ran in for the binoculars on the hall table, and focused them with trembling fingers.

Roz was one of the three. She was sitting in the stern beside the boy running the engine, and even from this distance you could tell she was laughing.

Jule ran back into the house again for something to wave; she snatched an old red sweater and went out and climbed up on the wide railing they sometimes walked like a tightrope. Holding onto a post, she waved the sweater. If Roz looked up at the house she'd see her, and certainly send the boys in to the rocks to pick her up.

But before they came abreast they made a sudden sharp turn away from the island toward the east and disappeared among the islands lying off there.

Roz had escaped. As quickly as that, she had gone.

Jule got down carefully from the railing. She felt hollowed out in skull, chest, belly, legs. Full of echoes. *She was alone.* She sagged on the steps, still holding the sweater. Mechanically she wrapped it around her.

After a time she got up, moving cautiously because of the empty head she was carrying. Part of her innards had returned, but her legs still felt strange and she was cold. The sun had left the veranda, it would be shining on Sunset Cove and slanting through the oaks to the buried granite road that led to nowhere.

All the places where she had ever been on the island now led to nowhere because Roz was gone.

She went into the house, into the library where the sun

still came in, and the spectre of Tony's tobacco was vaguely reassuring. She lay down on the leather sofa before the cold fireplace, pulled up the Hudson's Bay blanket, shivered for a while, and fell asleep.

14

SHE WAS THE RAGGEDY ANN DOLL left by some long-ago Benedict child, and Nana the dog nurse in *Peter Pan* was violently shaking her. At the same time the beast was saying clearly around a mouthful of Jule–Raggedy Ann, "My God! My God!"

Nana turned out to be Roz. "Are you *sick*? Did she *beat* you?" She tried to pull off the blanket to look for bruises.

"No to everything," said Jule, groggy and aggrieved. "I saw you in that boat. I kept waving but you never gave me a look. Never gave me a *thought*, did you? I thought you'd gone for good."

"I would be, if I'd made it to Port George."

Roz collapsed on the sofa, nearly breaking Jule's foot. Jule squawked and drew her knees up to her chest. Roz hunched over, staring at the hearth rug. "I found them down in Thistle Cove, and they look just like ordinary kids, you know. Summer people." She shrugged. "They asked some questions about the island and I answered, and then I asked them to take me to Port George." She fell into a brooding silence. Jule gave her a hard poke with her foot.

"Hurry up. What happened?"

"They said they had to stop at a cottage on Eagle Island for something, and they asked me if I wanted to come ashore. Well, I'd never been on the place, so I said yes. It turns out they thought I was willing. You know what I mean. When they found out I wasn't, I think they were going to rape me." She lifted a shaking hand. "Look at *that!*" she said. "I'm still scared. One kept trying to get around to grab me from behind. I must have had the strength of desperation," she said dramatically. "I got him in the shins with my heel and the other one I kicked in the crotch and disabled him. The limping one brought me back. He wouldn't take me to Port George. I guess he thought he was getting even." She gave Jule a cynical grin. "End of adventure. The Short Unhappy Escape of Roz Saunders. Wouldn't you know I'd pick a couple of apprentice rapists out of all the males on this bay?"

"I wonder if he's still doubled up over there," Jule said. "If he has to go to a doctor I wonder what he'll say. A horse kicked him, maybe. Do you suppose he's ruined for life?"

"I hope so. I wish I could've got the other one too, but I had to have somebody to run the boat. I don't know enough about outboards," she admitted modestly. "If I did, I've have gone to Port George like lightning."

"*Then* what?"

"I'd have left the boat at some wharf, and borrowed some change from Mr. Peabody for telephone calls, and walked up the road and disappeared."

"How would you disappear?"

"Start walking toward Limerock, get a ride with somebody who looked safe, a woman or a girl. I'd get them to help me telephone. I'd throw myself on their mercy." She assumed an appealing expression. "I'd say 'I've never made a telephone call in my life, and I have to reach a William Penn Benedict in West Newton, Massachusetts. It's a matter of life and death!' "

"What could he do, way up there? If he hasn't gone yet?" Jule was fascinated in spite of resenting Roz's imaginary freedom.

"I'd say I'd run away and ask what I should do. He knows people around Limerock and Fremont, and he could tell me where to go, and he could call *them*, and tell them about me. I'd be like one of those runaway slaves passed along the Underground Railway." She was quite carried away by the romance of it. "Once I was safe, and well away from here, I'd change my name, and nobody would ever find me again."

Jule must have been looking oddly at her, because Roz suddenly leaned over and gave Jule a pat on the shoulder. "Oh, I'd keep Billy B. informed, and he could tell *you*, and you'd have to run away too. I'd have a good job by then, and a place for us to live."

She bounced up, all her energy restored. "I was so close!" she lamented. "Where would I be now? In heaven! In lovely, enchanting Limerock. It would have worked, I know it! Oh, come on," she said, "I'm starved, and she can't have been sitting there waiting all afternoon with her portable rack and thumbscrews."

"What do you bet?" Jule got up and folded the blanket.

On the way out Roz got a handful of saltines from the pantry and they crunched them hungrily as they went down the meadow slope among the asters and goldenrod of late summer. "Remember, we spent the whole afternoon at Sunset Cove," Roz told her. "Just turn her off in your head the way you can do, and then you won't look guilty. Just stupid."

"Thanks," said Jule. I don't think I can live through many more days of this, she thought. The kittens died by water, the books by fire. What about *us*?

Jondy was sitting on the chopping block, whittling, obviously watching for them. He looked shrunken, as if they had been gone away long enough to grow much taller while he grew old.

He got up to meet them, his face crinkled into the familiar don't-be-too-hard-on-the-old-man grimace. "Well, I guess I really put my foot in it today. I can't tell you how sorry old Jondy is."

Jule hated him like this. He'd said the same thing about the kittens. She began picking at her thumb as if she had a thorn in it.

"How'd it happen, Jondy?" Roz asked him in a cool, adult voice.

"Look, it wasn't so much the books," he said pleadingly. "You know she never cared about you amusing yourselves that way, even if she can't put her own mind on reading. She wasn't always like that." He shook his head at them. "Your mother had a good education."

"Where was that, Jondy?" Jule forgot her thumb.

"That's nothing to do with now."

"Was she a minister's daughter, Jondy?" Jule asked eagerly. "Come on, tell us."

"And then we won't be mad with you any more," Roz said, "for getting our books burned, that Gentleman Billy Benedict paid out his own money for."

"It wasn't the books that set her off, it was what the note said about you getting your high school diplomas. It was like he was conspiring to steal away her babies. She was a wonderful mother to you when you were little, too bad you can't remember it," he said defensively. "Then you started to grow up and she's been in a ferment ever since. Can't you see how it hit her? She thinks it's a wicked nasty world over there." He waved at the mainland. "That's what she's trying to save you from, and she sees him like this serpent."

"In all the books I've read nobody was ever seduced by some man offering her a high school diploma," said Jule.

"Well, maybe you could compare it to the apple off the Tree of Knowledge," Roz suggested.

"Don't be irreverent," said Jondy, flustered. "The Bible's not to joke over."

"Who's joking?"

"Jondy, what do *you* think about us getting an education?" Jule challenged him. "Do you want to keep us here for the rest of your life and hers?"

He was confused, growing redder, his eyes watering. He began swallowing as if his throat were obstructed. Jule couldn't stand it.

"All right, Jondy. All right."

He loosened up at once. "Now, about what went wrong today. I dunno what came over me. I had a queer turn when I was coming into the cove. Blacked out, almost. Nearly rammed the wharf, then I came out of it and straightened her up just in time. Well, it confused me, I guess. Never had anything like that happen to me before. I've been dizzy a couple of times, but I think I almost passed out today." Suddenly his eyes were wildly frightened, and Jule felt the tightening of cramp in her midriff. Roz's hand nervously scratched a nonexistent bite on her cheek. "So I never thought to separate the mail. I'd planned to, but when this thing hit me I just—well, you two weren't here, and I just heaved everything onto the wheelbarrow without giving it a thought."

"Jondy, are you sick?" Jule asked sharply.

"Not now," he said with a quick grin like a tic. "Must have been some funny little kink somewhere. Back of my neck." He rubbed it. "Shut off the circulation. Don't mention it to your mother, she's got enough to worry her."

"But you said you'd been dizzy sometimes," Roz argued. "You'd better see a doctor."

"I can't do that. She'd wonder what I was doing all that while. Listen, forget it, babies, will you? I'm fine now! I just wanted you to know why I did such a fool thing about that parcel of books."

They wanted to forget it. The thought of anything happening to Jondy was ghastly. More confident, now that he had shaken them with his news, he moved between them, put an arm around each waist and squeezed.

"There's my ducklings. Go in now and get your supper. She's asleep. She was so worked up I made her take a couple of her nerve pills."

In bed that night, Jule tried to imagine Mummie bleary and blotched with tears, her flesh shaken with convulsive weeping, and Jondy with an arm around her shoulders holding a glass to her lips. "Come on, love, just for me. Just for Jondy." It was familiar because he'd said it so many times to her and Roz when they were sick.

She sat up in bed. Roz said in annoyance, "What ails you? I was almost asleep."

"I just thought of something. If Jondy dies she may go all to pieces and then we can take charge."

"Do you want Jondy to die?"

"No! *Never*! But if he did—"

"Will you pipe down and go to sleep? Who wants to keep this day going?"

15

AFTER THE DAY the books were burned, when Roz ran away, and Jondy told them about his blackout, a sort of equilibrium slowly returned but it carried the knowledge of an irrevocable change. If there was ever any answer to Mummie's letter, they never knew. Jondy didn't tell them, and he didn't sneak any mail to them now, only his little treats as if they were still children. It occurred to Jule once that he might never have mailed that pale blue envelope, but she wouldn't ask him. It was anguish to imagine Billy B. picturing them studying, quizzing each other, happily planning for their emancipation.

They worried at first about Jondy, but he was so much himself afterward that they convinced themselves the blackout had been a freakish, isolated incident.

Roz had not yet recovered from her experience that day. She was obsessed with the fact that she'd nearly made it to Port George. She went over and over her plans until Jule, her nerves exquisitely raw, flared out at her, "Oh, shut up!"

Roz went into a rage and didn't speak to her for the rest of the day. It was terrible. What if Roz began to be like Mummie and have silences? Jule couldn't rest until she'd coaxed her out of the black mood and showed false enthusiasm for her schemes.

Jondy gave up winter lobstering this year. Traps had to be set so far outside in winter that it wasn't good sense for a man to work alone; he should have someone with him, or travel always in company with another boat. Roz agitated for one of them to go as sternman, herself preferably, but she was graciously willing to take turns with Jule. It didn't work, but they caught the wistful spark in Jondy's eyes as he took in his gear during the heartbreaking Indian summer days.

He still had an escape. "Good day to work in the woods!" he'd say heartily, and the girls went with him, limbing out blowdowns for him to saw into firewood.

When he went to Port George to collect the mail and replenish the supplies, the girls usually had a fight. Everything was getting worse. Jule's dreams of killing or being killed came frequently, while Roz thrashed around in her own dreams, sometimes crying out in incoherent fury.

This year Jondy got the flu just before Christmas. He had always seemed tough and resilient, but not now, and to the girls it was very frightening. Jule remembered the wildness in his eyes when he told them about the blackout.

Mummie took all the care of him. She wouldn't allow the girls anywhere near him.

"The last thing I need is three of you down with it," she said. "If I get it, it won't be until after your father's up, and then he can wait on me. But I won't get it. I don't catch things," she added scornfully.

Mr. Peabody brought over the turkey and the mail-order parcels, but Jondy was so sick then that Christmas was treated as an ordinary day. The girls spent the afternoon at the main house, reading, playing records, eating what remained of the tinned delicacies the boys had left for them. A light snow fell and they coasted home in it at dusk. Behind the closed bedroom door Jondy might not have existed, they hadn't seen him for so long.

Waking in the night, straining to hear sounds downstairs, Jule wondered if Jondy was dying right now, or if he had already died while Mummie slept on the sitting room couch. Shivering, she waited for daylight, while Roz muttered and turned in her sleep. Jule kept remembering her own words. *If Jondy dies, then Mummie will go to pieces, and then we can take charge.*

She didn't believe that now. Mummie was so much in charge you couldn't possibly imagine anyone, least of all themselves, taking charge of her.

When in the morning she found out that Jondy was still alive, her relief was so great that for a while she was actually happy, a phenomenon that had last occurred back in July.

New Year's Day was fine and mild, and they took a lunch and went to Lindisfarne. The mansion had become so real to them that even for Billy B. to tell them it had never existed couldn't wipe it and all its people out. For a long while they hadn't been near the place, lest the loss would have hit them too dreadful a blow, but now they found it a refuge. Chickadees and little woodpeckers filled the woods with life, and sun shone where it could never reach when the oaks were in leaf. They did not want ever to leave.

But when they did, so late in the day that the stars were coming out, Jondy was sitting in his chair in the kitchen, dressed and shaved. "Happy New Year!" he greeted them in a weak but cheerful voice. They rushed to hug and kiss him, while Mummie rocked, smiling.

His convalescence was a long drawn-out process. There were weeks of high wind after the quiet spell, but they had plenty of supplies laid in. It was well into January when Ned Peabody came across one afternoon, while the weather had quieted down again to prepare for a fresh storm. He brought the mail, and the girls gazed greedily at the plastic-bound packet on the table, wishing they'd gotten it away from him at the shore. What if Billy B. had written?

He'd also brought some newspapers, a bag of Red De-

licious apples from his cellar, and his wife had sent a fruit-
cake, and a batch of new magazines to the girls; at least they
got these before Mummie could. Roz rushed them upstairs,
and came down looking smug.

Mummie was courteous in a dignified, remote fashion,
making the coffee herself. Peabody was a paunchy man with a
broad windburned face and a kindly smile. He sat back in his
chair and looked at the girls with candid pleasure. "You two
are getting to be real young ladies, and a pair of beauties. I
dunno but what you're doing the right thing, educating these
girls at home, Mrs. Saunders," he said. "You being a teacher,
you can do it. I've still got one in high school, and what's going on up there you wouldn't believe."

Jule, seeing Jondy's eyes sliding away from hers, realized
that he'd had to give some explanation of his unusual household arrangements. Roz winked at her.

Whenever Mr. Peabody spoke to Jondy his smile became
forced, or disappeared for an instant, and suddenly Jule saw
Jondy with his eyes: a meager little man with ugly bluish
shadows under his eyes, and tremulous hands. Yet it had
been over a month since he'd been sick.

"That bug is darned hard to get rid of," Mr. Peabody said.
"Folks been lying around half the winter. They get relapses,
and this virus leaves some people anemic. Now, Jondy, it's
flat calm this afternoon and going to stay so till the new blow
gets here. How about I take you across and drive you up to
Doc Partridge in Williston? He'll likely give you a pre-
scription for some special vitamins."

"Go on, Dad!" Roz urged. Ignoring Mummie's gelid gaze,
Jule joined in. "Please go, Dad." They hardly ever called him
that, and he visibly quickened at the sound of the word.

Mummie spoke. "There's no need of it, he's eating more
every day, and he just needs time. You needn't take the
trouble."

But Mr. Peabody was not conditioned to making the correct response. "It'll be no trouble, Mrs. Saunders. Would you like to go, too?"

"No." She turned her face away and stared out the window. Unseeing, Jule was sure. The girls got their father's warmest outdoor clothes. "Be sure you have some money," Jule said to him. He was grinning, and little skittish bursts of excited laughter came from him as he went into the big bedroom where the money box was. Mummie still never turned her head. When he came out he went over and kissed her cheek. "Anything special I can get you, Beatrice?"

"No." It should have flattened him, but he was like a man just drunk enough to be reckless.

The girls went down to the wharf to see him off. They were as exhilarated by Jondy's adventure as if it prophesied adventures for them. They stayed out for the rest of the afternoon, and when they got back, Jondy was home. He had brought them boxes of candy, for Mummie a package which she ignored. "I've got vitamins and iron to take," he said. "Something special and strong. He wrote out the prescriptions for them." He held up two brown bottles. "See? They've got some kind of weird names, but that's all it is, plain old vitamins and iron."

He talked on and on as if he'd been wound up. "I don't know what the matter is with me! It must be that shot the doctor gave me." He made a face and rubbed one buttock.

He described the ride, what he'd seen along the road, the changes in Williston, the nice girl in the doctor's office, and the young doctor himself. Then all at once he looked drained and exhausted, and went to bed.

"That interfering, meddlesome, stupid man has half killed your father," Mummie said.

But in a week he was building traps in the fish house on the wharf, even though he didn't go back in the woods to work on the winter blowdowns. He tired quickly, but didn't seem to stay tired for long. He said the vitamins were doing him good, and he did eat more; the girls could see that, and even Mummie showed some relief from strain.

Ceasing to be anxious on his account, the girls could now concentrate more on themselves. If there'd been any Benedict mail in that packet they never knew, but they had reached a solution that satisfied them at the same time it tormented them; Billy B. knew there was nothing more he could do for them until they were free of Mummie. Therefore he was waiting for their eighteenth birthday. He knew when it was, and somehow he would be at hand when they made it off the island. He would leave a message with someone at Port George if he couldn't be there himself.

Roz said, "But he'll be there. We'll get into his car and go away, and that's it. The End. But not for us. Only for her."

16

MR. PEABODY CAME ACROSS one calm morning and stood talking and smoking with Jondy on the wharf. Mummie wouldn't let the girls go down there, she kept them scrubbing the stairs and the hall. But she was obviously disturbed by the visit; she kept going to the windows and staring down at the two men in the February sunshine as if she could somehow beam Jondy straight up to the house by the power of her gaze. Finally she snapped at Jule, "Go down and tell your father I want a pail of water."

"I'll get it!" Roz shouted from the stairs.

"You will not. You keep at your job, and I'm going to inspect those corners with a flashlight."

Jule pulled on her boots and a jacket and went down the path to the wharf. "Hi there, Sis!" Mr. Peabody hailed her. "Don't you look pretty this morning!"

Jondy smiled. "You want something, duckling?"

"She wants a pail of water."

He frowned, perplexed. The girls got water all the time, and had been doing so for years. "In a minute," he said, and turned back to Mr. Peabody.

"As I was saying Ned," he went on, "I promise I'll give him a call the next time I come across."

"John, I want that water *now!*" Mummie trumpeted from the back doorstep.

"Morning, Mrs. Saunders!" Mr. Peabody lifted his cap off his bald head and waved it at her. "So long, Jondy. You keep that promise now. He's a mighty persistent young feller."

He went down the ladder into his boat and started the engine. Jule's heartbeat speeded up sickeningly. She wanted so much to cry out, "Take me with you!" that when he glanced up at her his expression changed just enough so she thought she'd said it, or looked it. "So long, Sis, take care!" he called.

Jondy shouted over the engine, "Thanks, Ned." He turned to walk up to the house. Jule watched the boat leave, and a wondrous supposition came to her. Who was the mighty persistent young feller who wanted Jondy to get in touch? Who but Billy B.?

She could hardly wait to get Roz alone, and this didn't happen until afternoon, when Jondy and Mummie retired to their room for a nap or one of those long mysterious conferences. The girls went up to the main house to fill the tanks of the kerosene heaters.

"He hasn't given us up," Roz exulted. "We know that now, even if Jondy doesn't dare call him—"

"How could he not dare?" asked Jule. "Billy could write a nice polite note threatening to have him fired."

"That's not Billy B.'s style," said Roz. "I wish it was. He probably hasn't told any of this to his parents. They'd be afraid of what he was getting mixed up in. We're not the kind of girls that move in Benedict society."

Jondy didn't go to the mainland the next day, though the weather held fine, and they decided to tackle him about it. "We'll threaten him," Roz said blithely. "If we have to make it off here on our own, we cut off from him for good. If he helps us, we'll always stay in touch with him, even if we ignore her."

It sounded possible until they were actually there in the fish house with him. He was heading new traps with the wine-red nylon trapheads he'd been knitting all winter. He looked around at them with a strained smile, and Roz's brassy self-assurance melted down at once. Jule said too boldly and too loudly, "We want to talk with you, Jondy."

"I've been wanting to talk to *you*. Find a place to perch."

They were actually going to talk about Billy B., and even Roz went pale with agitation. They sat side by side on a lobster crate as if they needed the reassurance of touch, and Jondy hoisted himself onto the workbench and sat swinging his legs.

His moccasins looked incongruously small. "I lied to you," he said abruptly, "and it's been on my conscience for a long time."

"If it's about the colonel's mansion, we know," Jule told him. "You just wanted to tell us a good story, that's all. But Billy B. told us there never was a house."

Jondy nodded solemnly. "I don't know where it all came from that day. I got carried away." He tried to smile, but gave up. "That's not what I wanted to tell you. And no matter how mad your mother makes you, don't you go spitting this out at her. This has got to be *our* secret." He looked long and severely into each face, in a manner strange for Jondy.

Awed, they promised with silent, eager nods.

"When I went to the doctor that time, I just kind of casually mentioned those spells I told you about, and he told me they could mean something real serious that could be fixed. Or not be fixed. He was honest about that. He said he couldn't tell anything without tests, and he wanted me to go into the hospital. Well, I couldn't do that, could I?" he appealed to them. "I *told* him, it's out of the question. Midwinter, I can't leave my wife and daughters alone on that island. He said, 'You wouldn't like to leave them forever, would you?'" He swallowed visibly. "Set me back a dight. But well, he's young, and dead serious, and he thinks everything else is.

Anyway, I told him I'd get in touch after winter's back was broken, so he's been chasing me up."

"Is that what you and Mr. Peabody were talking about the other day?" There was a heaviness in Jule's gut.

"Ayuh. Doc called him up and asked how to get hold of me."

"So you said you'd call him up next time you went a-shore," said Roz. "Are you going to?"

"Hell, no! I'm feeling better by the hour. I'm just telling you now because—well, someone like Ned Peabody might say you should talk me into going to the hospital, and I don't want you to be scared foolish. Why, with spring coming I feel like running and jumping like a new lamb."

Then he looked down at the toes of his moccasins and said, as if to himself, "About the colonel's mansion. It wasn't all a lie. There was a big house, and a stolen baby, but it was down east. Never mind where, the house isn't even there any more, most likely. It was a real old place, and it could have gone up in smoke one winter, the way they do."

"If it's not here, what does it have to do with us?"

His head snapped up. "You just listen, young lady. I've got myself charged up to this and I don't want to be stopped." It was a new manifestation of Jondy as someone who could lay down the law and expect to be obeyed. "I want to tell you about a young feller from the islands who was crazy about engines, and after he'd been away in the army driving generals around, and back home his folks were gone, he got a job as engineer on a big yacht that came into the harbor at Landfall one summer. The regular man had to be flown to the hospital on the mainland—gall bladder attack, something like that—so this young feller filled in; and ran those big beautiful engines all the way up to Bar Harbor. Of course the other man got his job back, but the owner—"

"Was this young feller you, Jondy?" Jule asked. He gave

her a sidewise glance, oddly reminiscent of Mummie, and she knew he wouldn't, or couldn't, tolerate a distraction.

"The owner introduced him to a friend of his, had a great big place. He went to work there, helped the gardener, but mostly did all the maintenance on the cars. The Mister was away a lot on business, and the Missis didn't drive, so he drove her, but that wasn't often because she was getting over the hard time she'd had when her baby was born. She wasn't young, and she'd been real sick, and afterwards too. Well, he drove the maids and the baby's nurse on errands and to the city on their days off."

"What city?" Roz asked, but she too was squelched.

"This nurse ... She was a mighty impressive young woman, handsome and elegant as all get-out. He'd never known anyone like her before, and he fell in love, arse over teakettle!" A faint twinkle. "If your mother heard me say *that*! Real uncouth, wasn't it?" Roz opened her mouth, took a breath, but he went quickly on.

"Anyway, this young feller and the nurse connived at a terrible thing, but it didn't seem that bad at the time. They'd never hurt the baby, and the boss had plenty of money to spare. They could get enough to start out somewhere on their own with a good nest egg for them and their—" He blushed deeply, and scowled down at those small, swinging moccasins. "Well, they were in love, and well, they kind of rushed things. They'd have to leave as soon as she started showing, but they got this idea."

The heaviness in Jule's gut was shot through with stabs of pain. Roz's arm against hers was stiffening into iron.

"So the nurse disappeared with the baby, and the ransom note said they'd both been kidnapped. The money was left but never collected because he got the idea the FBI was in on it, and it scared him. She went into hiding, and he stayed on working for a decent time. It was hell." Jondy's voice was alien in its harshness. "Some hunters found a baby girl's bones in a shallow grave and they were buried in the family lot under the baby's name. The skull had been fractured. . . . It was the last straw. The mother lost her mind."

Roz's arm began to shake violently. She said unsteadily, "Was that—"

"*No!*" he shouted. "I don't know anything about that baby! Some drunk must have beaten his own child to death. We never—"

He put his hand to his trembling mouth, and his eyes were watering. "They would never hurt a child. They never *did*. It was just because they got so scared that they didn't bring it back."

"Wasn't there some way you—*they*—could do it? Leave her at a church, or somebody's doorstep? *Somewhere?*" Roz looked like a paper mask, and Jule's own face felt numb.

"When you go into a panic nothing makes sense. You just want to run as far as you can. He had a place to hide her out, in a boardinghouse with a landlady who was half drunk most of the time and thought she was somebody who'd left home with her little bastard baby. . . . That was the story the nurse spun her and she believed it, she was always too drunk to read the papers anyway, and nobody else ever saw the baby. Good young one," he said with a horrifyingly affectionate reminiscence. "Six months old, healthy, happy as long as she got her grub each day, and the nurse was damn good at her job."

"If stealing babies was it, I should say so," said Roz.

Jondy ignored her. "When he left the job, he found a place for them all. He'd been looking for it on his days off. An old cabin way off in the woods. This Indian woman who used to come there for sweet grass and ash for baskets, that was about the only person she ever saw. He'd hike out on an abandoned logging road and backpack the grub in, but nobody at this little settlement ever asked any questions. They thought—he kind of made them think it—he'd run off with another man's wife." The corner of his mouth quirked up in a parody of mischief. "They thought I was a hell of a guy."

"And you were," Roz said. "Only they didn't know how."

They went on listening in fascinated horror.

"It was mighty hard on her, me being too yellow to pick up the ransom, after all we went through, but at least we weren't in jail. She had her savings and I had mine and we made the money last. She was healthy as a horse, thank God, for never seeing a doctor the whole time. The old Indian woman and I—" He broke off and thrust out his small jaw, tossed his pride into their stunned faces. "We brought my child safe into the world."

"Which was which?" Roz stood up. Jule thought she was going to grab and shake him. *"Which one am I?"*

He went on as if she weren't confronting him. "Thank God again, both kids were strong and healthy. She was a fine mother," he said earnestly. "You can't remember, but you were always sweet and clean as roses."

"Which was which?" Roz asked again. He looked past her at Jule. "Came a time when she said she was going crazy out there, living in the woods with small kids. Anyway, we went to Landfall. My dad had retired there, you see, and so I had this little house. It wasn't a city or even a town, but it was better for her than the wilderness, even if she never mixed with folks there."

"But didn't anybody—" Jule began. He shook his head.

"Nobody knew where I'd gone to work after I left the yacht. All they knew was I'd come back with a wife and twins, and I was going into lobstering. I fixed up my father's old boat."

"*Twins!*" Roz spat the word. "With one kid a year older than the other? How'd you explain that?"

"One was big like her mother, the other small like her dad." He winked at Jule. It was horrible.

She licked her lips, which felt glued together. "Didn't you ever feel any remorse? Working there, watching that poor mother and father, all the time knowing where their baby was when they thought it had been murdered?"

"I was what she called me for not getting the money, and what you call me without saying it out loud. A coward." He spoke with dignity. "If I told, we could both go to prison, and I couldn't stand that for her, and for me to be separated from her. She was the first woman I ever really loved, and the only one. Sometimes I had crazy ideas of sneaking the baby away and leaving it somewhere, but she got so fierce about it, like it was really hers, I knew it wouldn't work. *Well!*" he went on briskly, as if simply putting the rest behind him. "It was easy on Landfall. Nobody ever connected her with the newspaper story a year and a half before. With you young ones it was simple too. When you were old enough I took you to school in your new dresses your mother made for you, and Mrs. Crail just enrolled you. Nobody asked for birth certificates."

"Whose mother made the dresses?" Roz asked. "Which one of us isn't yours and hers? Which one of us is the rich girl? What's her real name?" Jule had the feeling that if Roz could have reached a knife she'd have put it to Jondy's throat.

His eyes glazed over, his small seamed face set like cement. "I don't remember any more. You're both my children."

"That's foolish! You can't have forgotten. Tell me the name!"

"Beatrice used to read a lot of Shakespeare. She wanted to be an actress once. She named you Rosalind and Juliet."

"The name of the *family!*" Roz shouted at him. He got

down from the bench and walked toward the door, where he stopped and looked back at them.

"It'll do you no good to know. The family's all broken up. The parents are dead. The heirs wouldn't even have the same name, most likely. . . . Anybody who showed up now they'd call an impostor."

"But they take babies' footprints in the hospital when they're born, I read that," Jule contributed. He shook his head.

"Their baby wasn't born in any hospital. She came ahead of time, at home. Took 'em all by surprise." He kept on going. They listened to his footsteps going away up the wharf; Jule wondered distractedly how he could face Mummie after all this; it should be plain on his face. Then they heard the axe as he began splitting kindling.

Roz seized Jule in a fierce hug. "God, my God," she muttered. "Jule, it *has* to be me! I'm taller than you, I had my period first, and I've always had this feeling that I never belonged to them." The masklike pallor had gone; Roz was a princess come into her own, glorious with the knowledge. "We'll get it all out of him, he can't stop at this!" She went out and Jule followed. Behind her stiff white face she was assessing the story and her own reactions. Roz's pounce on the prize was only to be expected of her, but she was wrong, Jule was sure of it, and her system was reacting so violently that she wondered wryly if she might drop dead of a heart attack right now.

She and Roz walked across the field toward the woods and once they were hidden from the house Roz cupped her hands around her mouth and shouted like the Valkyries on one of the old Wagner records at the house. The echo came howling back. She threw her arms up and screamed until she was winded, then collapsed beside the silent Jule.

"Now that he's told us, he can't keep us here. Not me,

anyway! All I have to do is get out of here and find my people. I'm an heiress, Jule. Can you imagine it?"

"He's not going to tell us any more," said Jule. "I could see it in his face. He's sorry he told us anything. He's more afraid of her than of us. And even if you could by some miracle find out *something*, and dig up some real proof, do you want to send them to prison? Wouldn't it be enough just to be shed of them?"

"Where have *I* been all my life but in prison? *She* wouldn't let him give me back. I'd say *he'd* always been good to me and that he was under her influence like somebody hypnotized."

"That still wouldn't get him off." Though Jule knew she herself was the stolen child, and Jondy's behavior revolted her, she still could not hate him. She couldn't change this quickly.

Now they had to go back to the house and look at the woman without giving anything away. Jule had learned how to keep a locked face and be called stupid or insolent for it, but Roz could be manic enough now to throw everything in Mummie's face the minute they walked in.

"Listen, Roz," she said urgently, "you've got to calm down. You don't know what will happen if you say anything."

"She might drop dead."

"I wouldn't count on it. She could take after us with a carving knife."

"We can run away in the boat. Listen, we'll do what I always said I'd do—locate Billy B. If he's not back from India, maybe his father would be even better, because he could remember the kidnapping, if it was famous enough. And I'll bet Mr. Peabody would lend us some money to tide us over."

"He's Jondy's friend. He'd be right over here to see what's wrong."

"I wouldn't care. They don't have a leg to stand on." Roz dug her chin morosely into the palm of her hand. "I wish she didn't keep the money box in her room. If we could only get into that. . . . They'd never dare chase us. You can see why she didn't want us to go away to high school, can't you? She was afraid they'd ask for birth certificates. I'll bet they aren't married, because when you go for a license you have to be identified, and her real name would come out. So you're probably illegitimate, Jule," she said kindly, "but they don't hold that against people nowadays, so I wouldn't worry about it."

"I won't," said Jule, wanting to laugh. Am I getting hysterical? she wondered.

Roz was winding down now, shivering in the cold shade. "Maybe I could leave them out of it, but I don't know how. I don't owe them anything but revenge for what they've done to me and my family, but still, poor old Jondy. . . . He's a rotten little coward, but he tried to make it up to me in his own weak little way. And I have to say, Jule"—she came up on one elbow—"that they never showed you any favoritism for being theirs."

Jule said with a surface calm, "I think maybe Jondy isn't lying when he says he doesn't know which is which. According to some of the stuff we've read, the mind does strange things. Maybe he can go thus far and no farther. And as for *her*, maybe she's pushed the whole thing so deep into her subconscious that she'd never admit it ever happened. She'd swear we were her twins and she could even remember how it was when we were born."

"Then it wouldn't hurt her to be arrested," said Roz. "She'd spend the rest of her life in a mental hospital."

"But there's Jondy. I wonder why he told us now."

Roz said, "He hasn't heard the last of this. I'm going to

drag every last detail out of him. I'll make him remember."

She was calm herself now. The two walked slowly back across the field in the late afternoon sunshine. Outwardly it was like a hundred other mild February afternoons. But the glass of time had been irrevocably shattered.

And Lindisfarne had been transported to unknown territory; now the granite avenue led only to a place they called Nowhere.

17

BUT JONDY, though outwardly the same with his little smiles, songs, and jokes, had changed. He stayed out of their reach so skillfully you couldn't really say it was on purpose. Roz seethed, but managed to keep in control. A few days after the afternoon in the fish house Jule woke to what they'd completely forgotten: the doctor was trying to get in touch with him. This now took precedence over everything else. He was going to the mainland that day, and she ambushed him successfully on the back doorstep when Roz was immobilized in the toilet and Mummie in the pantry.

He was pulling on his rubber boots and when he saw her, apprehension crossed his face; she said quickly, "I'm not asking you anything. Just reminding you to please call the doctor. Look, you wouldn't be long in the hospital and we'd be all right here. Mr. Peabody would check on us. So *please*, Jondy. Then you'd be all fixed up for the summer."

"I will, I will," he told her, and went off down the path light as a boy in spite of rubber boots. At the wharf he looked back and signaled her with the canvas tote bag. But she was sure he wasn't going to call, and she hadn't the nerve to ask him when he came back.

March began with weather so fine that Jondy was anxious to start setting traps. He picked a morning that had the pellucid calm and milky distances of summer, and the girls helped him load the boat.

As usual Roz said, "Can we go?" Someday he was going to slip up and say "yes," and they'd be on their way out of the cove before Mummie could sound the trumpet of wrath. Roz's thinking was as obvious as if written in letters of fire around her curly head. *Once we get him out there, I'll find out what I want to know.*

Jondy started the engine and said cheerfully over the noise, "Not this time, ducklings."

Roz threw back her head. "I think I've heard that once too often!"

Jondy cupped his hand behind his ear. "What say?" he shouted at her. He was laughing with pleasure at getting out on the water, at spring coming and the weeks of freedom alone with the boat. He's not thinking of us at all, Jule thought with sad resignation. Roz strode up the wharf, but Jule watched him back around with a flourish. The boat headed out of the cove, he waved, and she turned to follow Roz.

They were going to clean and fill the heaters at the big house this morning. They couldn't have borne being confined in the same house with the woman; even when she was sitting still, it was as if her presence kept ballooning out until they were pressed against the walls and fighting for breath. It had been bad enough before, but Jondy's history had effected terrible permutations. One of the girls *had* to accept her as a mother. Whatever their private thoughts had been, the horror and rejection were open enough now.

Roz took on the airs of a lost princess, Jule kept her own certainties to herself until she found herself actively hating Roz, and this was shocking in itself. She could hardly make ordinary conversation and she wondered sometimes why Roz didn't notice, but then why should she? She was too intoxicated with herself to notice anything different about Jule.

This morning while they tended to the stoves, a time

which used to be taken up with discussions of Billy B. and associated subjects, Roz talked about her prospects.

"What makes you so sure," said Jule, finally, "that you're the one? Being bigger, having your period first, doesn't make you older."

Roz sat back on her heels and stared. "I've always known! I must be just loaded with unconscious memories."

Jule carefully wiped up a drop of kerosene. "What do you say to the fact that I've always been sure that *I* didn't belong to them?"

"You poor kid! Who'd *want* to claim them? *Her,* anyway." The tone said, Sorry, chum, but that's the way it is.

"I've got my own good reasons for believing I'm the one," Jule retorted. "And you've got a widow's peak just like hers."

Roz struck at her, Jule dodged, fell flat on her back, and burst into tears. "I wish he'd never told us! No matter what happened, we had each other. It was two against the world. Now look at us!"

"Oh, listen, Jule darling." Roz patted her wet face. "It always *will* be two against the world. I wasn't going to forget you! Just as soon as I find out anything I'll get you off here, I swear. But I've got to get going *now,* I can't stand waiting."

"Not till we're eighteen next month?" Jule asked. "Or whoever's birthday it is we celebrate," she added ironically. "Maybe it doesn't belong to either of us." They sat on the floor, entwined, their backs against the kitchen cupboards.

"Jule," Roz said with unusual quietness. "You've been telling me all along they won't let us do it, and I've known all along that you're right. So I've got to take the chance when I can. They can't *all* be rapists out there."

The two broke into shaky laughter.

It was on this day that Jondy's boat was found laboring in wide circles out east of Port George's Lighthouse Point, and when it was boarded Jondy was not there. Some of the traps had been set. A rope was tangled in the propeller, which accounted for the impeded action of the boat. The man who first noticed the boat's behavior, and boarded her, shut off the engine and anchored her. Then with his own boat he followed the line of brightly painted buoys, hauling each trap in the chance that Jondy had been caught in a riding turn around an ankle or arm and had been dragged overboard. He was not found. The warp in the propeller suggested that he'd been leaning far out over the stern with a gaff, trying to catch the rope, and had toppled into the water. The gaff was missing.

The boat was towed into Port George. Mr. Peabody, who knew the doctor had been trying to get in touch with Jondy, said he might have had some sort of seizure and blacked out.

A community search for the body began, and a Coast Guard helicopter took part, but after a week it was called off. At Port George the rope was cut out of the wheel, and a Peabody son brought the boat back to the island.

Beatrice took the news in marble silence. The girls for once were alike in their reactions; stupefied to numbness. The busy boats and the helicopter had nothing to do with them; not speaking, they went about their chores, and Jule, at least, watched Mummie acutely for some signs of intransigent grief. They could see nothing that was any different from the profound stillness of her worst rages. Perhaps rage was what she felt now.

Pain came back into frozen limbs with Mr. Peabody's visits, bringing food from his wife and other women who behaved in the traditional way when there was a death in the community. Mummie looked at the food without visible reaction. It was the girls who thanked him and asked him to thank the others. Roz was very good at it, but Jule stumbled over the words.

He tried to talk with Mummie about details; she went into

her room and shut the door. The girls walked down to the wharf with him.

"The Benedicts ought to be notified," he told them.

"It's in West Newton, the address, but we don't know it," said Jule. "*She* does, but—" She didn't have go on.

"Ayuh, you don't want to bother her, she's in an awful state of shock still. The post office should have a forwarding address for them. If you want, I'll try to get hold of them either by mail or by phone."

"Oh, thank you!" Roz said with a faint sparkle.

"As a widow, your mother's due for social security benefits," he went on, worriedly. "But she'll have to stir herself a little for that. I don't know about you two. Almost eighteen, ain't you? He always mentioned your birthday."

"We'll be eighteen the fifth of April," Jule said. *One of us anyway. One of us may already be eighteen.*

"And we'll be leaving here and getting jobs," Roz said firmly. Her fire was reviving.

"I'll bet you're looking forward to that now, ain't you? Anything you need in the way of groceries, medicine, and so forth before I come out next week? I could send somebody over. I don't expect the family will rush you off here. Got to find somebody else, anyway."

"If we think of anything," said Roz, "Jule and I might come for it ourselves."

"That's the ticket!" he said enthusiastically.

As soon as he left the cove, Roz turned to Jule. The old glint was there. "Come on. Let's see if we can start the engine."

Out of habit Jule looked up toward the house but no large white face stared down at them.

Roz rowed the skiff to the mooring. It was a fine day with high clouds, the cove was translucent turquoise and outside it the water was dark blue marbled with green and white. While Roz started the engine Jule made the skiff painter fast to the ring on the stern deck, thinking at the same time, Was this where Jondy stood or knelt when it happened? Did he have time to *know*?

The engine, always scrupulously maintained, came to life, and Roz laughed for the first time since the news of his death. "We did it!" she shouted over the noise. "We're free! She'll *have* to let us do the errands, she hates him coming, and we can make all the telephone calls and mail all the letters we want! Come on, get up and cast off, and we'll take a little spin."

They circled the cove with Roz at the wheel, then Jule took over and they circled again. They were tempted to go outside but the crests were racing by the cove mouth, and even Roz knew better than to experiment out there today.

Jule rowed them ashore from the mooring and Roz exulted, "Who'd have *believed* it? Poor Jondy has made us free, Jule. She'll have to leave here because the Benedicts will want a man for a caretaker, and once we're on the mainland we can simply walk out and there'll be nothing she can do about it. I don't have to run away now, taking my chance with the rapists. I can afford to wait and find out everything so I'll know right where to go. That'll be better anyway," she said thoughtfully. "The more I know to begin with, the less trouble I'll have with the heirs."

18

IT WAS RATHER MAGNIFICENT for a week.
They alternated between fits of grief for Jondy, and an exalta-
tion which Roz embraced without doubts; Jule was more
cautious, but was beginning to believe in it. They practiced
with the boat whenever the windy weather allowed. One day
they went almost to Port George.

"Next time we'll go all the way in," Roz said, "and call the
Benedicts and tell them about the kidnapping so they can get
to work looking it up."

They agreed that Mummie would do nothing about social
security benefits because she and Jondy had never been married.
Even if they had been, she couldn't take the chance that somebody would recognize her real name. They agreed that behind
her blank, pallid face and dull eyes she was busily trying to think
how she could go on hiding. But even Mummie would have to
accept defeat, at least to the point of moving to the mainland.

"We'll have to support her," Jule said. "She'll have nothing."

"She's going to be locked up somewhere, don't forget.
When I prove who I am, there'll be no way to leave her out of
it, even if I wanted to, and I don't."

They were away from the house, up on the island, when
Mr. Peabody came one mild, misty day. When they returned,
the first thing they noticed was the emptiness of the cove. The
boat was gone, and her skiff. Their horrified eyes scanned the

scene as if a tidal wave had swept her off while they were away. The dory had vanished too. Without a word between them, they went in.

The house smelled of gingerbread, and Mummie was knitting. Knitting! They'd never seen her knit. The blue wool smelled of mothballs; she must have had it put away somewhere. She said serenely, "New caps for you."

Roz asked abruptly, "Where's the boat?"

"Ned Peabody towed it to Port George. He bought it, the skiff, and all the gear too. I got him to take the dory and sell it for me. He can get a good price."

"So he came out here to scavenge, while our backs were turned," Roz said.

"Not at all," said Mummie. "He was very surprised when I said everything was for sale. Then he bought the gear and boat on the spot, for his older son. He sealed the bargain with what he had in his pocket, and he'll bring the rest when they come out to get the traps. It'll keep us for a long time." Her voice flowed on, choking them like heavy oil.

"The condition is that he'll see we get the mail and grocery order once a week. He'll see that the kerosene and gas are delivered, and he'll also send someone reliable to do repairs you two can't manage."

"You sound," said Roz, as if around an obstruction in her throat, "as if we're going to be here forever."

"I think the Benedicts will be very satisfied with my arrangements," the woman said. "I wrote to them today. Jule, it must be time for that gingerbread to come out."

Mechanically Jule opened the oven, tested the rich springy brown surface, and took out the pan and put it on the rack.

Roz said, just above a whisper, "Whether or not the Benedicts are satisfied, I'm not. We're eighteen next week. We'll be legally of age. You can't keep us prisoners any longer."

As if she hadn't heard that, Mummie said, "There'll be a

couple of boats out here later today on the high tide, to take off the traps. You two are not to be down on the wharf."

Roz walked out of the room and upstairs. Mummie began to hum as she worked. Jule stood watching her, briefly submerged in objective curiosity. Then she left, and was not called back.

Roz was already over the first impact, and beautifully revitalized. "Listen, the Benedicts don't have to think she's wonderful, even if *she* does. And when Billy hears about it, he can influence them to fire her, for our sakes. I *trust* Billy B." She was all but incandescent. "Damn it, I wish we'd gone into the harbor that day! And never come back! But we didn't, so—"

She pulled Jule down beside her on the edge of the bed.

"When they come for the gear, you go right down there, and even if she calls you back, don't listen. Just keep on going. She won't send *me* after you, she trusts me even less around men." She laughed. "She'll have to stir herself and go out there, too, and I'm betting she won't take you by the ear or even order you back into the house with them for an audience. She'll just make sure you don't get a chance to talk to anyone alone. And I'll make a start in her room. There's got to be something I can use for evidence."

"She'll be able to tell!" Jule was panicky.

"No, she won't." Roz wouldn't have any arguments.

The thought of watching the gear go and of seeing someone else in possession of Jondy's boat was worse than Jule's physical fear of Mummie. But she went, not so much because Roz demanded it as from a knowledge that to watch everything go was preferable to coming suddenly upon an emptiness like Jondy's disappearance in death.

She darted from the house while Mummie was out in the toilet, and down to the wharf. The men spoke to her with kindliness and the boys with embarrassed or cocky grins. She stood there not knowing what to say or do, feeling like a fool.

She was relieved to see Mr. Peabody come out of the workshop with coils of rope looped over his arm. His ruddy face reddened even more.

"I'm sorry, Sis," he said. "I tried to get her to save the dory, at least, but she was bound and determined to get rid of the whole kit and caboodle. It seems like she's got her mind made up to stay here."

"She's still confused," Jule heard herself calmly saying, "though you wouldn't believe it. We just didn't think she'd sell everything so fast. At least not until we have a place to go."

Then she saw Mummie standing on the back doorstep. Jule deliberately walked out to the end of the wharf and sat on a crate near where the Peabody sons were working. The younger one was the boy with the thick yellow hair. She had a sense of power when she saw Mummie picking her way down the steep path. It was the first time that she had ever been able to make the woman do anything.

Roz was right about her not making a scene in front of this bunch. Ned Peabody might injure her prospects with the Benedicts if he took a strong dislike to her for bullying this meek young girl.

"Why, Jule," she said pleasantly, "I thought you were busy in the house. Mr. Peabody, would you like a cup of coffee and a piece of warm gingerbread while we finish the business?"

"Sounds good."

"Jule, run up and put the kettle on, will you?"

Jule left, but not running. "So long," the yellow-haired boy called after her. "See you around."

"I hope so!" she said with a smile, proud of sounding so ordinary. But halfway up the path the old terror overtook her, and she wanted to bolt the rest of the way. Holding herself back was one of the hardest things she'd ever done. The instant she was in the entry she yelled, "Roz! Get out of there! They're coming up!"

"All right!" Roz shouted back, but she didn't come at once. Jule ladled fresh water from pail into teakettle, her hands shaking. She spilled water over the kettle's shiny sides, spattered it on the floor. "Hurry, damn it!" she called, wiping fast.

Roz was suddenly there, her cheeks red as if with high fever. "I've been through just one drawer. I don't think I left anything out of place. There was nothing but Jondy's clothes. It was awful."

"If there's anything it'll be in one of those trunks, I'll bet." Jule slid a braided rug back and forth over the drops by the stove. "Are they locked?"

"I didn't look. I thought I ought to go through all the drawers first. How will we get another chance unless we knock her out?" She laughed wildly, and Jule grabbed her wrist in warning as the others arrived at the back door.

"Hello, Mr. Peabody," Roz said sweetly, and Mummie gave her one of those darting glances. Roz and Jule disappeared into the pantry and in silence took out cups and saucers, measured coffee, cut the gingerbread. Neither girl had the stomach to take even a crumb of it as the transaction was finished. He was paying by check, after the cash installment in the morning, and Mummie was now preparing the check for deposit in the bank. In her lady-of-the-manor tone she asked Mr. Peabody if he would be so kind as to drop the letter in the mail. Her behavior must have been catching because he said, "I'd be most happy to," instead of "Sure thing."

Mummie saw him out. "Going to come off to blow no'theasterly," Mr. Peabody said.

"And it always rips into this cove," Mummie said. "It will be a relief not to worry about the boats." She sounded perfectly serene.

"Good God, he hasn't been dead two weeks!" Roz said viciously. "Listen to her! Not a care in the world! And she's moved more in the last week than she has in the last six months. She's in another phase, and if I wasn't so furious I'd be scared silly."

"It's as if she ate him," Jule whispered. "She's absorbed him and got new life. He's gone as if he never *was*."

Mummie came in humming.

Jule was sweating with claustrophobia, not knowing what she was going to do next. Oh yes. Wash the cups and saucers. She couldn't do it with these shaking hands, so she headed for the stairs.

Roz didn't come with her. She was silent in the kitchen, while Mummie, still humming, settled in her chair.

Suddenly Mummie said, "Your face is very red, Roz. Do you have a fever?"

"Yes," said Roz. "I'm coming down with bubonic plague. You and Jule will quickly follow. Whoever comes next week will find three disgusting corpses."

"That is not funny."

"When they do come," Roz said quietly, "Jule and I are going back with them."

"You're delirious. Go to bed at once."

"I'm not delirious, and if I'm flushed, it's with rage. You see," she went on conversationally, "we know what you and Jondy did. He told us because he didn't want to die with your crime on his conscience."

Jule's head was buzzing so she could hardly hear; she was spinning with disbelief, hanging onto the bannister. She looked into the kitchen, narrowing her eyes to focus them. Roz's back was to her but she saw Mummie's face, lard-white, and she was pushing up from her chair.

"He told us," Roz said, "which one of us it is. We've known for months. He told us the *name*."

Mummie took a step toward her, and Roz stepped backward toward the hall. "We know why you tried to keep us hidden all these years." Her voice began to shake out of control. "Because you're a criminal! You're terrified that somebody will find out! Do you know it's *life* for kidnapping? What will the Benedicts say? What will everybody say? *Mr. French*, after what you threatened him with?" She began to laugh, and then she ran for the stairs, falling into Jule who clutched at her to keep them both from tumbling back down.

It was first a chaos of bruised elbows and knees and pure panic as Mummie came inexorably on. The scramble up the narrow staircase was like one of Jule's old nightmares of flight from demons or trolls, but no scaly claw grabbed her ankle, and they found themselves stumbling over the top step. Jule's shin hurt, and Roz hit an ankle bone. Mummie was two steps from the bottom, staring up. Jule wanted to shut herself in their room away from that face, but Roz, gone far beyond awe or terror, shouted at it. "We *know*! And *everybody's* going to know! And you can't do a thing about it!"

Mummie ponderously took another step upward. Jule jerked Roz into their room and buttoned the door. Anyone could push the button in with enough weight driven against the other side. "If she comes up we can pile the furniture against the door," Jule whispered.

Roz hugged herself, laughing; her eyes almost disappeared behind the golden fringe. "I got her for everything she's ever done to us all these years!"

"So here we are," said Jule. Exhaustion had followed chaos. "What do we do? She can starve us out."

"Or burn us out," said Roz briskly. "She's that crazy. Remember your reading, dear child. Ropes made of sheets! We get out the back window, where she can't see us from downstairs, and we run for Sunset Cove. *No!*" She hugged herself and rocked with joy. "We don't have to run, because *she* can't run. And you know how many boats take the western passage home, so we'll get something from the main house for a signal, and get somebody's attention, and we're gone. It's that simple."

Her fiery confidence encircled Jule. They began to strip their beds. All was silence downstairs.

"Come on, *pull*," Roz grunted. "Get these knots good and tight."

"Damn it, our warm clothes are downstairs," said Jule, pulling hard.

"We'll just have to load on sweaters and extra slacks and socks. We'll tell Mr. Peabody she's gone out of her mind and we had to run for our lives and we haven't got a cent between us. I bet he'll believe it."

"He might, at that," said Jule. "At least he'd listen." She was warming up now, down to her toes and fingertips. It was all so gloriously possible; freedom even without a penny between them was still freedom.

"Then we'll get hold of the Benedicts," Roz ran on. "Oh God, Jule, I can't believe it's here!"

They dressed for the escape, and stuffed pockets and two small zipper satchels with toilet articles and other little things they didn't want to leave behind. Downstairs there was a crash heavy enough to send a vibration through the timbers; the mirror trembled and a lamp chimney rattled.

The silence afterward was even more profound. "What did she *do*?" Roz whispered. "What *could* she do to make a noise like that?"

"Something big, falling." Jule put her fingers to her lips. "Do you think—? We'd better look."

"*No!* We're going *now*. She's done something to trick us, that's all."

But she didn't move. Jule unbuttoned and unlatched the door with exquisite caution, not making a sound, and went out onto the landing and listened. The loudest and most familiar sound was the mantel clock in the kitchen, until she became aware of the other noise, the heavy breathing, almost a snore. She went fearfully down the stairs, halfway.

Mummie lay on her back across the threshold between kitchen and hall.

19

THEY STOOD BY HER, whispering. "It has to be a stroke," Roz said.

"What are we going to do?" Jule asked.

"We're going to get out before it gets any darker. At least we don't have to run a marathon to Sunset Cove now, we can signal off the wharf. Then somebody can come and get *her*. I'd send the whole Coast Guard, once we were off the place."

"Look," Jule said, pointing to the windows. The fog was advancing steadily in a dark purple band; already the mainland and the horizon had disappeared. Roz groaned, then choked on tears.

"We couldn't have made ourselves seen even if we'd got away, the fog's come in so fast," Jule pointed out. "Come on, we've got to get her into bed."

"Maybe faith can move mountains, but we can't."

"Get me the afghan from the sitting room." Sighing and muttering, Roz fetched it; it was a gorgeous affair, never used, only displayed in a room where they never sat. Jule spread it over her, and stood up.

"If we can't get her onto the bed, we'll make the bed on the floor. Come on."

Roz didn't move at once. As always when she suddenly lost a high, she was physically and mentally depressed until she could reestablish her equilibrium.

"Roz!" Jule snapped. "At least *we're* in charge now."

They pushed the big double bed to the wall, and pulled the mattress off it. "Get that new plastic tablecloth out of the drawer."

Roz went to the pantry, stepping around the woman as if she were a large boulder in her way. When she came back she still managed not to look.

"One'll have to drag, and the other push," Jule said. "Thank goodness the floors are smooth. Do you want the shoulders or the feet?"

"Neither," said Roz. "Oh, I'll take the shoulders. I just won't look at her face." She was shivering and her teeth began to chatter. "Damn. I can't stop!"

"Build up the fire first," Jule suggested, "and put the kettle on, and as soon as she's settled we'll have something hot."

Roz brightened like a child. "*Coffee*," she said.

Mummie still didn't allow them to have it, and they drank instant coffee at the main house like secret topers.

When they had her lying beside the made-up mattress, Jule realized from the wet streak left behind that there would have to be some cleaning up done first. Roz was for rolling her onto the mattress and leaving her, but Jule, even though she was both physically and emotionally revolted by the prospect, felt it must be done. She didn't want to be ashamed when someone came to take Mummie to the hospital.

"Go stay in the kitchen if you can't stand it," she ordered.

"I can't," said Roz. "And I don't know how you can. I'll make the coffee."

Jule collected what she needed and set to work, her teeth set. But she found that once she had begun she could be objective, as if all this flaccid inanimate flesh belonged to no one she knew. Wasn't even human. She was amateur, but she was thorough. She then forced Roz to come in and help roll Mummie onto the made-up mattress. With her eyes shut Roz did her part, then escaped.

Jule got out one of the voluminous nightdresses, cut it down the back and put it onto Mummie's front and over the thick arms. When she had her tucked in with plenty of blankets, she carried out the cut-off clothes, and stuffed them into the trash box in the entry for burning. She rinsed towel and washcloth, emptied and wiped out the washbasin, and sat down to coffee and buttered gingerbread with Roz, surprised that she could eat and drink.

"What now?" said Roz, all fire quenched.

"We wait out the fog," said Jule.

The fog gave way to a three-day northeaster, which began with freezing rain and snow. They went to the well together because the icy curb was a danger. They had to shout to be heard above the roar of the breaking seas on the northeast shores and the echoing roar through the spruce forest. Between Port George and the island the sea was white and smoking as the wind blew the tops off the crests. Even Roz wasn't foolish enough to think they could get out onto the slippery wharf to tie Mummie's red corduroy bathrobe to the hoisting mast as a distress signal.

At first they kept expecting Mummie to awake suddenly and take command. Common sense said something different, especially to Jule, who had the cleaning up to do. She was sure this mountain of inert flesh wasn't going to wake up as Mummie.

Roz refused to go near her or touch her, except when Jule insisted on help to turn her so she could bathe her and change the bed. "It makes me sick to my stomach," she said. "It would be different if I loved her. How can you do it?"

"I don't know," said Jule. "Except that I just can't leave her lying there in the mess."

"I could clean up after an animal," Roz said. "A human being's different. Especially *her*."

She did the cooking, and it seemed as if they were hungry

all the time. They began to expand in the new breathing space. They listened to radio music, played cards, read while they ate their meals. At night Jule slept on the sitting room couch, reading late into the gale-ringing nights, then waking at intervals to go in and look at the snoring woman.

After the first twenty-four hours Roz walked into the bedroom and began going through drawers. At first Jule couldn't take part in the search; this would surely bring Mummie out of her trance, as if it had all been one long elaborate fake in order to trick them into a criminal act. But as Roz took out drawer after drawer from the deck bureau and chiffonier and set them on the bed, the woman remained so remote from them that she was impressive in her indifference.

The drawers revealed nothing. Neither did the trunks, The cedar chest was locked, but the key was in the money box and they'd found *that* key in one of the three little drawers across the top of the deck bureau.

"This is it," Roz said in a shaky voice as she sank to her knees before the chest. "This will tell everything about me."

Or about me, Jule thought. Roz's hands were trembling and she couldn't fit the key to the lock. Jule took it and opened the chest. "Now for the skeleton," she intoned in a sepulchral voice. "You know what happened to the girl in the Mistletoe Bough." Roz should have laughed. Instead she exclaimed hysterically, "Don't talk like that!"

Then they both looked over their shoulders at the series of mounds under the blankets. The breathing remained the same.

In the top of the aromatic chest there were two uniforms that Jondy had apparently worn as a chauffeur, winter and summer outfits. Under these were a woman's white uniforms, though when they held them up it was hard to imagine Mummie ever fitting into them. Two pairs of nurses' shoes had also been put away.

"Why did she ever save them?" Jule whispered. "I've never seen her wearing them."

"Who knows?" Roz said tensely. "What's this?"

It was a dress, a silky jersey print in shades of green, with soft flounces and bows. Wrapped in tissue paper there were green leather sandals with high heels.

"I wonder what these meant to her?" Roz said. "Can you imagine her ever being happy? Smiling, even *laughing*? I wonder what she was like when she wore this?"

"Maybe her life was good up until the time they stole—" Jule almost said *me*.

"Look here!" Roz brought out a flat cardboard box bearing the name of a store in decorative script. She opened it, and lifted the leaves of tissue paper. There were baby clothes, washed and folded. Tiny shirts, a slip and a dress of handkerchief linen, pale yellow, delicately embroidered. Small woolen shoes, hand-knit, with white daisies embroidered on the toes. The sweater and bonnet were of the same pattern.

Jule felt as if she were about to break into great, noisy, gulping sobs. She knew her mother had knit these things while she waited, hardly daring to move so as not to endanger the baby. After it came, she had added the daisies for a girl, during the hours when Mummie tended the child. If it had been a boy she might have embroidered ducks.

"This must be what I was wearing when they took me," Roz said reverently. Jule got up from her knees because she couldn't endure being that close to Roz; she hated her. She went into the kitchen and stoked the fire; a new gust shook the house, and sleet beat against the glass.

In a few minutes Roz came out with the box. She put it on the end of the table and patted it, smiling.

"Evidence," she said.

At supper she could talk of nothing else, and didn't notice, or want to notice, Jule's silence. Finally she groaned, "Oh

God! I can hardly wait to get off here! This damned wind! When is it going to *stop*?"

The next twenty-four hours were wilder than the first. The radio told of boats broken adrift and smashed to kindling, of wharves being torn away, whole lines of summer houses swept off their foundations as beaches disappeared in the southern part of Maine.

Roz brooded over the address book, but found nothing of interest except the Benedicts' address. Then she brought out the money box and went through that. There were sixteen hundred and forty-five dollars in cash; a checkbook in the name of Beatrice Moreton, with three hundred and ten dollars in the balance; a savings account passbook, also in her name. Roz whistled.

"Forty-three thousand, eight hundred seventy-five dollars, and twenty-two cents! And all we can touch is the cash! Jule, do you realize that if she'd gone before Jondy he couldn't have touched this either? It's all in her name, and she's *not* Mrs. Saunders. Which makes you—" She had the grace to stop.

Maybe you're the illegitimate one, Roz, Jule thought behind her eyes. "Well, at least there's plenty to take care of her in the hospital," she said.

"But I don't care!" Roz was laughing in victory, her eyes shining slits behind the thick lashes. "I'll have plenty when I get where I'm going. And I won't forget *you*, Jule darling."

"That's nice of you," Jule said dryly. She was seeing herself as a small dark solemn baby in yellow sweater and bonnet.

In the third twenty-four hours the precipitation turned to rain, and the snow vanished quickly. The wind still blew, and the air was smoky with blown spume. But the storm was blowing itself out; they didn't need the radio to tell them that.

Their birthday came, or the day that had always been

called their birthday. Roz made them a devil's food cake with thick fudge frosting, and they ate till they were sick of it, and wished each other a happy birthday.

"Jule, if she doesn't die of this," Roz lectured her, "you'll just have to put her somewhere so you can get out and *live*. The state should take over her care anyway. She's a criminal and everybody'll know it now."

Jule was tired, she felt unreal, as if she were delirious but knew it, everything was immense and frightening; now that the captivity was about to end, she could hardly wait, but she was also appalled because it was all so incredible. She felt herself paralyzed before the spectacle of a mountain beginning to move.

She got from hour to hour by concentrating on the thing at hand and dragging Roz along with her. It was rather like trying to tether a balloon, but she managed. They packed their own possessions, and Jule packed Mummie's and Jondy's. She set aside a small, smart, dressing case, which didn't look as if it belonged with the rest of the collection, to go to the hospital with Mummie. She put in the empty pill bottles so the doctors could see what Mummie had been taking. Jondy had always renewed her supply of pills, and she'd apparently been almost out when he died, and hadn't bothered to order more.

"For high blood pressure," one label read. And now she lay in her snoring sleep; she was losing weight, and the thin, arched, elegant bones were standing out on her face as the flesh fell away.

They stacked everything at one end of the kitchen, the money box on top. They were ready to leave. Only the wind was holding them there. Not Mummie.

20

THERE WERE BRILLIANT BURSTS of sunshine when the water turned blinding silver, then darkened to purple streaked with dead white. The water barrels were full, and Jule dragged out the galvanized tubs and washed sheets. Gulls circled and dived over riches churned up with the weed ripped from the rocks. The air was stunningly warm; it was as if spring had come in on the wings of the gale. Gradually during the afternoon the wind dropped to an ordinary breeze, southwest now.

Roz left the house wearing the scarlet robe, skidded on the muddy path, but kept her balance like a gull on a wind current, and ran out on the wharf. Jule watched her go. Before the day was out they could be walking up the wharf in Port George. She was suddenly overcome with love for Roz, and her eyes filled with tears. How could anything ever separate them?

She heard a sound from the bedroom. Slowly she went toward the moan or heavy sigh, expecting to find the green eyes alert with fearsome intelligence. She stopped outside the open door to calm herself, thinking, Even if she's waking up, she's not going to get up and begin battering us. She's a sick woman and we're in charge now.

She walked more confidently into the room. Mummie lay as before, and Jule crouched beside her, wondering if she dreamed endlessly in her stupor, or if there was nothing left that could dream.

The bed was wet again. Where did it all come from? She kept supplies in the room now, and she set to work. There wouldn't be any more of this after today.

She was bracing the woman on her side with pillows when Roz came slamming into the kitchen. "I didn't even have to fly it!" she shouted. "I saw a boat and waved the robe like mad, and he saw it! He's down at the wharf this minute!"

Jule laughed in joy. "Who is it?"

"Lyle Ritchie, his name is, from Saltberry Point. I don't think he's a rapist!" She giggled. "He's got his wife with him and they came out to check some gear."

"Is he going to call the Coast Guard?" Jule called out to her. "Is that what he's doing now?"

Roz came to the door, and averted her eyes from the sight of Mummie half-naked. "Listen, Jule," she said rapidly, "he's going to take me into Port George to make some calls, and bring me right back out again. I thought I ought to make a start on the Benedicts, the sooner the better, and try to get hold of that doctor whose name is on the pill bottles, and the hospital and everything—get it all lined up."

Jule sat back on her heels. "Roz—"

"No, look—we don't know when the Coast Guard will get here, maybe not till tomorrow sometime—they may have to come from Boothbay! And in the meantime we can get something started. He'll wait for me and bring me back and his wife'll help me with the calls. There's a booth right at the harbor."

She was obsessed with touching mainland if only for a few minutes, and Jule took pity on her. I am the older one, she thought proudly; I know it. "Go ahead. You'd better take some money for the telephone. And tell Mr. Peabody what's going on."

"Right!" Roz sang out. "Oh, I love you, Jule, and don't you ever forget it!" She rummaged noisily around in the kitchen, then called, "So long for now!"

The door slammed behind her. When Jule came into the kitchen later she thought she saw a dark red lobster boat halfway to Port George.

She did the rest of the washing outdoors, and the sunshine and the soft air went to her head. She laughed aloud suddenly, for no reason except that she was no longer awed by the complications of freedom; she felt as if she could tackle and demolish anything that confronted her.

The thought of soon seeing Billy B. filled her with a great tenderness. "Now look," she said aloud. "He may not be back in this country yet. And if he is, he may be involved in something he can't drop while he runs to you. It's *your* life, kid. . . . He told you that when you were eighteen you'd be on your own. . . . Anyway, you can't have everything at once, you'd die of shock."

She made herself a cup of tea—they'd rather overdone the coffee—cut a slice of the devil's food cake, and went out on the doorstep to watch for the dark red boat to come back.

The dark red boat didn't come that night, and neither did the Coast Guard. When it was dark and Roz still hadn't returned, she realized she was not surprised. Roz was Roz; she had ached for this for so many years that she just hadn't been able to make herself come back. She'd be there in the morning, probably with Mr. Peabody or one of his sons, if she could manage it, and she'd be full of apologies but not at all sorry. Of *course* it had taken time to make all the arrangements for the money; of *course* it had been impossible to locate the doctor who'd prescribed for Mummie so long ago.

"So the Peabodys got their doctor to take charge. Oh yes, I called the Benedicts, and Billy B.'s on his way!" She'd grab Jule and hug the breath out of her. "Oh, Jule darling, I just couldn't make myself come back last night. I knew you were all right, you always are. But I had this awful feeling that if I came back something would happen to keep us here. So I stayed all night at the Peabodys', and when I woke up this morning, all those idiotic ideas were gone and I was so *ashamed* of myself." Another suffocating hug.

Yes, that was how it would be. Annoyed, but not seriously, Jule slept well on the sitting room couch. But when she woke in the morning and thought about it, the real surprise was that Mr. Peabody wasn't worried about her being alone out here with a very sick woman. Roz must have made her out to be very well organized indeed. "Not a nerve in her body!" she'd say proudly. "In fact she *told* me she'd be better off without me. I've been a nervous wreck out there, and driving her crazy with my dithering."

After eighteen years together Jule could certainly forgive Roz for another burst of craziness, if only for the sake of those eighteen years. Roz deserved some kindness; she was in for a hard time searching for ghosts who might just turn out to be Jule's ghosts.

Why had Jondy told them there was no one left if it were not so? If they were to survive whole, it was better not to let the past become an obsession; Jule could not bear to think of her bereft parents.

The first swallows arrived that morning, but by noon no boat had come, and she was furious. She cleaned up Mummie for the second time that day, did the washing and then went to take the scarlet robe out of the dressing case; she'd packed it after Roz had gone. She'd fly her own distress signal and see how Roz wriggled gracefully out of explanations. But when she lifted the case from the stack at the end of the kitchen, it occurred to her that something was different there; she stood off and studied the way everything was arranged, counting in whispers.

Roz's zipper bag was missing. So was the flat box of baby clothes, which Roz had kept on the table so she could open it whenever she wanted to. Jule had touched the things only furtively, when Roz was upstairs at night.

She took the metal money box to the table and opened it. It was really not astonishing to find that only twenty-five dollars of the cash were left, along with a collection of loose change, and the bankbooks, of course; Roz couldn't make use of those.

"Thank you, Roz," she said aloud. "It was darling of you to leave me anything. But why the hell couldn't you have told someone about me out here before you took off for wherever you've gone?"

The most passionate weeping of her life burst from her with uncontrollable force, and the paroxysms wrenched at her belly muscles, seared her throat, clogged her nose so she couldn't breathe, and the tears ran as if something had broken loose and could never be fastened again. She heard the sounds she made and couldn't stop them; sometimes she thought of the woman lying in a stupor in the next room, sometimes she heard Roz laughing. Then she saw Jondy as she had shuddered away from seeing him until now, when she was defenseless and couldn't keep from seeing. He toppled overboard, trying to save himself and dying in the attempt. She saw his wiry little body swollen obscenely, the face eaten by crabs.

She fell suddenly into a sleep like a blackout from a blow. She woke up in the middle of the night with her head on her arms at the kitchen table, and could hardly move at first. She staggered drunkenly into the sitting room and collapsed on the couch, sank back into unconsciousness until a gull woke her at daylight. She thought in her sleep that it was Roz calling. She had arrived! Jule arose dizzily, tangled in her blanket and fell down, and woke completely.

No one was there but herself and Mummie. Shivering in the cold gray light, enervated by the heaviest sleep she'd had in days, she stumbled around the kitchen building up the kitchen fire. When she had it going she looked at herself in Jondy's shaving mirror by the sink. She still showed the signs of yesterday's tempest. She washed her face in cold water, held the dripping cloth over her swollen eyes. Then, in a need to do violence to something, she took the barber shears from the drawer (seeing many things she'd forgotten to pack, but who cared now), tied an apron around her neck, and slashed her hair off to the tips of her earlobes. The instant the long black hair went into the fire she was strangely but pleasantly giddy.

Then she went in to Mummie, apprehensively, in case this was the time Mummie woke up and asked her in a clear, glacial voice what she had done to her hair.

Mummie had not waked up. When she was cleaned and the bed made, Jule got herself some breakfast. With her hands wrapped around a mug of cocoa, waiting for it to be light enough for her to raise the signal, she knew just what had happened; she might have seen the whole thing acted out before her eyes as she slept in her trance of exhaustion.

Roz had given a perfectly plausible story about herself at Port George; an emergency trip to a doctor or dentist; or a chance at a job, the offer having come in the last mail. Whatever it was, she had to be somewhere at a certain time. Just *had* to. Mr. Peabody would understand, applaud, and assist in sending her to Limerock. Once there she'd take the quickest way to leave for Portland or Bangor or Augusta.

And of course she hadn't called the Benedicts, bringing awkward questions. But surely there'd be plenty of those from the lawyers. Was she crazy enough to think that nothing would be checked out? How could she present Mummie's evidence and omit Jule, who had just as much right to be the missing child?

"Oh, stop it, Jule!" she snapped at herself, and went down to hang up the red bathrobe. It was a misty morning with a strong southerly swash on the outer shore. The sun was a disc of muted silver over the gray-blue mainland. She could feel its humid warmth and thought optimistically, The fog will burn off as the sun rises.

She tied the sleeves into the line on the mast and hoisted it up and the wind coming over the point caught the robe and snapped it out. Looking up at the brave scarlet, she was assailed by a longing for Roz. All her reflexes, instincts, and impulses still knew Roz in the ways of a lifetime. She had been wounded beyond belief, but she *missed* Roz, even if she could not forgive her.

21

NOW SHE FELT HUNGRY, and scrambled some eggs and fried bacon. Just to know that by tonight she'd be among people and away from the responsibility of Mummie was enough to keep her going now. But the day dulled and the fog streamed in, and eventually she had to admit that no one could possibly see the signal in this. The robe hung limp and dark in the wet. With resignation she checked the fire, and stood for a time watching Mummie sleep. It occurred to her that Roz might have finally called someone, once she was well out of the vicinity. The fog wouldn't bother the Coast Guard, and they could arrive any time.

But no one came. It meant she wouldn't see anyone until Mr. Peabody's regular time. She didn't bother to eat anything more that day; she wasn't interested in food. She tended Mummie when it was necessary, and kept the fire going; she lay on the sitting room couch trying to read, but kept falling asleep. It was a relief when night came on, and one could hope for fair bright weather tomorrow. The batteries for the radio were exhausted, so she had no official weather report to go on.

She made a late supper of cocoa and buttered pilot crackers, and after that she didn't know when she fell asleep; there was no clear point at which she laid the open book face down on her breast and closed her smarting eyes to rest them. One moment she was reading and the next she was wide awake, sitting up, the book hitting the floor. The lamp was still burning and the room was too warm from it.

Someone had waked her. Someone had spoken.

"Roz?" she asked huskily, blinking sleep-gummed eyes toward the dark kitchen. No one answered. Nothing moved or made any sound, not even the clock; she had stopped it the first night after Mummie's stroke, because it broke up her uneasy sleep.

What had waked her was the silence.

She flung herself out of the bedclothes, took her flashlight, and ran into the bedroom. The snoring had stopped, and the woman's eyes were open, shining in the beam. "*Mummie*," she whispered in awe. She went back and got the lamp and set it on the chest of drawers.

The green eyes stared upward and the silence was entire. She had not waked up, she had died. Jule held a mirror to her mouth and nose, but no mist showed. Kneeling by the mattress, she had vague ideas about prayer. But all she could think of was the phrase, "To cease upon the midnight without pain." Was it fair that Beatrice Moreton should go so easily when she had put another woman through hell?

Never mind. She was dead. Shaking with awe or terror, Jule drew the sheet up over the face. Then she went out and shut the door behind her for the first time since the stroke, and wondered what she would do tomorrow if nobody came. Then she thought, I can walk to the big house again. I can go all the way to the road to Nowhere.

She was overcome by fatigue like a strong undertow, and she blew out the lamp, fell onto the couch fumbling for her blankets, and slept until morning.

It was still foggy. She made breakfast, all the time never looking toward the bedroom door, and afterwards left the dishes on the table in a conscious statement of independence. She gathered up the last books brought down from the main house, put them in a bag, and returned them. She scraped the wicks of the oilstoves, which they'd let burn out, and got them all to burning again with clean blue flames. She was tempted to build a wood fire in the library and stay there all day, but she suspected that the longer she stayed away from the house where the dead woman lay, the harder it would be to go back. She should have checked again this morning, she might have been too nervous last night to tell whether or not there was mist on the glass. But there'd been no sound. No sound at all. She hadn't felt for a pulse, but she knew there had been no breathing.

She took back with her *The Lord of the Rings*, an old favorite. Walking through the fog she resolved to look at Mummie the instant she got into the house. But she could not make herself go into the room. She listened with her ear against the panels, and silence roared in her ears.

She started the kitchen clock again, for its company. Then she moved Mummie's rocker into the living room and shut the door on it.

Back in the kitchen she settled herself in Jondy's chair, with her feet propped on the windowsill beside the hook on which he'd looped the twine for his trapheads. She read all day, getting up only to put more wood on the fire or go to the toilet, and once she went to the well. She fixed sandwiches for herself, and read while she ate. It was as if something terrible would happen to her if she left Middle Earth.

Before dark she took the bedclothes from the sitting room couch upstairs to her and Roz's room. Roz's empty bed was not terrible to her, she knew Roz was alive somewhere and enjoying it; if she felt any emotion at all about Roz right now it was a frigid resentment. She buttoned the door. *Against what?* she asked herself, but left the button turned anyway.

She read until blinking couldn't clear her eyes, then she

blew out the lamp and listened to the drip outside the open window. She was grateful for the ordinary sound of it, and for the hour and half-hourly chime of the mantel clock below.

She wondered where Roz was now; for some reason she always imagined her laughing, the curly head tossed back, the round chin tilted, the pretty teeth shining, cerulean eyes disappearing behind the golden fringes.

Scenes from their life together drifted through her head. They walked in a quiet snowfall along the road to Nowhere, or prowled the maple and birch woods in a summer rain, the raindrops hardly disturbing the leaves. She saw herself and Roz at either end of the old leather sofa in the library, with a fire burning. They ate apples and candy bars, and read aloud to each other.

This led her to the poetry she'd learned by heart because she loved the sound of it, even before the words made much sense to her. She went to sleep groping for and finding lost phrases of "A Thing of Beauty Is a Joy Forever."

She woke late. The fog was still thick, and she felt as if the world had ended in some giant nuclear dissolution, but the island had been flung free of the final Big Bang and was now floating in steamy space. She ran downstairs in her pajamas, and outdoors; wet silence hit her, but after a moment she heard first the foghorn at Manana and then the one from Lighthouse Point in their off-key duet. She sagged against the door, laughing weakly at herself; then sternly stopped the laughter before it could get out of control.

She read all morning, but now the closed door across the hall dominated her. She found herself looking up from her book to stare at it for long moments at a time. She moved her chair so she could see it without turning her head. All her life, whenever Mummie went into her room and closed the door, Jule had dreaded the reopening.

"She is not going to open that door now," she enunciated in a careful whisper. Nevertheless she did not want to turn her back on it.

On the third day, with the southerly swash still loud on the outer shore, she heard an engine in the cove; and when all at once she heard feet on the back doorstep and a knock, and there was Mr. Peabody in boots and oilskins, she burst into tears.

22

SOMEONE WAS KNOCKING at the door. The outside lights glowed softly through the drawn drapes and it was all foreign to her for the first instant, then she got up wiping away the tears with the back of her hand and stumbled dizzily toward the door, groping for a lightswitch, so she was half blinded when she opened the door.

Roz stood there. Neither spoke. Then Roz bundled her collar up around her neck and said shakily, " 'Saint Agnes' Eve—Ah, bitter chill it was!' "

"Oh, *Roz*," Jule choked on the word. She dragged her in and they hugged, collapsed on the side of the bed, stared at each other through tears, and laughed incredulously.

"We sound drunk as coots," Roz sputtered, wiping her eyes. "Oh God, I'm so *glad* you came! I was going to send for you as soon as I got my feet under me, but you have no idea what it was like—believe me, Jule, I never intended to simply cast you off."

"Shut up, Roz," Jule said softly. "Just *shut up*. Take a few deep breaths." She moved across to the other bed. The light behind Roz aureoled her head as light had always done. She looked the same, except thinner; yet her clothes and the way she wore them, the very way she sat, and above all her manner of speech, were only the first hints of the metamorphosis. How could she not be different?

So now she was here, *they* were here, and Jule felt curiously deflated.

"Did you get her into the hospital all right?" Roz asked.

"She's dead, Roz, and cremated. She died the day after you left and I was alone with her for two days after that. Mr. Peabody came on his regular day. He hadn't known anything was wrong because you never went near Port George. But couldn't you have called him?"

Roz suddenly doubled over as if she'd been punched in the belly. Then she sat up, seeming to spring back to a consciously beautiful posture. "But I *did* ask Lyle Ritchie to call the Coast Guard! If he forgot—oh, he *did* forget! I could *kill* him! Oh, poor Jule!" she cried. She reached for Jule, who drew back.

"He wouldn't forget a thing like that. Mr. Peabody asked him. All you wanted was to go uptown to a dentist, you told him, and you'd get a taxi back to Port George afterward. But never mind, Roz. It's over with."

"But you're still mad with me, aren't you?" Roz wouldn't be snubbed, she bounced across to the bed beside Jule. "I don't blame you. If you knew what I've called myself all these years! But I'll make it up to you, I swear."

"You can't," Jule said briskly. "Not those days, from the moment I realized you never intended to come back. But I've gotten over being mad with you except when I can't help it."

Roz was too shrewd to pursue that. "Tell me all about you, darling. You *look* marvelous. Not a day older."

"I know. Inside I'm rotting away like Dorian Gray's portrait. Am I supposed to say you look marvelous too?"

"Do I?"

"You always did. Now you look rich."

"I can't help that," said Roz. "Oh God, listen to me. Ten minutes with you after four years, and I'm already on the defensive."

"You deserve to be," said Jule candidly. "You've got a lot to be defensive about. Do you remember when you said goodbye? I was down on my knees cleaning up Mummie, and when you went out the door I was so happy I thought I couldn't stand it. The only time I've seen you between that day and this was when you showed up on Peabodys' television a week later. And oh yes, there was the story in the Sunday paper, telling how you got this Portland newspaper to help you go through their files. 'That's what a girl did in a book I read,' you said, smiling modestly. You read a lot of books in your tower, Rapunzel."

"Oh, for heaven's sake!" Roz got up and walked around the room, hands in her slacks pockets. She stopped by the mirror and stared at her reflection before moving on. "Don't quote *that* at me." She touched her hair and twitched at her sweater. "They fixed up a story to suit themselves. Thank God there wasn't much of it. Something else came along to divert attention. That boat sank off Monhegan—I read about it."

"I can understand why you wanted to be first with the evidence," Jule said, "when we thought it was just the baby clothes and the picture of Mummie. Because there was a chance I could have been the one. But when you found out there was a footprint, in spite of what Jondy said, and it was yours—what about then, Roz? Couldn't you have *written* to me? Wished me well?"

"I *told* you, you can't imagine what it was like! The pressures on me were terrific. There were times when I didn't think I could stand it. It was like landing on another planet—it was a whole new world so different from anything I'd ever imagined, and then there were hostile elements who resented me. If I'd tried to drag in hunks of my old life—well, I— I just *couldn't*, that's all."

She sat down abruptly again, squeezed her hands between

her knees and stared at Jule. "When are you going to stop looking at people like that?"

"I can't help it. It's the way my face is made. Didn't you ever wonder what happened to me? After you got used to being the princess?"

"I knew you'd be all right. People would want to take care of you, you always look so vulnerable until you pin somebody with those eyes. I expected that the Benedicts would have practically adopted you. How is Billy B., anyway? Did you two ever—"

Jule ignored that. "He's at the island for over Easter," she said. "I've never been back. Well, what I've been doing, since you're obviously frantic to hear, is working. I stayed with the Peabodys and worked for my high school diploma, and then I got a job with a group who were starting up a cleaning and maintenance business. We're called Clean Sweep, and we've done well. I swore I'd never do housework for a living, but this is a little different." She swung around on the bed and stretched out, hands behind her head. "I can see you're fascinated by the glamorous existence I lead. Remember when we believed that just to walk along Main Street in Limerock would make us feel like women of the world?"

Roz nodded. Her face was in shadow. "What did you come for, Jule?" she asked. "To tell me to my face that you hate me?"

"I've told you that I don't hate you now, except sometimes. I came for the money."

Roz said blankly, "What money?"

"My half from the money box. I need it for a deposit on a house I want to rent."

"What about the savings account?"

"That's still in limbo." *That word.* "For social security purposes I've been given identity. I'm Juliet Moreton, but when it comes to money, some real honest-to-goodness kin of Mummie's, a nephew and a niece, showed up and their lawyer says if they brought up one kid as their own and she wasn't, why couldn't the other kid be a stranger too?"

"Do *you* have a lawyer? Is he any good?"

"He's Mr. Peabody's lawyer. He's helped me from the start, when Mr. Peabody brought me off the island. He's still trying to find out where I was born, and every time I tell him to forget it he says it's a challenge and he can't turn his back on it."

"If you ever get the money you'll have to pay it all to him in fees," said Roz.

"Zack says no. It's a personal matter with him now." Jule shrugged. "Anyway, I never think about the money. I stopped that a long time ago. But I need that eight hundred, Roz."

"I needed every bit of it *then*," Roz said. "I used it all going to Portland and paying for my meals and my room there. Nothing was cheap, nothing decent, that is—I stayed in a nice hotel. Well, why shouldn't I?"

Jule didn't answer, and Roz rushed on. "I had to make long distance calls, and I had to have something fit to wear, I never took anything. Besides, I wanted something that *she* didn't choose from the catalogue or that we didn't stitch up on that damned old sewing machine." Jule didn't move. She sat there like a small image of stone.

"I wasn't going to forget you!" Roz shouted at her. "I was going to take care of you, the way I promised. But I *couldn't!*"

Jule snapped on a bedside lamp and saw Roz beautiful in her self-pity and distress, her eyes sparkling with tears that trembled like dewdrops without untidily spilling.

"You couldn't ask your family for it because they didn't know about me, is that it?"

"I *did* tell them you existed, but that we each wanted to

live our own lives and forget the past. They could understand how you'd feel about that. They've never questioned me about that life, or you."

"I can understand that. I'm practically a member of the criminal classes," Jule said. She was tired of the whole thing. Maybe she'd had enough to liberate her. "I'm not going to embarrass you. You must have your own checking account so you could give me the money and I'll go away, and that's it. I promise."

"I can bring it tomorrow morning." Then she tried to mask her eagerness with her new accent and mannered charm. "Jule, it's been so *wonderful* to see you. Don't let it ever be so long again. Do you have a phone number you can give me?"

Jule grinned. "Oh, come off it, Roz. You don't want my number any more than you'd want Dracula's, though you might have a go at him if it looked like fun. As long as you didn't let him kiss you." She swung her legs off the bed and went to the door.

Roz stood up. Her gestures were slow, pulling on the expensive coat, tightening the belt. She was preoccupied as if she wanted to say more, as if there should be more, but she didn't know what.

"Roz at a loss for words." Jule felt a small grim triumph. "Who answered the phone, a maid?"

"If she could hear you say that!" Roz came out of her trance. "That was Francesca Deverell, my cousin. One of the hostile elements that rushed to the scene when I showed up. She and her brother were the principal heirs, you see. *He* was all right, I suppose he thought if worse came to worst he could marry me." A swaggering assurance came back to her as she talked. "Fran's resigned to me now. Her boyfriend was worried for her and all that money, but he's the family lawyer, so once he knew I wasn't an impostor, he was fine. Easy to manage." Her smile was lovely; she bloomed like a gardenful of roses, if roses could be capable of pure vanity. She sounded incredibly like Jule's Roz. Was it possible?

"Your cousin must have been curious about the call."

"I told her you were someone who probably just wanted to say hello, you must be on your way somewhere. Mother and Dad are out for the evening, so is Piers. He's here on a vacation, and Fran's all wound up in some research project with Dad, she thinks she's indispensable to him."

"Is she?"

"I suppose so. I wouldn't know where to begin. She has a degree in Library Science, whatever that is." She shrugged.

"Did you go to college?" Jule asked.

"Are you kidding? *Me?* No, I finally convinced them I wasn't college material. Mother and I have done a lot of traveling, I help her with some pet projects, and I've made my friends and have my own social life. Well—"

The rough spontaneous embrace of their meeting was not to be repeated. They stood uncertainly in the open doorway. Roz's low car gleamed exotically beyond them. Jule had a sense of being lost in waste space between dimensions.

"Good night," she said.

"Good night. I'll bring you that check early tomorrow."

It was Jean Deverell who slid lithely into her car, started it into roaring life, waved, and cried—Jule could swear—"Ciao, darling!" She backed it around in a great reckless arc and went out with a powerful whoosh of expensive rubber on hottop.

The separation was real, and it was entire. Jule should be liberated now.

23

IF JULE COULD HAVE left then, she would have. What had she expected to find? How could Roz have still existed as she had known her? Roz had become what she was born to be. The goodbye on the island had been the final one after all.

Jule took a long warm bath, and then watched a mystery movie involved enough to absorb her attention. She slept heavily. Surfacing briefly toward dawn, she told Billy B. that it had worked, and sank again.

It was after eight when she woke up, and she was first incredulous and then pleased. She had never slept even as late as six. Now she was hungry, and eager to be on the move while the euphoria lasted. Eating the Lumberman's Special, she wondered maternally how Hodge was doing this morning.

She went back to her room, brushed her teeth, and wondered what she'd do until Roz came. She hadn't told her to mail the check to her because she didn't trust her to remember it. She'd forget it on purpose, the way she had forgotten Jule four years ago. If she doesn't come in an hour, Jule thought, I'll call the house again, and she'll deserve the embarrassment.

She had decided to take a walk in the direction Roz had driven last night when someone knocked on her door. She opened it not to Roz, but to two men. The motel owner was one of them.

"Nick here wanted me to introduce him and tell you he's all right. You'll be safe with him. As far as I know."

"Damning me with faint praise," said the man called Nick. He was a slim, very dark, young man in a pale tan trench coat.

The proprietor grinned. "Miss Moreton, this is Nick Winstead. Maybe I should say Nicholas, since he's got his office clothes on and his briefcase with him."

"How do you do?" said Jule politely. "What do you want to see me for?"

"If I can come in, I'll tell you." The delivery was clipped; not exactly rude, not hostile, but not friendly either.

"He really is all right," the older man assured her.

"I'll take your word for it," she said with a smile, and he left them. Winstead put his case on the desk. His narrow black eyes were not missing a thing about her. One eyebrow was tilted higher than the other and his nose was an arrogant beak; his long thin mouth promised nothing but trouble.

"I'm Scott Deverell's attorney," he said brusquely. Her gut seemed to twist, not with anxiety but with anger.

"If they sent you to get rid of me, there's no need. I came to see Roz, and I'm leaving the instant I hear from her this morning."

He didn't change expression. She was about to ask him to leave when suddenly he smiled. He had a long slash of a dimple in one lean cheek, and the black eyes sparkled beguilingly. "I haven't been sent here to get rid of you. I'm quite on my own. The Winsteads have been the Deverells' lawyers for several generations, and the sense of responsibility is inbred by now. May I take off my coat and sit down?"

"I don't know why it's necessary."

"You'll see. I've probably gotten off on the wrong foot and I'd like to correct that." He laid the trench coat over a chair. He was not much bigger than Jondy, elegantly turned out in a dark suit, wine-striped shirt, and dark red tie.

"How did you know I was here?" she asked. "Did Roz tell you?"

"I haven't seen her today, I just drove out from Bangor. Someone called me last night."

"Miss Francesca Deverell?" Sarcasm edged her voice.

"It doesn't matter," he said easily. "Could we sit down and simply talk?"

"All right," she said grudgingly. She sat down opposite him, folding her hands in her lap.

"Miss Moreton," he said, gentle now. "I do know more about you than Jean told, which was very little. On my own, out of pure but not idiotic curiosity, I talked with people at Port George. I heard nothing more than what Roz had told until someone very angrily blurted out that you two *hadn't* left the island together, set free when Beatrice died, but that she'd run out on you, left you alone out there with your dying mother and never let anyone know what the situation was. The woman died and you were still alone. How long was it before anyone came?"

"Roz didn't owe my mother anything but contempt," she said.

"But what about *you?*" he insisted, still with that deceptive gentleness. He must have used it to make someone give him the truth at Port George. "Didn't she have any feeling for you at all? She *said* she was fond of you, she believed for years that you were her sister."

"I don't need this," Jule said. Her stomach was beginning to protest in the old way.

"How have you been getting along? Has she ever tried to find out? Did you get angry after a while because you've never been able to forget those days alone with a dead woman? So you decided to give her a little trouble?" He leaned toward her, speaking softly. "Especially if you're hard up right now. . . . You might think she wouldn't want her parents to know how it really happened, and you'd be right. There could be other things she wouldn't want known about those island years. Didn't boys ever land on that island? They must have come like bees. Not where your parents could see, of course."

She stood up quickly. If there'd been anything handy to hurl into his smiling dark face, she wouldn't have hesitated.

"What about the son of the owners? The young gentleman from the manor, so to speak? She was a healthy, beautiful girl with a passionate nature."

He sat back with an air of triumph. "She wouldn't want all the fun and games brought to light, would she? Not after letting them think their baby came back to them as spotless as when she went?"

"Mr. Winstead," she said. "You have a filthy imagination, and a poor one if you can't imagine the shame I've had to live with. Do you really believe that I'd have the effrontery to threaten to go anywhere *near* those people when I know my parents stole their baby, and then let them think it was dead rather than return it? I came to talk to Roz about a private matter between us. It's not *blackmail*." She said it with loathing. Her small face was utterly contemptuous. "This will probably be the last time Roz and I ever meet, and it's our business and nobody else's. So will you please go away?"

His smile had gone. He was on his feet, looking concerned, and actually kind. "Not before I apologize. I've been abusive, and I'm sorry, but you probably won't believe it, I was only doing my job. But that's what Eichmann said, wasn't it?"

He picked up his coat. "You know something? When I

was in Port George I saw Osprey Island lying way off there. And I also saw *you*, down on Peabody's lobster car. You looked about fourteen years old, and you were buying lobsters."

She said unwillingly, "I used to tend car sometimes for Mr. Peabody when he had to go uptown." She'd loved it; she saw the harbor now on those late warm afternoons, the boats coming and going while her strain and anguish raveled out on the summer wind.

"I wanted to go and take a closer look at you, but I had no good excuse. I saw the black hair, I had no idea the eyes were so blue."

It was utterly disarming, and she didn't trust it, but he had evoked a time in her life that was always remembered in blue and gold.

"Will you accept my apology?" he asked, holding out his hand, and after a moment she put out hers. He held it firmly.

"Good Lord, I don't know when I've received such a blistering!" He laughed. "Not since my early days in the firm when my father peeled off my hide a couple of times." He whistled. " 'Effrontery!' I love it!" He wouldn't let her hand go. "I want to be completely honest with you, in excuse for my own effrontery. Francesca called me last night to tell me Jean had gone to visit a mysterious female friend at the Fernwood Motel, and had come back in a bad mood. She wouldn't talk, and shut herself up in her room. Francesca and her brother and I have always tried to protect a couple of very decent people who went through hell. For eighteen years they were victimized by impostors, fake mediums, and every other kind of criminal who battens on tragedy. So when buttons are pressed and bells ring, we get worried. Now their daughter is back, and if anything threatens her, it threatens her parents."

"All right," she said. "I accept that." She pulled her hand free and turned away, dismissing him, but he didn't go.

"They called you 'Jule' in Port George. I've never forgotten that. Listen, Jule, if you can't forget what *they* did, at least try not to think you're guilty by association. Nobody else sees you in that light. You were as much a victim as Jean was."

She did not want his sympathy. He was the Deverells' man and his presence brought shame into the room so strongly that she'd had to shut out the actual word.

She faced him again and tried to strike out and drive him away. She said defiantly, "I loved Jondy."

"What about your mother, or is that too personal?"

"It's none of your business!"

"I'll bet you thought you were the kidnapped one, right up until—"

"Will you *go*?"

"Goodbye, Juliet." His voice was tender, his grin mischievous. "Parting is such sweet sorrow when we shall not meet upon the morrow."

24

SHE WAS BADLY SHAKEN and was beginning to get the familiar stomach cramps again. She stood squeezing her elbows, wondering what to do. She wanted to get away, but pride clamped her rib cage in an iron embrace and painfully stiffened her neck. What would it look like if she ran as soon as the lawyer left her?

Damn Roz, holding her up this way. Wasn't she eager to get rid of her? Jule rubbed her cold arms with equally cold hands. She had to get warm. She pulled on her blazer and went out, to go across to the restaurant for a cup of hot tea.

On the way back she had to stop for a low, dark red Porsche swinging in off the road, and the man driving nodded and smiled through the tinted windshield. The woman beside him waved.

Jule waved back, waiting for them to drive by. Instead, the car turned into the slot opposite her door. The man swung out long legs in corduroys and scuffed moccasins. The young woman emerged from the other side. Smiling at Jule, they converged on her.

They looked alike in their slender height, the way the fair hair grew loose and soft from their ears and high foreheads. They both had wide, beautifully cut mouths, thin high-boned noses, cheekbones lightly spattered with pale freckles. Their smiles were alike, though his was broader. Their eyes were like Roz's the same acute blue of bachelor's buttons or chicory, set in thick fair fringes.

Deverell eyes, Jule thought. And where the hell is Roz?

"We're Francesca and Piers Deverell," said the girl. Her voice was low, but pleasantly suffused with warmth. "Nick Winstead arrived this morning absolutely radiant, to tell us all about you."

"Hello, Jule," Piers Deverell said.

"Where's Roz?" she asked bluntly.

"Still in bed when we left. I don't think she slept well last night." Francesca looked into Jule's face with a frank, steady interest.

"Why are you here?"

"To get you," said Piers. "You can't escape, you're ours. Tell her, Fran." He walked around, apparently aimless, with his hands in his pockets. He wore a bulky old Aran sweater.

"Our uncle and aunt want to meet you," Francesca told her. "They've always wanted to know more about you, but Jean has never wanted to dwell too much on that part of her life. Which is perfectly understandable."

Piers, squinting up at the sky as if tracking a bird's flight, said, "And it's also understandable that you wanted to begin a new life without any reference to the old, no ties, no connections."

"Yes, I insisted on that," she lied, compassionate for Roz. She must have felt under attack from the start by the effortless, invincible charm of the people who were there first. "I never wanted any part in her life. This is a kind of goodbye, that's all. I'm ready to leave as soon as I see Roz again."

"Nick said you were independent," Piers said admiringly. "But you can't go yet. You have to meet the aunt and uncle. They don't bite."

"But why?" Jule asked, beginning to sweat.

"They want to know you because you shared Jean's life for so long," said Francesca. "The lost years can never be made up, but they want to know everything possible to know about them, and you're an important part of those years."

"Roz can't want this," she protested. "She doesn't know you're here, does she?"

"She will by the time we get back," Piers said with a grin. "And in this case, it's what her father and mother want that's important. Get your bag, and I'll check you out." He wandered toward the office, whistling in the mild air. Francesca's expression was quizzical but friendly.

"Come along. It can't hurt, can it?"

Jule didn't move. For the moment it was a literal impossibility, and she thought the tea was going to come up then and there like a geyser.

"What is it?" Francesca asked in a low voice. "You're white. What are you afraid of?"

"What would *you* feel?" Jule retorted bitterly.

"The same way, I suppose. But I promise you, Jule, all they want to see, all they *will* see, is the girl who made life endurable for their child during those years. It won't matter who her parents were or what they did."

Once more unto the breach, dear friends! Then take the money and run. Think of your little house and cat, and no more dreams of Roz laughing. She'll be *out*. Exorcised.

"I could take the late afternoon bus for Limerock."

"Someone will drive you to Bangor in plenty of time. Probably Jean will want to."

After the first trauma, Jule was both amused and puzzled by the attention shown her. On the surface it was rather nice. They certainly had a gift for it, one a foil for the other, with a strong impression of teamwork. She decided to try to ignore what her intuition was telling her: that nobody, beginning with Nick, or perhaps even with Roz last night, was what he or she seemed. By late afternoon she'd be out of it, and in time she'd be proud of having met the challenge.

Piers insisted that she sit in front with him, and Francesca moved to the back. As they turned off the highway into the side road a man on a motorbike passed them on the way out, lifting a gauntleted hand. She hardly saw his face, which was dominated by the helmet and dark goggles, but she glimpsed a beard and a smile white in it.

"There's our resident biologist," said Piers. "At least he calls himself a biologist, but he could be masterminding a drug-running operation down there in the marsh. Who'd know? The stuff could be brought up the creek at high tide the way they used to bring the booze in the rum-running days." He grinned at Jule. "But he keeps his bike at the house, so he'd have to lug it all out on his back in the middle of the night, unless he's got a cadre of hikers lined up to backpack it; and they'd be likely day *or* night to be stopped by the Sheriff's Patrol, in case they're carrying off somebody's coin collection or old silver. So now I've talked myself out of Guthrie's life of crime and turned him back into an innocent, unworldly, marine biologist researching the exciting secret life of the marsh. Don't be afraid, Jule. You're not shut up with a manic-depressive. I never sink; I'm always manic."

"And boring," said Francesca. "After a while you simply learn to turn him off."

Sunlight twinkled through the red maple blossoms as they trembled in the breeze, making moving patterns on the road. She was excited, but with dread; she wanted to go on and on, yet the ride would end any moment now and she feared the ending. The glib self-confidence of the other two, the speed of the car, the alien landscape burnished with spring—there was no reassurance in any one element of the whole scene.

The road swooped around a long curve through spruce woods that gave off a cold resinous scent and shade. They went down a grade, broke out into sunlight, passed a mailbox on the left, and drove onto a narrow wooden bridge above a noisy stream splashing brown and white down a rocky gorge.

"We're on the property now," Francesca said. "The mailbox is at the line. This is Birnam Water, and we've been driving through Birnam Wood."

"If we ever look out some morning and see it advancing toward the house," said Piers, "we're in trouble."

Off the bridge and up another slope, the road forked. The left-hand way was only a faint double track disappearing into the woods. "That leads to the old orchard and the site of the original farm," Piers said. They went to the right, and came out to broad gentle surges of lawn broken by granite outcroppings and massive old oaks and maples. A tennis court showed beyond some magnificient blue spruces.

Too soon they reached the house. She realized she had been expecting a mansion, something stately and Federalist with a widow's walk, and an eagle carved over an impressive front door. This house was gray-shingled and gambrel-roofed; rambler rose canes starting to leaf out were trellised up either side and over the modest white-paneled door with its brass knocker and strips of small panes on either side. The house did not look very big, but once she stood in the hall she realized there was much more to it. She had an impression of airiness, much light, and an elegant simplicity.

Francesca was talking to a pleasant-faced middle-aged woman in a housedress and apron. Piers was going up the white curved staircase with her bag, three steps at a time, whistling. Light poured in from a broad arched window on the landing. He moved across it in silhouette and disappeared.

Where were *they*? Those who had sent for her? Doors stood open around the wide hall, she had glimpses of colors and polished woods as her eyes ranged from one opening to another; she was desperately anxious not to be taken by surprise.

"Jule," Francesca said, "This is Rodina Clement. Rodina, this is Jule, short for Juliet." Was it tact that made her omit the last name? The woman smiled and nodded.

From the stairs Roz cleared her throat and said, "Come on, Jule."

Francesca and Rodina Clement, talking, went past the stairs to a door at the back of the hall. Jule walked with Roz up the stairs toward that broad windowful of sky and clouds. Roz looked haggard, and was silent. From the landing they went up a short flight into a hall of white paneled doors, and met Piers on his way back. He grinned at them.

"Is this a dagger that I see before me? No, it's two gorgeous girls. Come, let me clutch thee."

"Funny, funny," Roz said.

Piers winked at Jule.

"Don't you like our little surprise, dear coz?"

"I always beware the Greeks bringing gift horses," said Roz.

"In this case, it's a rather pretty little pony."

"Thank you both," said Jule, reaching heady heights above ordinary anger. She whipped away from them toward the stairs, and simultaneously they each took an arm.

"Oh, come on, Jule," said Roz, sounding entirely natural. "Don't mind us!"

"Forgive us, first," said Piers. "Please. If you walk out now my aunt and uncle will have my scalp. Not to mention the painful way my sister will first remove it."

25

IN ROZ'S ROOM Jule's first reaction was relief at having a door shut between her and a sudden confrontation with the parent Deverells. The next was a conscious bracing to deal with Roz.

Windows of sky and sun blazed at her and she wanted to rush to them like a trapped bird. She turned around and said, "This wasn't my idea."

"Oh, I know that," said Roz. "Those two. Of course it was Fran. She likes to make trouble for me."

"Why is it trouble for you?" Jule asked mildly. "Do you think your parents will take one look at me and say 'We like that one better,' and toss you out?"

Roz ignored that. "Until I showed up those two had been the prince and princess, ever since those poor little bones were buried under my name. You'd think that after four years—well, I suppose you never get over losing a fortune."

"You mean they lived here like a son and daughter?"

"No, because they had parents and a home. But they spent vacations here so there'd be kids in the house. I can understand that," said Roz with an air of conscious generosity. "I'm glad they were here for Mother and Dad, I really am. But *I'm* here now."

"You couldn't really expect them to cut out entirely." Jule

turned back to the windows. "Your parents must be fond of them, too."

Roz didn't answer.

Directly below the windows there was a stretch of lawn, and a clump of tall white birches cast a network of shadows on the new bright-green grass. The turf was bounded by a stone wall, and beyond the wall the land descended in thickets, small copses, and rock outcroppings to the great tapestry of the marsh. Down there a bright blue creek appeared around a long low hummock to the southwest and meandered into a pool where a small dory and a skiff lay moored. They moved lightly whenever a breeze swooped down on the pool. Jule could see the gusts hit the water, sending catspaws shimmering across it.

On the far side, the marsh was bounded by rising and wooded ground; along a high ridge spruces pricked the April clouds.

"Fran called Nick, didn't she?" Roz said behind her. "Spying on me! What did he say? What did he ask you?"

Jule faced her with apprehension, but Roz looked quite good-natured. "Nick," she said indulgently. "The family watchdog. Terrier size." She dropped onto the four-poster bed; she wore designer jeans and a silky blue turtleneck jersey, and sprawled across the hand-quilted counterpane as if she had never in her life lived as anything else but the child of wealth and privilege.

"What happened to make him rush here afterward and tell them how wonderful you are?"

"Maybe it's because he found out how wonderful I am." Jule sat on the window seat. She couldn't keep from looking down on the marsh. Now she discovered a tent pitched on a wooded knoll off to the right of the tide pool. The biologist's camp, it must be.

"*Come* on, Jule!" That was familiar enough to hurt. She'd always said it like that.

"He thought I was here to blackmail you about your past as a nymphomaniac. He was going to save you and the honor of the family."

"Oh, wouldn't Fran love to find out something like that about me!" Roz rolled over, laughing. It was the way she'd always laughed, it shattered the glaze and made her sixteen again.

"I convinced him I wasn't a blackmailer, and then your cousins came and gave me a good reason for coming with them. I didn't exactly jump at the chance. If you'd gotten up earlier and brought me my check I'd have been gone by then."

"You like them," Roz said, "because they made such a fuss over you. I know just how they work it. They've always been that way to me. Cream and honey."

"Then why are you so paranoid about them? You're the daughter here, nothing can change that."

"Do you have to be so damn logical?" Roz sat up. "And I'm not paranoid, I'm honest. I've dispossessed them, and they're nice to me. And why? Piers taught me how to drive, how to play tennis, he took me to dances and parties. We've had a lot of fun together. But underneath is he *really* like that? After four years I don't know. Fran was all set to be Big Sister, except that I didn't need a sister. Fran," she said with fine sarcasm, "is always a lady. What was the reason she gave you for coming after you?"

"That your parents wanted to meet me because I shared your childhood."

"And you *believed* that?"

"It sounded reasonable, the way it was presented."

"But it's just to upset *me*."

Jule sighed. She was so tired of this her head was beginning to ache. "Thanks so much for the gracious welcome. It makes me feel warm and cherished, like the twenty-five dollars you left me. If you'll give me my money I'll be out of here so fast they'll think I was a hallucination. And *you* won't ever have to lay eyes on me again."

She got up from the window seat. "Come on, write me a check." She gestured toward the small elegant desk. "I'll go right now. I'll walk to the main road if you don't want to drive me."

"Oh, Jule!" Roz leaped up and caught her in a hard embrace. "Not yet! I'm glad you're here, honestly! You're somebody I can be me with, the *me* I grew up with. But it throws everything out of focus, can't you see? Even after four years I'm not half as sure of myself as I thought I was." She let Jule go, and got a handful of tissues and wiped her nose and eyes.

"It's funny," Jule said thoughtfully, "but all these years I've been seeing you swimming around in your proper element like a lovely blue and silver mackerel, right from the first."

"More like a blind cod in a school of herring." Spontaneously they laughed, and then looked away from each other.

"Jondy's expression," Roz said, "and I was always using it. They'd laugh, they thought it was colorful, but I trained myself out of it. Then let you show up and all that work is for nothing."

"I'm sorry, Roz," said Jule.

"Never mind. We'll get through today, we've survived worse." They walked back to the windows, arms around each other's waist, and stood looking down on the sunlit marsh.

"What about the men in your life, Jule? Do you go with any of those in your company?"

"Sometimes," Jule said.

"What about Billy B.? Have you made it to bed with him yet?"

Jule yanked away from her, indignantly. "For heaven's sake, Roz!"

"What are you blushing about?" Roz was delighted. "What's so terrible about the thought? I was dying to, but he would never give me the chance even to work on it. So come on, Jule, you can tell me."

"*No*," Jule said crossly.

"No talking, or no Bill and Bed? Didn't you ever *think* about it? Wish for it? Or is it strictly big brother and kid sister, and not the kinky kind, though I hear that's in nowadays. Simple home pleasures. Keep it in the family."

This was Roz all right, the Jean enamel was falling off in flakes.

"Have *you* been to bed with anyone yet?" Jule asked.

"Here and there. But not much, and very discreetly. Fools might rush in, but not me. I was a prisoner too long to let anyone put a lien on me now."

"What about the man down there?" She pointed at the tent. Roz backed off from her, genuinely shaken.

"Old psychic Jule. How'd you know?"

"You have a rosy aura whenever you think of him," Jule said solemnly. Roz's hoot of laughter was pure Roz.

"What have I been doing?"

"Staring at that tent. Willing him to appear. He won't, because we met him coming onto the main road as we turned off it."

"Gone to Orono, I suppose. He's connected with the U. of Maine. Jule, I don't know how he feels about *me*, but he's quietly passionate about his work. He's dedicated, and I love that about him and I don't want to interfere with his project or put his grant in jeopardy. When I find myself being that unselfish, I'm like someone who's had a mystic experience." She put her hands against her cheeks as if to cool them; the gesture was ingenuous and moving.

"I think I love him, Jule. I think it's real. I don't want to grab, shove, be greedy. I just want to be with him. The hours I spend with him I'm not Roz, I'm not Jean, I'm someone else. A really good and peaceful person. A person who is *good*."

She was touchingly fervent, and even her ears were scarlet. It was quite a phenomenon. "I wouldn't have told anyone else this, Jule. Only you. The minute you show up I regress five years."

Jule said dryly, "Your secret is safe with me, but don't you think anyone else has noticed?"

"They all know I like him, but they all like him too. And even if they thought I was crazy about him, they can't guess about the rest of it . . . his effect on me. All I pray for is that when he finishes his study here he'll take a good look at me, and at himself and discover that he's been falling in love with me all along. Just like those books we used to read, believing every single, solitary word."

"In the meantime why don't you get a job?" Jule suggested. "The time'll go a lot faster."

"Are you kidding? And miss out on a chance to tramp devotedly behind him while he makes his observations on what's happening to this or that?"

"Sounds fascinating," said Jule, and they both giggled.

"*He* is. Seriously, if I had any qualifications for a job, it would have to be away from Tremaine, and the parents like to have me around after all those years when I wasn't."

"Then you could get some education, so you'll be ready to hold your own in case you're the one who wakes the Sleeping Prince."

"The Sleeping Prince . . . that's my Dave all right, with his Marine fatigues and his baseball cap," she said tenderly. "Listen, Jule, I'm living one day at a time where he's concerned. I know in the old days I existed on plans. Now it's different. I don't dare plan because I couldn't stand the disappointment. So I just hope."

There was a scratching at the door, and Roz opened it. A small shaggy brown terrier scrabbled in and threw himself at her.

"Joey, love!" cried Roz, bending down so that the terrier could flick her nose with his tongue. "Well, the parents are back. They've been out walking around with Nick and having conferences. At least there are a few things that darling Francesca isn't in on. We'll have to get ready for lunch."

The word put a block of hardening cement in Jule's stomach. "I can't meet them."

"Yes, you can." Roz dramatically opened a door. "Can you imagine how I felt about having my own bathroom? With pink tiles? I still adore it. Come on in and wash, and comb your hair, and fix your lipstick. The first thing I did in Limerock that day was buy a lipstick."

"You remembered that, anyway," said Jule.

"If you're going to keep needling!" They confronted one another in the broad mirror.

"Excuse me," said Jule to the glowing image of Roz. "I'm not at all happy about this." She saw her face dark and tight, and turned quickly away from the mirror. "I can't eat in this house. Roz, this is where it happened. Where my parents planned it. I can't go and face yours."

"Oh, stop vaporing," said Roz. "Nobody can hold you responsible. You're here, thanks to the spy network, so let's make the best of it. If they think I'm upset about it, they've got another think coming."

26

JOEY RAN AHEAD OF THEM along the passage and down the short flight to the broad-windowed landing. Roz held Jule firmly by the arm. The hall below was like a stage setting, with the terrier the only creature unconscious of the drama. Piers and Francesca stood in an archway to the left, Piers watching the girls on the stairs. Francesca looked not at them but at the man who stood at the foot. Jule thought that Nick was off to the other side somewhere, but it was only an impression caught on the periphery of her vision. The scene belonged to the man waiting there, watching the girls descend the stairs toward him, his hands behind his back. He was a tall man with bulky shoulders, his tweed jacket was a warm rust against the cool blues and greens and ivory of his background. His thick brown hair was graying. His mustache and slightly tinted glasses made his lifted face a blank to Jule. She was unnerved by the silence and the inhuman scrutiny of lenses that seemed only to hold reflected light. She was more than unnerved; she was almost suffocatingly afraid.

If he can bring himself to speak politely to me, she thought, it will be worse than being ignored.

They reached the next to the last step. "Dad, this is Jule," Roz said blithely.

Now she saw eyes behind the lenses but she couldn't tell the color, just that she wanted to break away from them, and only stubbornness kept her from yanking free of Roz. The back of her neck was wet.

Just as she thought she could bear it no longer, he inclined his head toward her with a courtly air and put out his hand. Her own moved uncertainly to meet it, and was imprisoned.

"I'm glad you let them persuade you, Jule," he said. He could have been being gracious and indulgent toward any of his daughter's friends. His voice was not as deep as she'd expected.

"She had no choice," Piers said, coming forward. "She wasn't persuaded, she was snatched." It was an appalling joke under the circumstances but it didn't seem to bother anyone but her.

"Caroline!" Mr. Deverell called, still holding Jule's hand. She couldn't have got it away without a struggle. And there's not enough time to chew it off, she thought. The water ran down her back. A tall woman came through the door at the back of the hall, and walked toward them with a swift stride, the terrier bouncing around her feet.

"Here I am," she said, smiling amiably down at Jule. *Another of Roz's little friends, how nice!* the dispassionate side of Jule's brain said, while the other part ached to wallow in panic. Her helpless hand was transferred from Mr. Deverell's to his wife's. She had such a jolt in her chest she wondered if she was going to have a heart attack and die dramatically at their feet. It would be a relief.

The dark eyes that looked earnestly into hers were set deep in a long, plain face with an outdoor complexion. Her dark red hair was lightly stranded with gray, looped in a thick twist at the nape. Her smile began around her eyes and the plainness disappeared; one doubted that it had ever been there.

"Welcome to Birnam Marsh, my dear."

How can I be welcome? Jule wanted to cry out to her, wanted to make a scene, wanted forgiveness, and blessings, not merely generosity from people who could now afford to be generous.

Her hand was pressed, then gently released. As if on cue, Francesca came up behind her uncle and gave Jule a reassuring nod past his big tweedy shoulder. Piers said dreamily, "What a day of beautiful surprises! And to think I didn't want to get up this morning." He gave Jule a beatific smile.

"Shall we eat?" Mr. Deverell said. He and his wife walked toward the dining room.

Roz's—or Jean's—natural buoyancy was back. She tweaked a hair on Piers's neck and said, "You didn't think there was one good-looking girl left unknown to you in the whole state of Maine, did you?"

"Ah, but I knew her in my dreams," said Piers.

If it was a conspiracy, what was it for? Nick Winstead was there, saying, "Now Jule, just run up the stairs again so I can recite 'But hark, what light from yonder window breaks? It is the east, and Juliet is the sun.' "

"I thought of that, but I'm not such a show-off," said Piers. "Jule, I'll lead you to the food." Nick took her hand and pulled her arm through his.

"I discovered her, so I'm taking her in."

"You're rotten, did you know that?"

"To the core, as they say. Come along, Juliet."

"Ah well, I'll latch onto my foxy cousin," said Piers, "and my lovely sister."

"A thorn between two roses," said Francesca.

With her arm held snugly against Nick's warm hard side, Jule felt as if she were being towed rapidly beyond her depth and any moment now would be released to drown. The terrier scampered around their feet and she thought that if she could scoop him up he would be like the cat, a touchstone to fetch her back to reality with a jarring but welcome jolt.

The senior Deverells sat at either end of the long oval table. There was a good deal of lazy foolery among the younger three; Roz was Jean here, and no resentments or insecurities showed through the lacquer.

Food was constantly passed to Jule, but no one insisted that she eat, which was a relief, considering the state of her stomach. She was at Mr. Deverell's right, and his manner toward her would have pleased her if she hadn't been so conscious of her identity. She couldn't keep from sneaking glances at Mrs. Deverell, she wanted to look at her without hindrance, but whenever she did, the deep-set brown eyes always seemed to be expecting it, and Jule would look away quickly.

With dessert and coffee there was a discussion of afternoon plans. Roz began enthusiastically describing the walk she and Jule were going to take. It sounded as if she intended to keep Jule away from the house until it was time for her to leave, and Jule was willing.

"I'd better look up my bus first," she said. "I have to get one back by tonight."

There was a complete silence. Then Nick said, "*Have* to?"

Flushing, she appealed to Francesca. "I thought it was understood—"

Mrs. Deverell rescued her. "Someone will drive you to Bangor in plenty of time, Jule. So enjoy your walk with Jean, get caught up on your news, and then we'll have a cup of tea together before you leave." She laid a hand over Roz's. "Don't keep her out too long, Jean dear. Your father and I want to visit with her for a bit."

"I won't lose her anywhere," Roz said. She hurried Jule toward the stairs. "Let's get a good distance away," she muttered. Up in her room, she said, "I don't mean get away from my parents. It's that secret society of the other three. Though I like Piers, and Nick's all right, except that he's Francesca's property."

Jule laughed. "Leaving just Francesca that you can't stand."

"Why not? Obviously she can't stand *me*. That's why she's so damned nice to me. It's practically an insult. Here." She tossed a pair of jeans at Jule. "You'll have to roll up the legs a bit. Here's some socks too. Your shoes will have to do; you couldn't possibly wear my sneakers."

"I have rubber soles," Jule said absently. Roz handed her a scarf to use for a belt, and gave her a warm pullover.

When they went into the hall, the house sounded and felt empty until she heard a distant typewriter. Roz flicked a hand at doors as they passed them. "The parents have the big room and bath just across from me, on the front corner of the house. Mine's the nursery suite, by the way, where *she* and I lived until she stole me. . . . Next along, beyond the parent's two guest rooms. Nick always uses the same one when he's here so it's practically his."

They passed the stairs to the landing. "Francesca's on the other front corner, and Piers behind her, facing out on the side, next to this little sitting room and the back stairs. Handy for his comings and goings."

Joey's basket and a television set were in the small sitting room. "They won't have one in the living room, spoils the decor. I like it up here. Piers and I watch old movies. You can run down the back stairs and get things from the kitchen. Or scamper out, if you have an assignation."

"With a biologist in the marsh?" Jule asked, and Roz giggled.

"Don't I wish it! But I told you he's dedicated."

Through the sitting room they came to a landing on the back stairs. The servants' suite, part of the kitchen wing, opened from here, but only Rodina lived in, and she and the cook were out for the afternoon.

They went down the back stairs and into the kitchen, where the tea trays were already laid. Jule averted her eyes as if from the sight of torture instruments, and outdoors she breathed like someone escaping from a dungeon.

There was a roomy garage with several cars parked outside on the hardtop, various other outbuildings, and a woodpile whose symmetry was a thing of beauty. Beyond the buildings there was a newly ploughed kitchen garden, and a small orchard laid out in precise rows. Forest filled in the sky to the east, but the southwest was open to the great stretch of the marsh.

"There's a man who comes by the day to keep up the grounds but Dad works with him," Roz said. "Rodina's been with the family for years. She knew Mummie and Jondy; she was here when they took me." She spoke without drama. It had all become an accepted part of her life, but each mention bruised Jule like a flung stone.

They crossed the lawn and followed the stone wall into the woods at the western side. Roz led through a gap in the wall onto a path that descended to the marsh through poplars, alders, birches, and wild cherry. Blackberry vines wreathed thickly among them.

At one spot the track ran close to the edge of a rocky ravine gashed out of the hillside. Ferns, now slender and curled, would soon fill up the steep sides and hide the boulders at the bottom, and the tiny watercourse that ran among them. The whole hillside resounded with birdsong. The air was scented with earth, and green growth.

They came out onto open ground and followed a hard-beaten track through blueberry and juniper and then onto the actual marsh and the tough tussocky grass. A sea smell was blown to them on a southwest wind. The white dory and skiff now lay on mud flats.

In the west and north the land rose in dense woodland, and to the northeast the house stood above the hillside against a dappled sky. Jule couldn't seem to take her eyes off it. This was where it had all begun. The house began to assume a personality, a knowing presence. Fine tremors ran over her skin.

Roz was talking. "That's my dory, Jule. I don't know how many times I've been all the way to the shore, sometimes alone, if I could manage it—not very often because they worried so much at the first. But I've gone with Nick and sometimes with Piers, sometimes Fran's gone too. Or all of us at once. But the fact is, it's *my* dory. No one can take it away from me and sell it." She was not Jean but Roz, nourished by the knowledge that she had something that Mummie couldn't touch.

"Do you know what this place is called? The Jean Deverell Memorial Preserve, and it goes all the way to the sea. Can you *imagine* it?" Her blue eyes, Roz's eyes, implored Jule to be impressed, and Jule tried to look it. She was impressed, but not in the way Roz imagined.

"The only thing I don't like about the name is the word Memorial. I really hated it at first, it made me feel dead. The same as those poor little bones buried under my name." She hunched her shoulders and shuddered. "They changed the stone, but I still haven't seen it."

"It's astonishing," Jule murmured.

"What is? Tell me exactly what you're thinking! I can't stand it when you're so quiet."

"All this light, all this space, and you in the middle of it like a little figure in a glass paperweight. The Lost Princess returned. If we turn it upside down, will it snow? My head's spinning as if I were turning upside down. I won't take it all in until I'm far from here."

"Oh, I know how you are," Roz agreed happily. "You'll mull and you'll brood until you get everything in place for you."

It was the phrase *far from here* that made Roz so happy, Jule was sure. "Come on over to Dave's tent," Roz ordered.

27

JULE WOULDN'T GO into the tent while he was not there so Roz contented herself with talking about him.

Jule sat on the chopping block while Roz ranged back and forth, going on about Dave's devotion to marine biology, his scientific mind, his fine character, his good humor. Jule only half heard her. She listened to the wind blowing through the uneven old pines around the tent. The air smelled so fresh and wild down here, and there was something so safely familiar about being alone in it with Roz, even though the setting was as foreign to her as the moon, that she hated to go back to the house.

Suddenly Roz said, "Do you really want to go into the house and drink tea, or would you rather walk some more and be alone with me?"

"I think I'd like it if you gave me my check and then drove me to Bangor," said Jule.

"I *can't* give you a check for that much money." Roz grew red. "My checking account's very low, and I'd have to ask for an advance on my allowance. Then if I used it all up in one fell swoop I'd be broke again, and it would look very strange if I asked for more right away."

She sounded as if Jule were asking the impossible and being unreasonable about it. Jule controlled her own reaction.

"If I had rich parents who adored me I wouldn't be afraid to ask them for money to pay an honest debt," she said moderately. "You don't have to say you took the money behind my back. They don't have to know about how you left." It wasn't the time to tell her that Nick knew. "You can say I a-greed you should take it all to finance the search, but I was supposed to have my half back."

"And then they'll wonder why I made you wait four years! But all right, I'll get it for you, damn it!" She ran down off the knoll.

Jule didn't try to keep up with her. She was glad to be go-ing away but full of unworded regrets which she couldn't sort out, at least not now, and perhaps she would never want to face them.

She climbed slowly up through the trembling light and shade of the copse. Where the path skirted the ravine she stepped carefully around and under the tall blackberry whips, held onto a mountain ash trunk and leaned far out until she could look down to the bottom and see a minuscule splashing where a bird energetically bathed in the little stream.

Roz sat on the stone wall at the top. She got up when Jule came, ostentatiously avoiding looking directly at her but strode on ahead. When they came into the kitchen she stopped so abruptly that Jule almost walked into her.

"I could say I want to loan it to you."

"*No!* I won't have them thinking that's what I came here for!" She stared at Roz in revulsion. "Roz, how can you be so—oh, damn, I don't know why I expect you to be anything *but* insensitive. You're all set, you've got everything, and now you're not only trying to wriggle out of this but to make me look like the worst kind of leech—parasite—brazen—"

Color went out of Roz's face, she kept nibbling at her lower lip, her eyes had the hard shine of glass. She left before Jule could finish. The door still swung in the wake of her pas-sage, her voice was raised in the dining room. No, it was Jean Deverell's voice.

"Mother, where's Dad, do you know?"

Jule didn't hear the answer. She went up the back stairs to Roz's room. I can't possibly drink tea with that woman, she thought. It's all right for them, they were the victims, they can be gracious to me and think, How magnificent of us. But it would be a hell of a lot more honest for them to say, We can't stand the sight of Beatrice's whelp, innocent though she may be. Get her out of the house.

She could go out the back way again, and head for the main road. She was a good walker, she had walked hundreds of miles in four years, having never recovered from the first rapture of being able to go wherever she wanted with no devil to pay when she got back.

To hell with the money. She could pay Billy B. back little by little. Why had she ever jibbed at it? Because she wanted an excuse to see Roz. Well, she'd seen her, and knew now that some dreams were preferable to reality.

The tumult in her stomach ceased. She breathed easier. She put her handbag and raincoat with the overnight case and went to the bathroom. While she was washing her hands, Roz came back and slammed the door. When Jule returned to the bedroom, Roz was sitting on the side of her bed with her curly head bent, staring at the floor.

"Never mind it, Roz," Jule said quietly. "I'm sorry I ever mentioned it. I'm leaving now, and I don't want anybody to drive me. I need to be alone. I'll call a taxi from the motel."

"Are you crazy?" Roz asked dully, without looking up. "It's at least ten miles."

"Is that your bike out by the garage? I could take it and you could pick it up later."

Roz lifted her head. The tears were there, as Jule expected, turning the blue to purest, bottomless azure. "Why are you trying to make me feel like a criminal?" she asked.

"That's your doing. All I want to do is get away without

any more conversations with a Deverell, including you. I must have been out of my mind, coming here."

"Nick and Fran were in the library with Dad," Roz said, returning to her study of the carpet. "I couldn't talk to him alone, then."

"Forget it! Remember some of the stuff we memorized? Some we put tunes to?" She sang softly, " 'Farewell, and forget me, for I too am free—' I sing that often with my guitar. My cat is particularly fond of it."

Roz said drearily, "It's Fran's bike. I'll drive you to Bangor."

"No," Jule said. "The motel is far enough."

"*Bangor*," said Roz. Her voice gathered strength. She stood up. "Nick will say he'll take you, because he's going back anyway, but I'm going to do it, Jule."

No quarrel there, if she must be driven. At least she and Roz could be silent on the way. Roz would also think she was keeping Nick from discussing her with Jule. Not that Jule would allow that, but Roz was far more insecure than she had expected. There was the tea session to be endured first, but she had gotten herself into this and couldn't blame anyone else. Roz went into the bathroom to wash her face and repair her makeup.

Once more unto the breach, dear friends, Jule repeated to herself as she and Roz started down the stairs. Joey was waiting for them at the foot, twirling in circles, a ragged cloth rabbit in his mouth. Roz walked on through the archway to the left, but Jule spoke to the dog, sitting down on a step and putting her hand out to him. He pretended to give her the rabbit, then snatched it away, his eyes blazing with the fire of the game. Off beyond the arch someone began to play the piano.

On the island the only piano they'd ever heard had been the out-of-tune one in the Benedict house. Since then she'd heard good music on records, at local concerts, and in one house maintained by Clean Sweep. It always moved her. But to hear it here in this house, with all its other associations, was almost unbearable. She shut her eyes. It was such a beautiful, sensuous sound, you could all but touch it; it would run through one's hands like phosphorescent water at night.

Joey pushed his head under her arm trying to get her attention, the damp rabbit flopped into her lap. He nosed her hand toward it and made sounds of frustration.

The music stopped, and Mrs. Deverell said, "There you are, dear. Where is Jule?"

Hearing her name in that voice Jule wanted to run, not away but toward it, and imagined herself mute and grinning like a fool.

"Communing with Joey," Roz said.

"Hey, dear coz, I've been waiting for you," Piers said. "Bob called me about Joey's booster shots. I'll drive him in if you'll go with me and hold onto him. You know how he rages around challenging everything on the road, climbing over the wheel or my head because of some kid on horseback."

"I suppose so," said Roz without enthusiasm. They came out where Jule was still sitting on the stairs, and Piers said, "Hello, Little Sally Water."

Roz was sulkily nibbling her thumbnail. She had expected to monitor all conversations with Jule.

"I owe you for my motel room," Jule said.

"We'll take that up later. Come on, kid. Want to go for a ride?" Joey snatched the rabbit and left Jule in a rush of frantic paws and barking all the way out to the kitchen. "We'll be back in plenty of time," Roz called back to her. "Don't go with Nick. *Promise.*"

"Promise."

Alone in the hall, she tried to concentrate on the scenes in the landscape paper to calm herself. Then all at once she realized that Francesca and Nick should be at tea, too, so she wouldn't be alone with Roz's parents.

Mrs. Deverell came out through the archway and said, "Would you help me with the trays, dear?"

28

JULE FOLLOWED NUMBLY to the kitchen and stood in imbecilic silence while Mrs. Deverell measured tea into the heated blue and gold pot. "Now for the cozy . . . ridiculous thing, but useful." The cups were flowered and translucent, napkins small and fringed; lemon in thin slices, and little frosted spicy cakes. "Scott's favorites," she said. "I hope you'll like them too, Jule. Now if you'll take that tray; it's the lighter one."

Jule emerged from her trance. "I can take the heavy one, my hands are very strong."

"If you're sure, dear."

"I'm sure." It was the one thing she *was* sure of. She followed the tall straight back through the dining room into the hall. Nick and Francesca were just going out the front door.

"Goodbye for now!" Francesca called. She had binoculars hung around her neck.

"Fran's convinced there's something exotic in the old orchard," Nick said. "Blown off God knows what flyway. If we don't come back, it's carried us away. The keys are in my car, and my father knows where my will is."

"We'll take care of everything just as you'd have wanted it," said Mrs. Deverell. They went out laughing, and Jule was left alone with the Deverells, not even a Joey to help her. And it had all the signs of having been arranged. She began to sweat down her back again, and the tray shook enough in her hands to make the cups rattle.

Mr. Deverell met her at the arch and took the tray, and carried it to the far end of the room, where chairs and a sofa covered in flowery linen were arranged to take in the afternoon sun and the view of the marsh.

"Come and sit down." Mrs. Deverell patted the sofa beside her. "Do you prefer milk or lemon in your tea?"

"Lemon, please. I heard you playing. It was lovely."

"They used to tell me," Mrs. Deverell said, pouring tea, "that I'd be glad someday that they made me keep up my music lessons when I wanted to leave them for tap dancing. Well, they were right. At my age I can look infinitely more graceful playing the piano than tap dancing."

She handed Jule her cup. Mr. Deverell, moving quickly for such a big man, set a small stand at her side for it. She said nervously, "Roz and I used to pore over pictures of ballet dancers. They were so beautiful, but how could they stand on their toes? Then Billy B. told us about the special slippers, and how it hurt until you got used to it, and even then it could still hurt. One of his cousins was studying."

Mrs. Deverell, erect and long-necked, must have looked like a Burne-Jones maiden in her youth. She arched her brows. "Billy B.?"

"William Penn Benedict. Didn't Roz—Jean ever tell you—?"

Mrs. Deverell shook her head. Her husband leaned slightly forward, attentively, and their hunger touched her.

"His family owned Osprey Island. He used to come to stay in the big house sometimes, and we saved up all our questions for him. You wouldn't believe some of the things we asked him. But nothing ever fazed him." She smiled at her and Roz and Billy B. "Well, almost nothing. . . . He was our connection with the world. He told us over and over again that when we were eighteen we—"

Self-conscious all at once under the two pairs of eyes she looked down into her lap like a child.

"Jean has told us very little about that life," Mr. Deverell said.

"Can you blame her for wanting to forget it all?" Jule asked with some spirit. "And *me*?"

"Jule, please understand this," Mrs. Deverell said. "I am not seeing you as anyone's child but as the girl who shared Jean's childhood. Her father and I lost all those years, and if she won't talk about them, how can we ever find out anything to fill the blanks?"

"But if you have her back, what does the past matter? She may talk sometime—she couldn't be Roz and *not* talk. But even now, even after four years, she's not sure of herself. I guess anyone would have to go through what we did to know just how long it will take. It's quicker with me, I think, because my responsibility is only to myself."

She saw the truth as she spoke the words. "But I still have bad dreams. When Roz grows into it, when she knows it's real, knows it even when she's sleeping, then she'll be able to see the past at a safe distance and talk about it."

"This is something we haven't understood," Scott Deverell said. "But you make it lucid in one paragraph. And why not? You've known her most of your life, and we haven't." He smiled at her. "We're most grateful, Jule."

She saw now that his eyes were the same vivid blue as Roz's and the cousins'. He sat back in his chair, the thin cup fragile in his big hand. Mrs. Deverell held out the plate of cakes to Jule.

"We've always been a bit uncomfortable about the way Jean left you. Nick told us you were alone with your mother until she died, and afterward."

In her indignation Jule shook her head at the cakes. "If you know that about Roz, you should tell her, and that *I* didn't tell you." She wished Nick were there so she could let him know to his face what she thought of him.

Mrs. Deverell said gently, "She would have to know who told us, and it would make strain between her and Nick, and drag Francesca into it too, I'm afraid. . . . It makes no difference in the way we feel about her. You're very loyal and understanding, by the way."

"I wasn't very understanding at the time," Jule admitted. "But we're adults now. She was going to send someone for me, I know she was! But she must have been so confused and dazzled and excited all at once—we were so ignorant, you see, we'd never ridden on a bus or even made a telephone call. Everything must have gone out of her head. Then, after she found you, she was pretty sure Mr. Peabody had come to the island by that time, and got me. I can't blame her for wanting to shut it all out." She swallowed tea to moisten her lips and throat. "She couldn't have known my mother was going to die just then."

The two older people listened without moving. His eyelids drooped and with the vivid eyes hidden his broad rugged face was impassive. His wife sat very straight, her head slightly tilted on the long neck.

"Besides," Jule added, "Roz didn't owe *her* anything."

"But what did she owe you?" Mrs. Deverell asked softly.

Jule's cup shook wildly. She put it down. "Mrs. Deverell, she doesn't owe me anything except for what I came for. When she left she took what money there was in the house. She needed it, I knew that later, and I knew she intended to give me back my half. Well, she forgot. But I need it now, and that's why I wanted to see her. I never wanted to come to this house."

"But we wanted *you*," the woman said, "for the reason I gave you."

"Jule," Scott Deverell said, "my wife and I would like very much to have you stay on a bit with us. We'll also see that you get your money. This isn't a bribe. You'll have it whether you stay or not."

"I can't see why you'd want me, considering what my parents did," said Jule bluntly. This time he looked away first, toward the sunlit marsh.

"You're not accountable for anyone else," he said.

"It would be for Jean's sake," said his wife. "After all, who knows her better than you? If she's under stress, perhaps you could help her. You were her twin to all intents and purposes until four years ago."

But she doesn't want me or need me, Jule answered mutely.

"What about your job?" he asked her.

"I'm taking some vacation time," she said unwillingly, puzzled by her cooperation, however reluctant it was. "But there's my landlady, and my cat. They're expecting me home tonight."

"Then you shall call and tell them it won't be for a few days yet." He added dryly, "Does the cat have his own telephone?"

She grinned. "He'd probably love one. The Mickey Mouse kind." The others laughed, and Mrs. Deverell asked what kind of cat he was. Halfway through the story of Hodge's debut in her life she thought, What am I *doing*? What have they made me do? Roz will have my scalp for this.

It was too late now. They had accomplished their purpose. As if he had been orchestrated like the others, someone walked into the far end of the room and came down toward them. He was lanky in many-pocketed fatigues and an old, stretched, handknit pullover. He carried a limp baseball cap in one hand, and he was smiling in his brown beard.

"Dave, it's good to see you here," Scott Deverell said, rising to shake hands.

Mrs. Deverell said, "Come and have a cup of tea, dear, and do something about these things. Nobody's making a dent in them, and Martie will feel rejected. Jule, this is Dave Guthrie. Dave—Juliet, known as Jule."

He looked down at her from a bony height and said, "Hello, Jule. I came in on purpose to meet the new girl."

She discovered in the next five minutes why Roz was so drawn to him. He could have been Billy B.'s brother. He had the same accent, the same loose-moving rangy build with long arms and legs, the same amiable way of paying attention, of seriously considering, and of being unexpectedly funny.

All the other men could go by the board. Those in the cigarette and liquor ads, the yachtsmen watched through glasses, the handsome young lobstermen and clammers; Piers, with his fine-drawn blond distinction and charm, Nick of the dark good looks shot through with glints of mischief like fireflies in a black night; whoever the males were with whom Roz had been discreet. Not one of them could spin a thread, to use Jondy's term.

Whether we like it or not, Jule thought, Billy B. was and still is our first love.

29

HE BROUGHT WITH HIM an immensely comforting atmosphere. While he and the Deverells talked about the study in the marsh, she drank two cups of tea, and ate three tea cakes. She sat in her corner of the flowery linen sofa, half listening to the voices and gazing out at the shift of colors across the marsh as the afternoon moved toward evening.

But when the grandfather clock in the hall struck five in counterpoint with a mantel clock here, she rose up like Cinderella. Mrs. Deverell directed her to the library and the telephone.

She swung luxuriously back and forth in the leather-cushioned chair behind the desk, waiting for Mrs. Baynes to answer. Papers and open notebooks were spread out on the desk beside the typewriter, and scrupulously she kept her eyes away from them. It was shadowy enough in here now so she couldn't read the bindings on the shelves, which made them all the more provocative.

Mrs. Baynes, who had no idea of her errand, told her to have a good time with her friends. While she waited for the veterinarian to answer, Nick and Francesca appeared in the library, and the instant they were inside they were in each other's arms.

Obviously they hadn't seen her. She whirled the chair

around so her back was toward them, just as Dr. Ames answered in Limerock.

"This is Juliet Moreton," she said. "I'm going to stay where I am for a few days, if it's all right with you."

"No problem," he assured her.

"Thank you, and give Hodge my love."

"I shall. Enjoy yourself."

She turned around to replace the telephone. Nick sat on a corner of the desk lighting a cigarette, and Francesca was busily cleaning the lenses of her binoculars. "So!" Nick exclaimed. "All is discovered! Who is Hodge?"

"A cat," she said.

"Oh, God. I'm disappointed."

"So you're going to stay a while," Francesca said. "We all cleared out so they could work on you."

I'll bet Roz didn't know that's why she went, Jule thought. "I'm staying just a few days," she said.

"Enjoy the library," Francesca said. "Take down anything you'd like to read." She switched on lamps, told her how the categories were arranged. "Nothing's off limits and there are no closing hours. Jean learned to be a great reader in that strange life of hers. How about you?"

"We struck it rich on Osprey," Jule said. "The main house was full. There was a little of everything, and we were like those ants that eat anything in their way. We read it all, from Shakespeare to Harold Robbins."

"What did you think of Robbins?" Nick asked.

"Not as good as Shakespeare. Who'd want to memorize him?" The others laughed. She was inclined to like Francesca no matter how Roz felt about her, and Nick in Francesca's company, fresh from her arms, was less a lawyer than a lover. She was no longer angry with him. Perhaps it was the influence of the books, or whatever it was that Dave Guthrie had brought in with him. In any case it was all illusory. Being who she was, she could not ever be genuinely at ease in this house.

As she was going upstairs the piano began again, something simple and meditative. She felt unutterably sad and weary, and she did not belong anywhere.

She napped deeply on Roz's bed, with the western light muted to deep amber by the shades, and dreamed that Mrs. Deverell was her mother and that Roz had stolen her place from her, as Jacob had stolen Esau's. She cried in the dream and woke up sobbing.

She rushed into the bathroom to wash her face with cold water before Roz could catch her. Her coming here had wakened something better left asleep in its sea cavern.

"You don't have to put up with it," she said aloud, belligerently. "At least you know what the monster is. You can face it. That's better than tiptoeing through life like the man that on a lonesome road doth walk with fear and dread because he's afraid of what's behind him. If you have to vanquish your frightful fiend in hand-to-hand combat, *you can do it*." She was so ferocious in the mirror she had to laugh.

She heard the terrier's sharp bark downstairs, and a few minutes later Roz was in the room. "Hi! Have you been lurking up here like a mole all afternoon?" She tossed packages onto the bed. "Piers told me you'd be asked to stay to dinner and I knew you'd like something different to wear, so I got you a little present. Call it a belated birthday. Hurry up and see."

There was a slip, and a sheer dress patterned with little red roses. The long full sleeves were gathered at the wrist, the collar was round and innocent, the belt was a sash of red velvet ribbon. It was charming. It was also very young. If I had long hair I'd look like a brunette Alice in Wonderland, Jule thought.

"Well?" Roz demanded eagerly. "What do you think? There's a really nice little shop in Tremaine. I thought it looked just like you, and so did Piers."

I wish Piers had told you the rest of it, Jule thought. "It's nice," she said slowly. "It's the prettiest I've ever had."

"Try on the shoes." They were red sandals. "I remembered your size. I hope your feet haven't grown any more."

They hadn't. "Thank you, Roz," Jule said. "Is this really a present, or are you taking it off what you owe me?"

"It's a *present*! Can't you be gracious about it? And as far as your money goes—I'll take care of that once and for all." She started for the door.

"Don't hurry," Jule said. "I've been asked to stay for a few days, and they know about the money. So you won't have to make any explanations."

She couldn't tell which statement upset Roz more. She grew very red, as she always did, as if she had trouble with her breathing. "How did you manage it?"

"The money came up by accident. I made it sound all right, don't worry."

"But why do they want you to stay? You, of all people?"

"It's for your sake," said Jule. "They think you'd like it. I couldn't very well tell them the truth, could I?"

"It's just so damned confusing! My two lives mixing up and I don't want even one scrap of the other one. Can't you see?"

"Maybe you don't want it, but you can't pretend you were born five foot eight with bosoms and designer jeans."

Roz gave her a tortured grin and bolted into the bathroom. "You'll be sleeping next door!" she called back. "You can find it!"

Jule took her things and went out into the hall and along to the next door beyond the bathroom. In which of the two rooms had Mummie slept? Was this the glass into which she gazed with the green, heavy-lidded eyes while she brushed and did up her long black hair? All redecorated, Roz said airily, so probably this wasn't even the same furniture. She hoped it wasn't.

At dinner Roz began in low key, but improved to concert pitch. She'd reconciled herself to Jule's presence for a couple of days, and then all that part of her life would be over with. If anyone could convince herself that she had been born fullgrown, it would be Roz. But part way through the meal Jule became aware that Roz wasn't totally the center of the stage. Nick Winstead was watching *her*; when she caught him at it, he winked. It was so funny and unexpected she couldn't hide a small grin.

After dinner he was driving to Bangor, and Francesca decided to ride to the gate with him and walk back. Roz and Piers were going to watch a television special, and Piers invited Jule to join them, but she was tired of Roz's showing off, and worn out by the burden of the day. She excused herself to go to bed. She had chosen three books, and the bed was superlatively comfortable.

When she put out her light she drifted on the music of the peepers out over the marsh, where the tide was creeping silently up the creek in the dark. It was a lovely escape until doors opened, and a light from the bathroom blazed in on her. She flopped over crossly to get away from it.

"Are you asleep?" Roz whispered.

"Yes," said Jule. "Go away." Roz giggled. She put off the bathroom light and bounced onto the foot of the bed.

"You know what I thought of just now? Our one birthday party. The time when she was sick with shingles, and Jondy snuck us away on the west side of Landfall and gave us our first and only cookout. I can still feel that flaming marshmallow on my upper lip."

Jule didn't answer. Roz quieted, and asked somberly,

"Jule, what was it like? Was it terrible, being there with her dead?"

"Her being dead wasn't terrible." Jule turned onto her back. Roz's head was a dark shape against the pallor of the window. "But being alone was, in all that fog. As if nobody in the world knew I existed."

She felt Roz's shudder against her feet. "I can't forgive myself."

"Oh, go ahead, have a try at it. Fight your better instincts. *I've* forgiven you, and anything I can do you can do better."

"Is that a slap?"

"No. It's over, Roz. What's gone, and what's past help should be past grief."

"*A Winter's Tale*," said Roz. " 'We were as twinn'd lambs that did frisk i' the sun, and bleat the one at the other; what we chang'd—' "

" 'Was innocence for innocence,' " Jule joined in. " 'We knew not the doctrine of ill-doing, no, nor dream'd that any did.' "

"At least not the kind we found out about later," Roz said. "Jule, she was your mother. How did you feel?"

"Why do you want to know?"

"Because I do. You know how I am, I want to know everything. I haven't changed that much."

"I'll tell you this. I never felt as if she was my mother, and I didn't feel it after I found out she was. I would look at her and try to imagine being carried by her, inside as well as out, and I just couldn't. Maybe because I can't remember being rocked or cuddled by her, only by Jondy."

"She was a cold bitch," said Roz. "No, that's an insult to dogs."

"Now, at a distance from it, I can be a little sorry for her," Jule said. "She did a terrible wrong, and it didn't pay off. So she wanted to punish the Deverells for her crime against them, and by keeping you she put herself in prison." Jule rose up on her elbows and tried to look at Roz's face in the gloom. "She was far more miserable than the rest of us. Jondy worshipped her, in spite of his bad conscience, and that made life bearable for him. You and I were young and we'd get away sometime, unless she killed us to keep us there."

"Oh, God, I was really afraid of *that!*" said Roz. "The way she was after Jondy died. I used to have nightmares about it. When she went down like a tree I couldn't believe it. Then I couldn't get away fast enough."

Jule didn't answer, and after a moment Roz said, "I suppose everybody talked about me, and the awful way I acted."

"Not for long. You were a nine days' wonder and then it was over. The *Limerock Patriot* called the Peabodys about having an interview with me, and I refused, and that was it. I don't want to live in either your shadow or your glow."

"Still, the Peabodys and other people back on Landfall must have expected I'd do a lot for you."

"All I want—"

"Is eight hundred dollars," said Roz.

"I wasn't going to say that," said Jule with dignity, "but I'm glad you're keeping it in mind."

"No chance to forget it now that you've told *them.*" She didn't sound angry. She yawned. "I went down and visited Dave tonight. The television and the back stairs are a real help to Piers and me. I don't think *he's* back yet. He has a string of enchanted girls."

"Was Dave enchanted? Or enchanting?"

Roz laughed. "He had a lot of paperwork to do, and he made me feel like a ten-year-old pest that he's too nice to be rude to." She got up off the bed. " 'Night." She felt her way to the bathroom door, still yawning.

Jule had to put on her light and read two chapters of *Nicholas Nickleby* before she could begin to float again.

30

WHEN SHE WOKE UP she knew at once where she was. It was after seven, and very quiet except for the birds, outside. There was one peremptory robin high up in a big birch on the lawn. Jule knew before she went into the next room that Roz was gone. She had always hated getting up early, so the motivation now had to be a powerful one. Dave, probably. She wrapped herself in Roz's robe and went to the windows. The creek bed was a dark winding line across the rich texture of the marsh, and nothing human moved down there.

Just below the windows, Mr. and Mrs. Deverell walked arm in arm on the damp, house-shaded lawn. Joey ran along by the stone wall pushing his nose into crevices and ardently wagging his short tail. The Deverells stopped and talked, heads bent. Jule's stomach, until now quiescent from the narcotic of heavy sleep, was unpleasantly aroused. She had the feeling that they were regretting their invitation, that they had discovered in her some maddening resemblance to either Mummie or Jondy and now could see nothing else but that.

She washed, dressed in her skirt and blazer, and went downstairs in a silent house filled with sunshine. In the dining room she saw three places set for breakfast, and wondered what she should do. Then she heard Francesca's voice out in the kitchen, so she went through the butler's pantry. There was a good-natured discussion going on, and when she knocked, someone in the midst of a laugh told her to come in.

Francesca, Rodina, and a thin young woman with short red hair and outsize glasses sat at the table with their coffee cups. "Hello, Jule," Francesca said. "You know Rodina. This is Martie Foster. Juliet Moreton."

Martie arose to shake hands. She had a hard grip. "What will you have?" She went briskly down the list. Jule made her choices, and wondered if she should go back and wait in the dining room.

"Would you like to eat out here?" Francesca asked. "Do you mind, Martie?"

"Nope," said Martie.

"Did you sleep well?" Rodina asked her.

"Oh yes, thank you." What did this woman think of Beatrice Moreton's daughter? Her pudgy, amiable face could hide a good deal. She took her cup to the counter and said, "Well, I must get on with my work." She left by the back stairs.

Martie set cranberry juice and oatmeal before Jule. "If nobody minds, I guess I'll restock the bird feeders," she said. She went out the back door, thin and straight in blue slacks and a gingham shirt.

Very self-conscious now, Jule sipped her juice and stared at the pattern on the cream jug.

"Would you rather be left alone?" Francesca asked.

This disarmed Jule, who said at once, "I shouldn't be here."

"They wouldn't have asked you if they hadn't wanted you."

"But how can they stand even to *look* at me?"

"They're strong people, Jule. When they asked you to stay they'd thought it over very carefully beforehand."

"But being here isn't doing me any good," Jule argued, "or Roz either, no matter what they think. . . . I shouldn't have asked for this cereal."

"It'll go out behind the garage tonight for the raccoons.

How about some coffee and toast? Martie bakes all the bread here." She took the dish away, and sliced bread from the brown loaf on the wooden board. "Look at it this way, Jule," she said. "You think you're of no use here, but couldn't you just give them the benefit of the doubt for a few days? That's what they really want."

Why she should trust Francesca, she didn't know, but knots were being untied, harsh wrinkles smoothed out. The toast was good, the coffee reviving. Martie Foster returned, saying with terse satisfaction, "Just saw a male cardinal." She and Francesca each got fresh coffee.

After her second piece of whole wheat toast, Jule asked Francesca where Roz was.

"I haven't seen her this morning. She's probably making the rounds with Dave." They went through the dining room to the sun-filled hall. "I'm going into Tremaine. The historical society keeps its records in the public library, and I've got to do some digging in them. I'd take you to town with me except that I use a bicycle here, and you'd have to ride on the handlebars. The local police frown on that."

Jule laughed. "I'll take a walk."

"If you go to the old orchard this morning you might see a deer, as well as a lot of incoming warblers. Take my binocs, they're in the library. But you'd better change out of that lovely skirt first."

Jule walked out to the garage with her in the cool bright morning. "Nick will be out tomorrow for the weekend," Francesca said happily. "We've been talking about a picnic at the shore, and the weather report sounds sensational. We row down the creek on the outgoing tide, and come back up with it as the moon rises. We're glad you'll be with us."

"I am, too," Jule said.

She meant it. Let Roz go scratch her maddest spot. If the rest of them wanted Jule around she'd get what she could out of it. She had wanted to like Francesca from their first meeting, even while she was being recalcitrant. It could be that the resentment and jealousy had always been on Roz's side.

She watched Francesca ride off down the driveway, and then returned to the front door, intending to change into the jeans. Joey hurled himself at her; the Deverells were conferring by the hall table.

"Good morning, dear!" Mrs. Deverell called.

"I'm going into Tremaine for a haircut, Jule," her husband said. "Would you like to come along? It's not very exciting, but there might be something you want."

Jeans and sneakers of her own for the picnic. "Can I have five minutes?"

"Oh, take ten."

"He's being the crusty but kindly old squire this morning," Mrs. Deverell said.

Alone in the station wagon with him, Jule was attacked by a juvenile and nearly paralyzing shyness, and looked very hard out her window as if she had to memorize everything she saw. By the time they'd crossed the wooden bridge and passed the mailbox, taken the rising turn and had almost reached the main road, he still hadn't spoken, and she still kept her head turned away, but she saw hardly anything. Her hands tightly held her bag.

Suddenly he said in his light, agreeable voice, "What have you done since your mother died, Jule? How do you live? What's your work?"

She told him briefly. It was easy to tell facts. "Clean Sweep sounds like a going concern," he commented.

"It is. It provides essential services, and no one needs to buy the whole package. We'll send someone to do just windows or shampoo carpets, for instance. Yard work. Snow cleanup. We can always provide part-time staff for these jobs in addition to the regular team. Some of that has changed as

people move on to something else, but I'm one of the origi-
nals."

"Have *you* ever thought of moving on to something else?
Not that I'm downgrading Clean Sweep, but I'm curious."

"Housework was the thing I could do well when I came
off the island, and I had to begin earning my living. But no
matter how successful an idea Clean Sweep was, I never
thought of making it my life's work. I do have more education
than high school, I took university extension courses, and by
now I've accumulated a pretty good liberal arts education with
almost enough credits for a degree. But my mind is too scattered, somehow." Why was she telling all this? She kept for-
getting he was one of the victims. "I can't seem to make any
long-range plans. As long as I know what I'm going to do tomorrow, or next week, I feel—" She hesitated.

"Safe?" he suggested.

"That's the word. That's it, I think. And sometimes I hate
it! On the island we were forever planning out our lives. The
world and the opportunities in it were limitless to us then.
Now I'm off, and—" She made a gesture with her hands to ex-
press futility. "Of course for a long time I had no legal existence. I was officially a nonperson and that had a demoralizing
effect on me, I think. But that's no excuse now."

"Your mother," he said, "was a woman of some education.
Well-read."

"Jondy always said that. But there was never anything to
read in our house but the almanac and the calendar and
Jondy's mother's Bible. On Landfall we read through the
school library over and over. On Osprey we did all our reading in the Benedict house."

"But you were named for two of Shakespeare's heroines."
He sounded bemused. "Didn't that ever puzzle you?"

"Yes, but it could have been a coincidence. We didn't
know anything about her," she said. "Jondy told us all about

himself. Well, almost everything. But we could never get him to talk about her except what he said about the—" Her throat blocked.

"The kidnapping. You can say the word."

"He did say she was a very handsome young woman."

"She was, I suppose," he said absently, stopping to let some cows cross the road. He and the farmer exchanged greetings, and some spell was broken inside the car. Jule decided they'd gone far enough with Mummie and Jondy. She still couldn't believe the Deverells really wanted the pair's daughter here, and if they were being nice to her for Roz's sake, how could she make it clear to them that if Roz had succeeded up to now in burying Jule along with the rest of it she certainly didn't want her resurrected now?

Riding along, staring out without seeing anything, Jule felt sickish and depressed. She wanted to be away from here; she thought, with a weak childish sensation of tears in her throat and nose, of holding Hodge in her arms, of the office on Linden Street and the others coming and going; of the small house in view of the harbor. I was the worst kind of fool to come here, she thought. And this is what I get for lying to myself.

31

THEY DROVE ALONG MAIN STREET under an arch of elms in translucent leaf, past white houses where the General Tremaine Inn and the post office faced the business block. There were not many people about this early. He pointed out the dress shop to her.

"The car will be unlocked, so you can put your things away. I may have to wait a bit at the barber's, and if you get bored waiting, they have some fine paintings at the public library, by one of the local boys who became famous." He told her where the library was. "Francesca will show you around."

He went along to the barber's, greeting and being greeted on the way. She went into the dress shop. A stout, pretty woman with curly white hair had been watching them through the door. She said thoughtfully, "Scott Deverell always makes me think of Richard Cory. Without the sad ending, of course. Do you know that poem? Or don't they teach Edwin Arlington Robinson these days?"

"Oh, I know about Richard Cory," said Jule. "Yes, it fits."

"And Mrs. Deverell. Such a lady! We couldn't believe that something so terrible could happen to them. And now to see this beautiful girl of theirs. . . . Well, you know all about it, don't you? You must be the friend she bought the dress for yesterday. A birthday gift."

"Yes, and one of the prettiest I've ever had." She could be sincere about it.

"It must suit you. She said you were small and demure."

Jule repressed a grin which would have been anything but demure. "What I'd like now is something for a long weekend. I hadn't planned to stay even a night."

It didn't take long to pick out what she needed, including another change of underwear and, as a present to herself, a two-piece dress in fine gingham checks of blues and greens.

"That could have been made for you," the woman said. "It's a sample, so I'll take ten dollars off."

Jule thanked her, wondering if being seen with a Deverell often led to such favors.

She went to the drugstore next, picked up a few useful items and some postcards with an aerial view of the marsh and creek at high tide on an autumn day, the roof and chimneys of the house just showed through the golden foliage at one side. Across the street in the post office she wrote a note to Billy B. on a card and mailed it to him at Port George. She said simply that she was here for the weekend and would tell him all about it later. She wrote one to the Peabodys also.

Then she went looking for the library, a short distance beyond the business block. It was one of the old white houses, with maples on the lawn. From a certain angle as she approached, she glimpsed a grassy yard beyond it, with lilac and forsythia, and fruit trees. Two persons were sitting on a trestle table under a huge old cherry tree. Then the corner of the house hid them. She went along the brick walk to the porch, where Francesca's bike leaned against the railing. A modest sign beside the door identified the house as the Tremaine Public Library and the Ira Getchell Homestead, built in 1736.

Inside there were white paint, low ceilings, and morning sunlight and shelves of books, and the glow of the paintings.

"I just heard about these," she said to the girl behind the desk.

"Help yourself," the girl said with a smile. "They begin here and they're all through the rooms."

Her euphoria was increasing by the moment. This was a lovely place; it was worth coming to Tremaine for. She took her time looking for Francesca. She walked around carefully examining each painting and reading its title. In one room, some small children around a low table chattered softly among themselves while their mothers browsed in the next room. Windows gave on the deep yard, with its rustic wooden chairs set around for outside reading, and there were the two people sitting on the table under the cherry tree. The woman's hair took the light that came down through bare twisted boughs. She was graceful, motionless. The man swung his legs, and was smoking a cigarette. He was Nick Winstead, and the woman was Francesca.

Jule froze in place, then moved swiftly backward out of the line of vision. Nick wasn't expected until tomorrow; something had brought him out early. She bore with her an instant reprint of their expressions, solemn and absorbed.

A lovers' meeting, because he couldn't wait until tomorrow? Or a lovers' quarrel? How could that be, after the passionate embrace in the library yesterday? Feeling extremely tactful and kindly, wishing them well, she left the library.

When she came back to the car, Mr. Deverell was putting some packages beside hers. He turned and saw her, and smiled. *Richard Cory.* And Roz could claim him for a father! The torture of jealousy could be a matter of choice, and she didn't choose. She'd afford it no house room.

"I saw the paintings," she said. "I could have looked at each one for an hour, I think."

"They're Tremaine's most precious treasure. After General Tremaine, that is. When we get home, go in and look at the painting over the fireplace in the living room. Did you find Francesca all right?"

"I saw her bike, but I didn't ask for her. I thought she was probably busy."

"The Historical Society collection is upstairs." The policeman came out of the drugstore and held up the sparse traffic for him to back out. "Thanks, Bob!" Mr. Deverell called. She thought perhaps the Deverells were considered a local treasure also.

He drove without speaking until they'd left Main Street and were in open countryside again. Then he said, "Tell me about John." It was not peremptory, but it wasn't tentative either. Well, he deserved the best she could do. And whatever they thought of Beatrice's daughter they'd know she was no coward.

"I think he was always sorry," she said, "but he didn't know what to do about it. I know now he had limits, he had to be as off-track in his way as she was in hers. But sometimes he could manage her. She had silences . . . depression. He'd send us out and sometimes we'd be gone all day. That saved us, because it gave us a chance to blow up." She saw, not the country road through the windshield, but the two of them running, whooping, cursing, threatening, or walking silently through a winter wood.

"When he was gone—" Her palms slammed soundlessly together, fingers locked in pain. "He was good to us," she said gruffly. "He tried to make fun for us. And it was so quick, the way he went." Her nose clogged. It was dreadful, to betray herself after all this time. She struggled obstinately. "One day he was here, and the next—"

No good. She groped hopelessly through her bag. A handkerchief appeared before her, fresh linen from his breast pocket.

He asked her nothing more, and she had time to straighten

her face out before they reached the house. She was afraid her eyes might look strange, and whoever was there would notice even if it was not remarked upon; she felt as if she were helpless under a microscope, and the apparent benevolence that went along with the concentrated attention was harder to take than Roz's frank reactions to her presence. She *knew* Roz; the wealthy young woman was still her old cellmate. They couldn't have been any more twinned unless they'd come from the same egg.

The wealthy young woman did not wish to be reminded of the fact that the instant they were alone together they were cellmates again. Theoretically they could do as they pleased. *It* was all over. But it required an act of will greater than the two of them could perform to bring it to a close, and until then it would never be all over.

Jule had such a pure and lucid view of the situation, saw it bathed in the exquisite light of logic, that she wished she could make it clear to the quiet man beside her. But she hadn't the words; she was inadequate for everything except to endure. Wasn't that what she'd always done?

"Roz was always the schemer," she said suddenly. "She always had plans. She'd go over and over them, take into account every possible unexpected circumstance. And when she had the chance she acted, and it worked, just as she knew it would."

"I don't think," he said, "that she has been so daring since."

"She's not desperate now, except in the way I tried to tell you yesterday."

"Jule, what about these people you stayed with at first?" he asked.

"There couldn't have been a better place to go," she said. "It's a big family. There was a baby grandson and I adored him, I'd never been around a baby before. There was a dog. I adored *him*. There was one son, still at home." She laughed. "You can't imagine what it was like for a girl like me to be living in the same house with a teen-age boy. He accepted me the way the dog and the baby did, and he was the first friend I made who was anywhere near my age. He's an all-around good person, like his father and mother."

"You've been lucky in your friends."

"His baby calls me Aunt," she said proudly.

32

NO ONE except for Rodina and Martie were about when they went into the house. He asked her if she would like a cup of coffee. She wouldn't have minded one in the kitchen with the women, but she'd spent enough time alone with him. She hadn't realized the strain both emotionally and physically until she got up to her room and had to fall on the bed.

"This is ridiculous," she said aloud to the ceiling. "I'm keeping myself vulnerable. It's not a road to Nowhere for me now, it's a road to anywhere, and it's my own fault if I don't take the one that leads out of limbo." She grinned. "I really should call my new house that. Welcome to Limbo. Come to a housewarming in Limbo. I'll have stationery printed up and the first letter will be written to Billy B. I beg your pardon. *Bill.*"

The foolishness helped. She got up and put away her new clothes. She'd get through the weekend the way she always got through things, even when she didn't expect to, and be thankful to leave on Monday.

Francesca was home by lunchtime, but Nick hadn't driven her out, and no one mentioned him. So it had definitely been something between lovers, and if Francesca wanted to ignore it, Jule was certainly glad to forget it. She couldn't tell if Francesca was depressed or worried; Roz had accused her cousin of being able to keep up a smiling front.

Roz hadn't come upstairs to talk to her before lunch. She'd been with Dave all morning, and at the table she discoursed eloquently on his discovery of a probably rare plant, and strewed botanical terms throughout like rose petals.

"Hey, you may have something terrific named after you," said Piers. "How about the Deverell Fleabane? Or Jean's Liverwort."

"I'd be proud," said Roz haughtily, and then laughed.

"Care to play tennis after lunch, Jule?" Piers asked. "Fran'll join us—won't you, love? And Joey makes a great ball boy. Of course you have to fight him for the ball each time, but that adds guts to the game."

"Oh, Jule has no use for tennis and she doesn't mind saying so," Roz said.

"Funny, I didn't hear her say anything," Piers said.

"Oh, she can read my mind," Jule said. She could feel Roz's relief, possibly gratitude, but in spite of the moment of communication, she wasn't surprised when Roz didn't come into her room after lunch. She hurried to change into her new jeans so as to get away from the house without meeting anyone else in this quiet hour, but when she went out Piers was sitting on the front doorstep, wearing blue shorts and a rugby shirt, bouncing a tennis ball on a racket. Joey was poised to pounce if the ball missed.

Piers looked up. "What are you thinking behind those solemn eyes? What do you make of this place?" He patted the step beside him, and she sat down. He tossed the ball for Joey.

"It's a happy house," she said.

"It really is now. But when we were kids our aunt and uncle made us *think* it was happy. We always loved to come here in the summer, it was the only heaven we wanted in our prayers." He laughed. "When I was small I had our Father which Art in Heaven confused with Our Uncle Which Art in

Tremaine. We never knew the horror they'd been living with, until Fran found out by accident. She was about twelve, and some summer kid told her. Imagine, all those years, and nobody we knew in Tremaine ever told us. That's the way these people are. They have a true delicacy." He looked seriously at her with the blue Deverell eyes. "We'd never even known there'd been a child. . . . Anyway, then we got the whole story from our parents, but we never let Uncle Scott and Aunt Caroline know. But they must have guessed we'd found out, because we changed; we couldn't do enough for them."

Joey came back and kept trying to push the ball into Piers's hand, then resisting his efforts to take it. Suddenly color swept into Piers's face. "Forgive me, Jule," he exclaimed.

"No, go on," she said. "I'm glad when someone forgets for five minutes who I am. *I'd* like to."

"Oh, Jule!" He gave her nearer knee a hard squeeze and a shake. "That's not a pass. Well, I'm not going on and on with the hard details. I'll just say that when we reached our teens our parents didn't see any need to keep it secret if Uncle Scott was having a new fake investigated, or if Aunt Caro was going to a new medium. For a long time Fran and I dreamed of miraculously finding our cousin and bringing her home in triumph. But that vanished with most of the adolescent dreams. It seemed absolutely positive that the poor little bones buried under Jean's name were hers. Aunt Caroline gave up the mediums long ago, after sure proof of fakery, and gave herself over to good works in the name of Jean Deverell. And then Jean Deverell came back."

"If she hadn't shown up," Jule said, "you and Francesca would be the heirs."

"*They're* happy beyond imagining. Don't you think," he asked quietly, "that for my sister and me it's worth forfeiting any inheritance?"

From behind the screen door Roz said merrily, "What are

you two planning, an elopement?" She came out, tall and golden-limbed in shorts, carrying a racket. She appeared to be just what she had always known she was; the gloss of wealth and maturity seemed to renew itself miraculously after each assault on it.

"I thought that was what you and I had cooked up." Piers wrestled the ball away from Joey. "Do you think I'm bigamous? I'm still trying to talk Jule into playing tennis."

"You'll never convince her."

"Actually, I'm a pretty good player," Jule said mischievously. "But what I'd really love is to go down to the creek and row that dory."

"The tide's going too fast, it drains out completely in no time at all," Roz said.

"I could talk to Dave, then. I want to know more about what he does. I might want to be a biologist."

Roz said rapidly, "He won't be there. He said he had to go to town."

"Funny, he hasn't been up to get his motorbike," Piers said, blandly innocent.

"He was going to walk out. You know that old track that goes through the woods."

Roz was on the brink of an emotional outburst, foolish as it was, and suddenly Jule found the whole scene distasteful. She got up. "I'm going away to explore."

She set off rapidly along the driveway. The terrier ran to catch up with her, but Roz called him back.

Even the dog, Jule thought. Never mind. Some time I can have my own dog, if Hodge allows it.

Then a voice called unexpectedly from an upstairs window. "Jule, don't get lost." It was Mrs. Deverell.

33

THEY ALL SCATTERED after tea: Francesca back to the library, Piers to give his uncle a hand in his workshop, Dave to the marsh. Roz would have gone with him, but Mrs. Deverell asked her to stay and talk. At this, Jule experienced a now-familiar wound of envy, but subdued the pain to a twinge.

She went up to her room, put her pillows at the foot so she could lie reading by the westering light, and read *Nicholas Nickleby*. When the light began to go she lay listening to the start of the peepers' night chorus. She felt weightless and detached until Roz slammed into her own room and came charging through the bathroom, snapping on lights.

"I wish they wouldn't keep talking about my future when I'm still trying to catch up on my present!"

"Poor little rich girl," murmured Jule.

"Don't be vicious!"

"Have I ever been?"

"Often," said Roz haughtily. "Only the Shadow knows what lurks behind that docile facade. Vicious Violet, the Venomous Virago."

They stopped laughing when they were out of breath. "Jule, there'll never be anyone else in my life that I can be such an idiot with," Roz said. "Whooping and hollering at nothing like a pair of fools. Promise me we'll always be friends."

"Yup," said Jule, waiting. It came.

"Even if we don't see each other more than once a year, you'll never change toward me?"

"Nope. Is the once-a-year going to take place in between your launching destroyers and reviewing the troops?"

Roz threw a pillow at her.

Some family friends called just after dinner, and Jule slid away through the dining room while coats were being taken in the hall, and went up the back stairs. She watched a movie in the sitting room, joined by Martie and Rodina, and was in bed reading when Roz finally came up. She put off her light and pretended to be asleep. She was dedicated to keeping Roz in a good mood for the rest of the weekend, and was taking no chances tonight.

The staff's weekend began after breakfast on Saturdays. In midmorning Francesca commenced the picnic preparations, and Roz became single-minded about working on her weak backhand, so Jule helped Francesca. This was no sardines-and-crackers affair, neither did it depend on frankfurters or hamburgers. Francesca was wonderfully organized. She talked of picnics past, and how the first one down the creek each year was always the most special one.

Presently Nick walked in, dapper in jeans and sweater, bringing wine, pears, cheese, and chocolates.

"Good Lord!" said Francesca.

"No, good Nick." He took her in his arms and kissed her on the mouth. She struggled but without conviction, her laughter stifled against his lips.

Then, with a pleasantly Satanic gleam of dark eyes, he put his arm around Jule, gave her a squeeze, and kissed her cheek. "I was born too late," he said. "I should have been an Edwardian lecher."

The senior Deverells left before noon to drive to Augusta for the day and return at night, and lunch for the rest was eaten around the kitchen table. Joey was to go on the picnic too and knew it, militantly guarding the tote bag that held his water jug, food, and dish. Dave came up to see what he could carry, and Roz cornered him outside, so they came in with her hugging his arm.

"We'll take the skiff and all the food," she announced. "That'll give the rest of you plenty of room in the dory."

The men carried the coolers down the steep track, the girls carried the tote bags and extra jackets, and Joey danced back and forth among their feet, trying to keep everybody together.

"Watch where you step, Jule!" Roz called to her. "If one of us trips we'll all go down like dominoes."

"And the picnic will be held in the brook in the gully," said Piers.

Out on the open ground a pungent coolness rose from the marsh, tempering the unseasonal warmth. The human voices seemed tiny and shallow in all this space.

Roz had the skiff hauled in before Piers untied the dory line, and was hurrying Dave with the loading. He was enjoying everything, he saw no need to rush, but Roz was in a fever to be alone with him on the creek and out of the others' hearing, if not sight.

"Either he doesn't know what's going on," Piers said to Jule, "or he's playing hard to get."

Jule smiled. Whichever it was, Roz thought she was perfectly safe. It was Billy B. all over again, with no competition, and no Mummie.

The dory took the other four very comfortably; Joey sat in Jule's lap. Piers rowed first, and the dory glided on the outgoing tide as if she were taking herself down the creek to the sea. There was either a meditative silence or the contented, fragmentary conversation of people who are used to each other. Piers whistled softly sometimes. Sitting in the bow with the terrier in her lap, Jule was very nearly blissful.

It took an hour, of which Nick rowed the last half. The skiff was always beyond shouting distance or out of sight. It had disappeared when the dory reached the place where the creek opened into a delta. The light sea air strengthened to a chilly steady breeze; bright blue crystalline streams ran off through white sandbanks moored by coarse grasses. The dory kept to the main stream of the creek and finally beached out where the silvery ribs of an ancient wreck thrust up against the spring sky.

The skiff was already there, and the gear unloaded, but there was no sign of Roz and Dave. This was not surprising.

"Jule!" Piers put out a hand to her. "Come on up and see." He pulled her along with him to the top of the sandbank and around the wreck. "This is the old *Marianne*. She was here when Uncle Scott was a boy. Now look."

Before them a broad stretch of sand was marbled with the sparkling rivulets of outgoing water until it ended with the long line of surf at the sea's edge. Gulls cruised high over the area, round and round like ice skaters.

"All this *sand*," Jule said. "We only had rocks. It's lovely! It makes me want to run around barefoot—it makes me wish I was about six, with a pail and shovel! It *excites* me!"

"I haven't a pail and shovel for you, but you can go barefoot."

She took off her sneakers and socks, sitting on one of the satin-smooth timbers, and when she looked up she saw Dave and Roz wading an azure stream a little distance away.

"Hi!" she shouted, just for the joy of shouting.

"Hi!" Dave called back. "I'm going to show Roz the nesting grounds of the least tern. It's safe now because they haven't arrived yet. Come along!"

"Go ahead, I'll keep your sneakers," Piers said. "Listen, you two!" he yelled at the others. "No coming back empty-handed. Bring some wood!"

The area where the least terns nested, a broad stretch of sand and fine gravel, was not spectacular, especially when there were no birds there; if there had been, Dave wouldn't have allowed them near it.

"Isn't it marvelous?" Roz cried.

Dave slanted a quizzical glance at her over his glasses. "I didn't think it was all that terrific," he said. "Well, we'd better start gathering any wood we see."

When they got back with their loads, no one was at the picnic site. Nick and Francesca walked slowly along a sandy ridge, their arms around each other. Piers came from the direction of the marsh, his arms full of wood. Joey was with him, his rough coat damp and sandy. Piers dropped his load beside the stack and said to Roz, "Sweet coz, hand me a can of something, I don't care what. And somebody put water in his dish."

Roz handed him a can of beer from the nearest cooler, and Jule poured water for the dog.

"Come on, Dave," Roz said, "let's go somewhere else and look for wood. Piers is wearing himself out and we can't have that, he's such a fragile creature. Stay and talk to him, Jule love. Dave shouldn't have *two* girls."

"I don't mind," said Dave with a grin.

"I hadn't the slightest intention of coming with you," Jule said, but she didn't know if Roz heard, she was already towing Dave away, saying, "We might see some more fascinating birds. I just can't get over those plovers you showed me. They're fantastic!"

"Let's you and me go out to the fantastic, fascinating beach, Jule," said Piers.

Joey ran on the damp firm sand while Piers and Jule strolled. The sound of the waves breaking and retreating filled their ears. The sunlit marsh and blue-hazed forest looked to be miles away. At the end of the long beach they came to a rocky promontory where bone-dry driftwood littered the sparse turf, tossed up by a winter of storms. They filled the canvas tote bags and carried larger pieces in their free arms, and wandered back at a pleasurably slow pace, wading dreamily through little brooks warmed by the sand.

Francesca was organizing a table from some planks and old lobster crates. Roz was half-heartedly assisting, attempting to keep her eye on Dave at the same time in case he took flight. He and Nick were whittling kindling. They were both extremely efficient with their clasp knives; Dave even carried a small stone to keep his knife honed. They were reminiscing about their days as Boy Scouts and the impossibility of starting a fire by rubbing two sticks together unless they happened to be matches. Roz watched them jealously, and finally gave up her rather aimless motions around the table to go and hunch down on the other side of Dave.

Fran was trying to level up one of the crates and Piers rummaged through the fuel pile for a small block of wood. "Here, try this," he said.

"Jeanie with the light brown hair," said Nick. "Let's you and I go for a walk. Why does it have to be Dave all the time? Follow me and wear diamonds."

"What for?" Roz was delightedly curious. "Why should I go for a walk with you, apart from the diamonds?"

"I made up my mind I was going to take you for a walk out here, and by God, I'm going to." He shut up his knife.

"But what about Fran?" Roz asked in a meek, silky little voice.

"Why should I mind?" Francesca said. "I know he never commits seductions on weekends."

"I don't think I'd be that sure of him." Her voice was still dulcet, but Jule had seen that certain smile before; it had convinced her that Mona Lisa was expressing pure vanity.

"She has perfect faith, dear child." He took her elbow.

"And so have I, in her. So Dave's quite safe too. That leaves just Piers and Jule for the high jinks. Come along. I've got some favorite spots of my own out here, where I'm the only wildlife."

"Soon to be an endangered species," said Roz. "I'd better not lose my last chance." They jumped down into a damp gully and followed its winding course between deepening banks, disappearing around the base of a miniature dune.

Francesca was taking food from the cooler. She looked as usual, her fair hair almost blinding in the light, her profile fine and serene. But it was as if Piers's place had been taken by an older and cynical relative who gazed at the spot where the other two had vanished. Just what was it Roz had said about Piers and her?

"Need any help, Dave?" Jule asked over-brightly. "I'm a good kindling-maker."

"I'll bet you're a good anything. That sounds funny, but it started out as a compliment."

"And was taken for one. But I guess you've got enough kindling there to patch hell a mile, so I'll go help Francesca." She sounded too loud, too silly, but Dave didn't seem to notice anything.

Piers spoke in his ordinary manner, "Has anyone opened the wine?"

Still disturbed, Jule climbed up among the ship's timbers and looked off at the sea. A seiner with a tail of dories traveled eastward. In the late afternoon light the horizon line was almost violet against the porcelain pallor of the sky.

A weather-breeder, she thought automatically. That's what today is.

"Great place, isn't it?" Dave had come up.

"I love it. I'd like to see it under a full moon."

"I have, at the last one. I came down the creek and wandered around half the night, too excited to sleep. I didn't want to miss anything. I bunked at the edge of the marsh finally, and Canada geese went over in the biggest skein I'd ever seen, and a bull moose walked around my sleeping bag."

She was enchanted. "Were you scared?"

"Primitively, but not intellectually, if that makes sense. They're harmless except in the rutting season, which is in the fall. But that was a tremendous beast looming up in the moonlight."

"Hi up there!" Piers called. "Come down if you want to eat!"

Roz and Nick were back, and Nick was leaning over Francesca to kiss her. Roz went to Dave at once and put her hand possessively on his arm. "Did you miss me?"

"Yes. I'm starved, and now we can eat."

"Is that all her return means to you?" Piers asked. "Where are your spiritual values?"

"Everything vanishes before the sight of food," said Dave. But he patted the hand on his arm. "After I eat, then I can be spiritual."

The sun went down behind the dark bank of western woods, and the stars began to appear. Silently the tide crept over the sands, and the air chilled so that the extra jackets felt good, even though the fire warmed their faces and their feet. Joey sprawled in sleep. The moon, in its first quarter, climbed higher and higher.

"It's not rising," Dave said. "*We're* moving. Everyone concentrate and see if you can get the sense of moving."

Everyone did, or pretended too. Piers yawned, Roz said the mere thought made her dizzy. Francesca and Nick, sitting close together, said nothing. The firelight flickered on their peaceful faces and sparkled in their eyes.

The boats, which had been lying on wet sand below them, began to move gently and knock against one another. They were afloat. It was time to go back.

34

"I'M TAKING JULE IN THE SKIFF," Nick announced. "I'm spreading myself thin among all the girls today and now it's Jule's turn."

"Are you honored, Jule?" Francesca asked her.

"Should I be?"

"Many a nice Maine girl would think so," said Piers.

"Simply because they don't know *me*."

"I didn't think there was a girl in Maine who didn't know you," said his sister.

"Jule hasn't said yet whether she wants to go with him," Piers said.

"Of course I do. Maybe he'll let me row."

"Oh, he'll love that," said Francesca. Nick took her into his arms and kissed her. "Later, my adored one," he said with a languishing look.

Rowing up the creek on an incoming tide under the stars and by faint moonlight was a superb experience. There was no effort involved and the skiff was borne swiftly on the moving water. Nick entertained her with stories of the old smuggling days, from the time when enterprising locals set out to beat the embargo and the blockade of 1812, up through the Prohibition era. "They haven't used it yet for pot and cocaine, as far as anyone knows, but there are plenty of spots along the way where they could unload small shipments and get them across the marsh. Some ridges are high and dry enough to support a jeep."

"I'd rather think of the old-time smugglers. They're cleaner."

From behind they could hear faintly the singing from the dory. "Doesn't it sound beautiful like that?" she asked dreamily. "Once a yacht anchored off the island and the people sang on it that night. Roz and I knelt on pillows for hours by the window. We thought it was the most beautiful thing we'd ever heard."

"Tell me more about your life back there."

She was no longer dreamy. "I didn't mean to bring it up. It was just the combination of night and music . . . I'd like to float along like this and not think about anything."

"But Jule"—he was gently persistent—"what if *you* weren't their child either? Did you ever think of that?"

She pulled steadily on the oars, sometimes looking over her shoulder. A heron took off with a loud discordant cry and a sound of great deliberate wings.

"What difference does it make now?" she asked at last. "I hardly think about it now, unless someone reminds me. I guess all I want is what Roz is going to pay me back." She asked nicely, "Now can we talk about something else?"

His face was an interesting study in chiaroscuro. "Supposing she wasn't your mother, but John was your father. That would explain a good deal, wouldn't it? The lack of maternal feeling and so forth? She's stuck with one baby which she won't give back but doesn't have the courage to kill, and he brings home a little by-blow."

She gave a sudden exasperated jerk on the oars so that one jumped the oarlock. "*Please!*"

"It's my relentless legal mind. Or else I'm a suspense novelist at heart. Forgive me, Jule."

The dory glided into sight astern, like a ghost dory bearing the spectres of early smugglers.

"There's no escape!" Piers shouted. It echoed weirdly across the marsh. "The Viking long ship is about to overtake you! It's rape and pillage time, kiddies!"

"We'll fight to the death!" Nick yelled back. "Change places," he ordered Jule. She'd been letting the tide carry them; Nick put his back into the job, and the skiff shot ahead. In the dory Roz gave her Valkyrie whoops. Joey was barking. Oars flashed in and out of the black water.

The skiff touched the bank first and Jule scrambled out over the coolers in the bow with Nick after her, calling, "Sanctuary! Sanctuary!"

The dory slid into the mooring pool. Piers said petulantly, "Oh, *darn*! No bloodbath tonight, chaps."

"Now, that's what I call a damn shame," Dave said. "I always thought I'd be pretty good at that Viking stuff. Making the blood eagle, and so forth."

"They're a couple of spoilsports," Francesca agreed. "I wanted to be a battle maiden, and Joey was going to be a dog of war. You know—'Cry Havoc! and let slip the dogs of war.'"

"Gosh, I'm sorry," said Nick penitently. "How about a spot of human sacrifice? We could draw lots, if nobody wanted to volunteer."

"Well, maybe that's all right," said Dave, "if we could have something to eat first, to get our strength up."

Piers and Francesca groaned. "I *told* you he had no spiritual values," Piers said. "Food, food, always food!"

Roz, after her war whoops in the pursuit, was silent. The dory nosed the bank and Jule left Nick tying the skiff into its lines and went to hold the dory's bow steady. Roz was the first one out, with Joey under her arm. The fingers of her free hand dug savagely into Jule's braced shoulder.

"I want to talk to you," she said under her breath. The hostility was shockingly obvious.

Wouldn't she, though! Jule thought. Wouldn't she *just*! I can't have this much fun without her wanting to ruin it.

Dave followed Roz and took the painter from Jule, making some remark she hardly heard, though she heard Roz's warm responsive laughter. She wanted to go up to the house and lock herself in her room to keep Roz out for the rest of the night. But damn it, the house was locked unless the senior Deverells were back, and then she'd have to encounter their solicitude.

There was a good deal of good-natured confusion due to Joey, who had slept all the way home and now was as wild as a child staying out after dark. Fran had his leash because he must not be allowed to dash ahead into the woods and perhaps meet a porcupine. Jule caught him finally by kneeling down, and he bounded happily into her arms.

"Why can't you and I make coffee at your place?" Roz asked Dave.

"Because my coffee is terrible," said Dave happily, "and Martie's cookie jar draws me like a magnet."

"Ah, Jean," said Piers. "Don't deprive us of the sunshine of your smile."

It would always work on Roz, even when she didn't want it to. Flashlights were handed out. Jule felt safe enough now; Roz wouldn't start anything on the way up. Nick and Fran went first, Roz lighted the way for Dave, and Jule illumined the dew-slippery path for Piers.

When they passed the ravine, something rustled below, and she tried to see what was down there. "Something having a drink," Piers said. "A porcupine, a raccoon, maybe a fox. Does that make you nervous?"

"Gosh, no! I wouldn't even mind wolves or bears, if I

could just get to see one."

"I wish I could make it possible for you," he said. "I really do." He sounded quite serious, for Piers, and she remembered the new side of him that she had glimpsed today.

Mr. and Mrs. Deverell were home. They all drank coffee or chocolate around the kitchen table and it was not only Dave who helped lower the level of the ginger snaps.

Roz was on stage. In the presence of her enchanted parents and three attractive young men she was like one of those Japanese paper flowers that open in water. Only Jule knew how hard Roz was working, and why. Since nobody seemed to be able to take eyes off Roz, Jule got away without being noticed except by Francesca. But as she went up the back stairs, she heard Mr. Deverell say, "Where's Jule?"

"Oh, she was tired," Francesca said easily. "She said goodnight, but nobody heard her but me."

Jule appreciated the lie. She took a quick hot shower and got into bed, reading *Nicholas Nickleby* until she heard voices in the hall. "Good night, Mother and Dad," Roz called sweetly. Jule snapped off her light and burrowed down, hoping Roz's successful performance downstairs had sweetened and tranquilized her.

But Roz was "slatting"—Jondy's term for being rough and noisy. Drawers were wrenched open, slammed shut. Doorknobs attacked instead of gently turned. Shoes kicked off. Shades snapped up or yanked down. She opened the door into Jule's room before she took her shower, and clashed or rattled anything movable in the bathroom. Only an idiot would have believed Jule to be asleep after this performance. She came in on a steamy whiff of lily-of-the-valley soap, put on the light, and addressed the back of Jule's head.

"*I* wanted to come back in the skiff with Dave. You *knew* you were sticking me with the Deverells. And *why*?" She gave

Jule a powerful dig in the small of her back. Jule groaned and turned over.

"It wasn't *my* idea to come back in the skiff. It just happened."

"Oh no it didn't. You worked it that way with Nick to show me what you could do."

"You're a bore, you know that? A paranoid bore. Just because you scheme all the time doesn't mean everybody else does."

Roz lunged forward, landing on one knee on the bed, hand raised to slap, and Jule caught the wrist. She tightened her grip and had the satisfaction of seeing tears in Roz's eyes, not of pain but of frustration. Jule was smaller; she wasn't *supposed* to be stronger.

"What's the matter with you, Roz?" she said softly to the wild face close to her own. "You were with Dave, weren't you? *I* wasn't. And you say you can handle Piers. So why couldn't you enjoy yourself? Fran was the one who should have been uncomfortable, she probably wanted to be with Nick."

"As for Fran," Roz whispered venomously, "she's a little too smug about her precious Nick. *Old Nick's* more like it. She'd better watch out."

Jule let her go so suddenly that Roz lost her balance and almost fell backward off the bed. "Roz, I'm as sick of you as you are of me," she said. "I can hardly wait for Monday morning."

Roz stood looking down at her, rubbing her wrist. "What's the matter with tomorrow?"

"Questions. I'm not thinking up any lies, Roz. If you can come up with some good reason to explain why you want me to leave in a hurry, I'll be happy to leave in the morning. You just give me my eight hundred dollars."

"I know how you've been buttering up my father."

"Oh, don't be such a damn fool," said Jule.

Roz gave her a long smoldering stare. "You—*you*—!" She had no words. She gave up and went away, slamming the doors between the rooms.

Jule was shaking. Everything she'd eaten that day seemed about to come up in a fountain. Roz had succeeded in ruining what could have been one of the most precious memories in a life that so far had very few of them. Now she couldn't sleep, but she could do something to take away a little of the nastiness.

She dressed in her jeans and sweater, took her jacket, and let herself silently out into the hall. The passage was sufficiently illuminated by the pallid moonlight coming in through the landing window. The house was so quiet now that she imagined everyone either contentedly asleep or on the verge of it; Roz too would drop off quickly, she always could.

She went into the small sitting room and immediately smelled warm and recently damp dog. Joey sat up in his basket, growling. "It's all right, Joey," she murmured. He came to her, wriggling from stem to stern, and she leaned down and rubbed his back. "Go back to bed, that's a good boy," she whispered.

But Joey didn't obey. The door was kept open onto the landing, and Joey was down the stairs and into the kitchen before she'd begun the descent. She could hear him drinking, and then polishing his empty food dish.

The heavy brass bolt of the back door gleamed in the dim light. She tried it, expecting a struggle, but it moved with ease. Behind her Joey noisily searched the floor for crumbs. Outside was the freedom of the night, not dead with sleep but alive with the peepers, and whatever walked through the woods, scouted the lawns, drank at the bottom of the ravine, and prowled the marsh. A raccoon or a fox would put a seal of gold upon the day. She didn't dare to hope for a deer; she'd settle for a porcupine, if nothing else.

The door swung open with hardly a sound, just enough for her to slide through.

And Joey. She hadn't heard him coming, but he was out before she was and across the porch with a frantic scrabble of toenails, the growl boiling up in his small throat. He streaked around the corner toward the marsh, with his bark snapping out behind him like a train of firecrackers.

She panicked. *Porcupine.* A mouthful of quills, he could die, and it was her fault. She wanted to run herself in another direction, away from the scene of her crime and never come back. First her parents, and now herself! It would have been heaven to die of shame on the spot. But reason is always the enemy of escape, and she remembered Francesca hanging up the leash, collar still attached, on a hook near the door. She forced herself to see and feel through the murk of panic, and found his leash.

The chilly sweet air was quiet, as if something had quenched the peepers. No terrier barking. Did that mean he'd already engaged the porcupine and was silenced by the agony of a bloody mouthful of quills? *Please, please!* she prayed as she ran, without knowing where to run until she saw where he'd left a track across the wet silvery grass to the woods.

Once she was inside the trees she called his name. He began barking again, down below. No mouthful of quills yet. But what was he barking at that could hurt him, if he angered it enough? Her calls were ignored; he was probably afraid to turn his back on whatever faced him. She started down the path. The faint light from the sky was almost extinguished by the arching branches, but the trail seemed clear enough, and with sneakers you could feel your footing. Her soles were wet and she skidded several times, but saved herself by grabbing at the nearest tree. Down on the marsh Joey's bark was hysterical, as if he were terrified, and she tried to hurry, yet keep the ravine in mind.

She came to it too soon; she'd thought it was farther down, and she'd forgotten an abrupt jog in the path. All at once there was a sense of space about to open up under her feet. When she backed away a branch caught her between the shoulders, and threw her off balance. One foot slid as if on grease into a tangle that seized her ankle like fingers, she flung out both hands and grasped space with one and a dry bough with the other, she felt it snap, and knew with a peculiar resignation that she was falling.

She went end over end through the wet growth, bouncing off hidden boulders, clutching at thorny canes, trying desperately but vainly to slow her descent toward the boulders at the bottom.

Something brought her to a jolting stop. It was an alder, partly dead so that branches broke away under her weight, but there were enough live shoots to brake her fall so that she rolled slowly to the bottom.

She didn't know whether she yelled or not. She couldn't yell now, she had no breath. She lay uncomfortably on her back across an edge of rock, her hands both ached and stung, she felt bruised and raw all over. She stared up at the high arch of trees until her vision cleared and the roaring died away in her ears. The sound of Joey's barking came to her as if from miles away, and she thought, Oh, God, where is he *now*?

She tried to sit up and get off the sharp ridge. There was no jab of internal pain as if she'd broken ribs. She was one big vibrating pain, but it all seemed to be on the outside.

Joey was abruptly silent. Something's killed him, she thought. It was too awful for tears, and there was no way she could disappear; she would have to find his little body somehow, and take it home, and face the consequences. But how could she get back up the side of the ravine?

In the new stillness she heard water running close by her. She'd completely forgotten the little brook where an animal had been drinking earlier. The jagged rock had kept her from rolling into it.

Something was moving up above. Creeping. Planting one foot with infinite certainty, then another. Stalking something. *Her?* She'd read about rabid wild animals who lost their natural instincts and attacked human beings instead of running from them. She felt as if she were imprisoned in a night of terrors that would never end.

Was the rustling nearer? It would stop, and her heartbeat filled up the vacancy; then she thought she heard it again, nearer. She stared up with watering eyes into the dark. A cautious sliding. A pause.

Joey barked out on the marsh. He was alive, and it gave her the impetus she needed to get going.

She accomplished it, crawling on hands and knees in places, on her belly in others, in and out of the water, whispering "Ouch, ouch, ouch," sometimes swearing in her head, afraid to speak out loud, in case it brought something down on her back, whatever it was.

When the marsh opened up before her under a broad starstrewn sky, and she could hear nothing behind her, she sagged flat on her belly sobbing in relief. Maybe she'd imagined it. No, she hadn't. But it was probably innocent, an animal wanting to go down to the brook and knowing an alien was there.

Joey sniffed loudly around her ears and put a cold nose against her neck.

"*Jesus*," said a man's voice. "Who is it? What in hell's wrong here?"

With an effort she heaved herself onto her back. Joey

anointed her face with warm wet kisses, and she tried to hug him with her lame arms.

"Jule, for heaven's sake!" The towering man was Dave. "What happened to you?" He hunched down beside her.

She told him in fragments; she was short of wind, she ached, and she was so glad that Joey was alive she wanted to howl.

"Do you think anything's broken?" he asked.

"No, or I couldn't have crawled out of there. Oh, damn, I dropped his leash somewhere."

"That's all right, he's not going anywhere but home." He helped her to sit up.

"Oh boy," she said. "I don't think I missed anywhere on me. I bounced off rocks all the way down."

"And if you'd hit just right you might have broken your back or fractured your skull." He didn't sound severe, he was simply stating facts as Billy B. would do. "I'll help you back to the house."

"What was Joey barking at?" At the sound of his name, Joey pranced at her.

"I don't know what he heard the first time, when he left you. It could have been any noise in the woods, or just the scent of something that had gone by. But when he reached the marsh he saw me standing by the creek and he didn't know what I was." He laughed. "The Phantom of Birnam Marsh! He was making so damn much noise about it I couldn't make him hear me, until he stopped for breath. Then he was over-whelmed with joy and relief. I knew he'd sneaked out some-how, so I was taking him home when he shot off over there. The sight of a body shook me up some," he said moderately.

"I'm sorry." She made motions about getting up, and he lifted her easily to her feet. "I'm just afraid of losing him again."

"I'll take him under one arm and steer you with the other, and with any luck the three of us won't go crashing into the gully."

She giggled weakly. When Roz found out about this she'd probably accuse of her of arranging the whole thing.

35

JULE WASHED HER FACE and hands very tenderly, and patted them dry with paper towels. Joey had another drink and resumed his search for crumbs as if he hadn't been anywhere. Dave opened the nearest cupboard. "They keep first aid supplies in here," he said. "Are you bleeding anywhere?"

"I'm scraped but not really bleeding."

"You're going to be lame as hell in the morning. You should have a long hot soak now, then put iodine on the worst places, and take a couple of aspirins."

"I don't want to wake up Roz," she said. "She'd never get settled down again." Let sleeping tigresses lie, she thought. "But I'll take the iodine and the pills. Thank you very much, Dave. I'm glad you're not the Phantom of Birnam Marsh."

"Who knows, I might be? In daylight a mild-mannered biologist. By night even the werewolves are nervous about me."

"By the time of the full moon you should be a sensation," she said faintly.

"You're bushed. Can you make it up to bed all right?"

"What are you doing?" asked Nick from the back stairs. "Propositioning her? I'd never have believed it of you, Dr. Guthrie. I'm shocked. A midnight assignation." He came on into the kitchen. On him a bathrobe should be called a dressing gown, she thought, dreamy and giddy. This one was in vertical stripes from deep brown to gold. He looked faintly Biblical. Joseph and his coat of many colors.

"What happened to *you*?" he said abruptly.

"I went out for a walk, Joey slipped by me and I went after him and tumbled down the ravine. Dave caught Joey on the marsh, and saw us both home. End of story."

Nick was quietly but impressively enraged. "You could have killed yourself! You had no business being on that path alone in the middle of the night!"

"It was my fault that Joey got out." She was suddenly too weary to talk.

"I think she'd better get to bed," Dave said mildly.

"How did you get out of the ravine?" Nick was accusatory, as if questioning her about a crime.

"Along the brook, so I'm wet in places, and I'm going to bed and warm up." She stood up, managing not to wince while the two watched her. As she turned toward the stairs she staggered slightly. Nick exclaimed and reached for her arm.

"I'm all right," she protested. "Not light-headed or anything. A little lame, that's all."

"Wait here, Dave," Nick ordered. "I want to talk to you." He put his arm around her.

"Good night, Dave," she said. He was sitting on a high stool with his feet hooked over a rung, his big hands dangling between his knees. His baseball cap was on the back of his head. He smiled and said, "Good night, Jule."

It would have been easier going upstairs alone, even if it took her longer, and she tried to say so, but Nick was determined, and he had a grip like steel. It was a relief for several reasons when she reached her room. The whole episode was far too humiliating for her to take any great satisfaction in all this male attention.

He opened the door for her. "Thank you," she whispered. He didn't release her at once. With his free hand he brushed her hair delicately back from her temples. "When I think what could have happened to you—" He kissed her forehead and cheekbone with a light brushing of his lips. Then he let her go. When the door shut between them she could hardly believe the little incident had occurred; Dave on the stool back in the kitchen was much more vivid.

She got out of her clothes somehow, allowing herself to gasp all she wanted to now that she no longer had an audience, and crawled into bed without remembering either the aspirin or the iodine. No bed ever felt so good to her as that one, at that moment. By some delicate adjustments she could cosset the sorest places, and exhaustion took over like a drug. Later she awoke and heard rain spattering on the windows.

She struggled to recall the hours on the sands among the azure streams, as if it were something from very long ago. She resented having the Elysian afternoon so far removed from her. Stolen, really. And it was her fault, letting Joey out. No, Roz's fault for lighting into her that way. She drifted off again, and dreamed the fall.

The darkness was there, and the weak moonlight, the dog barking far away, the attacking boughs and stumps, the thick vines like fingers around her ankle; the accelerating slide and tumble over wet leaves and slippery rocks, nothing to hold onto but twigs that ripped free in her grasp.

"Someone was there." The voice that said it was very clear but she couldn't recognize it, yet she knew she should. Billy B.? Could it have been his voice because he was always in her mind even when she didn't consciously think of him?

She realized that she was awake and hurting. A southwesterly storm battered the windows, and the room was filled with the lonely gray light that belongs to a house where you are the only one awake and miserable. After some cautious stretching and flexing she slid out and went to the bathroom, got some water, and swallowed the aspirin. They wanted to dissolve in her throat, which was horrible, but she kept gulping water, which in its own way was horrible, and finally washed the bitterness down. She put on her lamp and focused her attention on *Nicholas Nickleby*. The combination of Dickens and the aspirin worked, and she fell asleep again, this time not to dream.

Roz came in and woke her, but Jule wouldn't turn over and answer her.

"*I don't care,*" Roz said loftily, "but Nick's got this fantastic story about you running around outdoors like an idiot in the middle of the night, and Dave bringing you home. My mother wants to know if you're all right."

Jule heaved herself over, and Roz said in a different tone, "What *happened?*" She came closer and stared.

"Nick must have told you why I was running around like an idiot. Because like an idiot I let Joey out. Of course he didn't know why I was up in the first place. Because like an idiot I let you bother me. Thank your mother, and tell her I just want to keep out of sight and be forgotten for the day. Or better still, until I leave this place for Bangor," she added.

"There's absolutely no chance of anyone being ignored around here," said Roz gloomily. "So even if I could do it, don't count on the rest of them. What a rotten day for Easter! And I'm expected to go to church." She went to the windows, apparently trying to make out Dave's camp through the blowing rain. "Want some breakfast?" she asked absently.

"No, thank you," said Jule. She did, but she knew the question hadn't originated with Roz, who wouldn't care whether she ate or not. "You might be interested to know, though you probably won't believe it, that I didn't throw myself down the ravine just to get Dave's attention. That was an accident too."

Roz spun around. "Did Dave carry you home?" she demanded.

"Dave carried the dog home. I'm tired, so go away, Roz."

"Gladly." Roz floated off, through the bathroom.

She had been right about the impossibility of being ignored. After she had gone downstairs, Francesca came in carrying a breakfast tray, and Mrs. Deverell was with her, looking more than ordinarily tall and stately, and she was so solicitous that Jule's midriff knotted and she felt like the idiot that Roz had called her. When Mrs. Deverell offered to help her sit up Jule hastily did it herself, even though it hurt; when she arranged the pillows behind Jule's back, Jule felt a boiling wave of heat, and then broke into a sweat. Francesca set the tray across her lap.

"How are your hands? Do you need any help?" she asked. Jule wished she had come alone.

"No, my hands are scratched but I didn't sprain anything."

"You were lucky to bounce."

"Luckier than I deserve."

Mrs. Deverell's deep-set eyes were both quizzical and concerned. "How so, Jule?"

"Because I let Joey out. I didn't mean to," she explained anxiously. "I was too restless to sleep and I thought I might see a wild animal. We didn't have even squirrels on Landfall and Osprey. But he was so quick."

"He's done it to all of us, Jule," said Mrs. Deverell. "The next time you'll be prepared. Just put him on the stairs and shut the door into the kitchen. He'll go back to bed."

There'd be no next time, of course. "Eat now," Francesca said. "I brought hot milk for your coffee. It makes it rather special, I think, when you're under the weather."

They left her and she found that coffee with hot milk was indeed rather special. She wondered if she had said "Thank you," or had been too dazzled by the visitation to remember her manners. Mrs. Deverell in her room. . . . She'd remember that always, like the piano music and the afternoon on the sands.

When she thought everyone must have left for church, she took a long hot bath and went back to bed to read. She was just getting settled when there was a scratching at the door. She opened it and Joey, the author of her misfortune, bounded in without a trace of shame.

The book and the rain lulled, and Joey felt like Hodge by her feet. She was almost asleep when someone tapped at the door and Joey roused with a growl. Nick said in a low voice, "Are you awake?" Joey relaxed.

"Just about," she said.

"Can I speak to you a minute?"

"I'll get up," she said, not enchanted by the idea.

"No need. I'm quite safe." He came in without waiting. "Why are you smiling that enigmatic smile?" he asked.

"It's not meant to be enigmatic. I was just admiring your clothes." He was wearing fawn-colored corduroys and a dark wine turtleneck sweater. "I thought you'd gone to church too."

"I'm not a Deverell, so I don't have to be a pillar of the Tremaine Federated Church." He pulled the chair away from the dressing table and sat astride it with his arms folded on the back. "I want to ask you something, little Jule. Without alarming you, if possible."

"If you want to elope, the answer is no. Not in this weather."

He grinned. "I guess you don't scare easy. Listen, do you think there's any possibility that you could have been given a little shove last night? Or tripped? Or *both*? You were listening to the dog, you mightn't have known if anyone was near you—why that expression?" He looked contrite. "I *have* scared you."

"No," she said slowly. "I'm not scared. It's just that I had a dream early this morning, and I heard the words 'Someone was there.' " She was more intrigued than worried, safe here, with warm food in her stomach and Joey at her feet. "I wasn't frightened, I was more interested in trying to recognize the voice. I remember thinking last night that those tough vines were like fingers around my ankle, but I'm sure they weren't."

"But they may have been, and whatever prodded you in the back could have been a hand. The voice in your dream could have been inside your head, your own recollection of what you were too startled to notice at the time."

It was rather like a good suspense story. "Why are you asking me these things?"

"Well, Dave and I took a walk around the place last night. You know, we were careful to lock up the house before we all left yesterday, but nobody thought of the garage and the workshop. We had the definite impression that things in the workshop have been moved around. I can't be sure if anything's missing until I talk with Mr. Deverell about it." His dispassionate attitude was a compliment to her. "My glove compartment's been gone through and some loose cash taken and a lucky coin someone gave me, an old five-dollar gold piece. I'll have Piers and Mr. Deverell check theirs when they come back from church. My guess is that some teen-age crook, or a couple of them, left a car on the old wood road down below, and hiked in for an evening's reconnaissance and to pick up anything they could carry. If they're local kids they know Martie and Rodina are off this weekend."

"Do you think that's what Joey went after?" she asked.

"We don't know, Jule." He creased his lower lip between thumb and forefinger, his sharp face gone vacant as if he were trying to will himself into the imagined scene. "If there were two, and one had already gone down and Joey picked up his trail—but another one was just out of sight up here, and started off as soon as he thought it was safe and went down the path and found you still on it—" He shrugged. "Hoodlums, and vicious."

"But Dave was out down there. Wouldn't he have seen?"

"Not if they scooted around the edge of the marsh within the fringe of the woods. And don't forget, when Joey saw this mysterious figure in that weird half light he couldn't think of anything else."

"The Phantom of Birnam Marsh," said Jule. It was a relief to laugh.

"Dave was going to check over his stuff thoroughly when he went back down last night. He's got some expensive equipment there, but he keeps it locked up to protect it from the damp, so they'd have had to lug off his foot locker, and he knows that was still there. But these kids will pick up anything they can put in their pockets and sell for a few dollars, while they're trying to get into the Big Time."

"Are you going to tell all the family about this?" she asked.

"No only Piers and Mr. Deverell. They'll have to do some checking. Tools are a big item for thieves, and Scott Deverell's been just too trusting. Tremaine isn't what it was—no place is, really. How he's still so innocent all these years after what happened to them—" He stopped, and she saw him disconcerted for the first time, his black eyes flickering away from hers.

"Don't say 'Excuse me,'" she said tartly. "I didn't know anything could embarrass you, Nick."

He got up from the chair and swung it back to its place. "When I first met you, Jule, I could have said anything, and I did. Then you knocked me out with your dignity. 'Do you think I'd have the *effrontery*—?'" He had to laugh. "By God, I never heard that word used outside a courtroom! But little Jule flattened me with it. And ever since—" He came and stood by the bed.

It was unnerving, because she wasn't sure how to react. She didn't want to simper or freeze, so she simply gazed back at him, wondering objectively if he was going to kiss her again. But he didn't move from where he was, and kept his hands in his pockets. There was a short silence during which a new gust of rain and wind beat noisily against the windows. Then he said, "They'll be back soon. Goodbye for now, Jule. . . . Oh, I'll take your tray down, shall I?"

He did, balancing it neatly on one hand while he opened the door. "If I'm ever disbarred I can always qualify as an Italian waiter. Buon giorno, Signorina."

36

A PROWLER JOSTLING HER off the path either by accident or intention was not half so important to her as her desire to get out of this place without a cataclysmic blowup with Roz. If she stayed in bed until tomorrow morning, perhaps Roz would be grateful enough to get her another book from the library when she finished *Nicholas Nickleby*.

Roz didn't bother to visit when she came back from church, but Mrs. Deverell looked in, her hat in her hand; she was subtly scented with violets.

"How are you, dear?"

"Oh, less lame all the time but washed out. Will it be a bother if I stay in bed?"

"Jule?" Mr. Deverell appeared behind his wife's shoulder. "Next time let Joey go. But we're putting up a railing tomorrow. Should have been done long ago." He disappeared.

"It's no bother at all, dear," his wife said, "except that we'll miss you. Perhaps you'll be ready to have dinner with us tonight." She didn't give Jule a chance to negate that possibility, but went quickly across the hall to her own room.

Jule's forehead was damp. Staying away from Mrs. Deverell seemed as necessary as staying away from Roz, if this emotional upheaval was to take place at each contact. She looked the truth in the face: she was jealous of Roz for having this mother. Now that she had admitted it to herself, in so many words, she should be able to deal with it. *Only not in this place.*

Piers brought up her lunch tray. The tape deck had been stolen from his car, but he wasn't as disturbed about that as about some things in his glove compartment.

"It's funny how the loss of something that couldn't possibly have any value to anyone else can make you murderous. Good God, he just cleaned the place out without stopping to pick and choose. He'll throw away what he doesn't want, and I'll never find it again." He said it too quietly. She saw again the version of him she'd seen for just an instant yesterday morning.

"What is it?" she asked.

"If I tell you," said Piers, "don't laugh. I know I'm a case of arrested development but I'm sensitive about it." His eyes shone with water. "Peter's collar and tags. My first dog. I picked him out at the shelter myself. He was a little of everything, and funny-looking with it, and I loved him more than anyone else in the world, even my family. He was my *child*, you see."

He turned away toward the streaming windows, took out a handkerchief and blew his nose. "I saw him killed by a truck out on the main road when I was twelve years old. Nobody was home that day, and I brought him back and buried him in the old orchard before anyone else knew. I bawled myself blind and speechless, and then everybody thought I was over it. But I wasn't. Losing him was what made me suffer so for my aunt and uncle when I found out about their baby."

The kittens. He kept his face away from her. "I can't stand thinking of Peter's collar thrown out somewhere with the trash. It would be like—" He stopped and she finished silently for him. *Throwing Peter out with the trash.*

She had to blow her own nose. Piers looked around at her

with those blue Deverell eyes. "If you tell anybody I'll kill you."

"I'll never tell."

"And I wouldn't really kill you. I'd just feel stabbed to the heart." His forced laugh was painful to her.

"I'd tell you something that happened once to Roz and me, except that I still can't bear to talk about it."

"We could have a good cry together," he suggested. "Experiments in non-erotic communication. Seriously, I feel better already for having told you. It's something even Fran doesn't know. She'd be worried for fear I'm permanently locked up in the emotional makeup of a twelve-year-old." He sat down on the window seat. "Go on eating. I didn't mean to spoil your lunch. Uncle Scott didn't lose anything from his car, they must have gone through ours before he came back. But they lifted as many small tools as this guy or guys could carry. He's lucky they didn't come in with a van and take everything else. But just to salve our consciences—locks don't make much difference to these types."

"What can Mr. Deverell do?"

"Have a security system connected with the police station, which so far he refuses to do. Or try to persuade Coney to live on the place, so there'd always be someone here, but Nick pointed out that there's a hell of a lot more violence these days, and Coney could be beaten up or shot. But Uncle Scott still refuses to believe Tremaine's gone bad because of one isolated incident."

"Maybe he's right."

"Maybe. Or he's trying not to contract the Great Plague of the times, anxiety. Now that I've cheered you up I should leave you to collect the tatters of your nerves."

After he left, she let herself drift on thoughts of Billy B. Oh Lord, to have all this behind her and everything all right, which it would be when she heard his voice again, in reality, not just in dreams.

In the late afternoon she woke up rested and much less lame than she'd been in the morning. Her hands felt better. The wind had quieted, though the rain was steady. In spite of her resolutions, she couldn't bear to be confined any longer. She took a shower, and for the first time saw her bruises. On her face the scratches, a few small bruises on cheekbone and jaw, a scrape on her nose, didn't look bad, and she wasn't light-headed. If she went downstairs but kept out of the way, and returned early to bed, Roz should be pacified.

They were all in the living room. Mrs. Deverell was at the piano, and Piers was turning pages for her. Mr. Deverell was reading by the fireplace and Joey lay on the hearth rug facing the fire. Francesca had her feet up on a hassock and was writing in a large notebook propped against her knees. At the far end, where the curtains had been drawn across, Dave and Nick sat in a pool of lamplight playing chess; Roz perched on the edge of a chair drawn close to the table, her chin in her hands. Her hair entangled the light, her profile was perfectly outlined with it.

Jule hoped to move unobtrusively to a dim corner beyond the piano, but Piers saw her and gave a little salute past Mrs. Deverell's head. She was frowning at the music but as if she sensed movement, she looked up and nodded at Jule across the length of the piano. Jule gave a small wave, and went on toward the lighted library. She had lost her courage about going into the living room. Everyone had looked so peacefully absorbed, and she would be the warring element, a battlefield in herself even if nobody else guessed.

Mr. Deverell followed her into the library; she knew it without seeing him, by the scent of his tobacco smoke. Joey was with him.

"What are you looking for?" he asked.

"More Dickens."

"He's a great favorite of mine, too," the man said.

She put up a cold hand and moved it across the bindings. Grab one and get away, you imbecile, she told herself. She took *Our Mutual Friend*, murmuring, "I haven't read this one yet." She turned to go, holding it against her breast. He was sitting on a corner of the desk, holding one end of Joey's rubber bone while the dog tugged growling at the other.

"Jean tells me you insist on leaving tomorrow," he said.

Roz would. "It's time for me to go. I never intended to come to this house, it was against—" She wasn't sure how to finish.

He let the dog have the bone, took off his glasses and began to polish them with his handkerchief. "Against your will, you were going to say."

"Yes, and against hers." He might as well have the truth first as last. "I told you that she doesn't need me here, Mr. Deverell, she wants nothing around to remind her of her old life."

"I disagree," he said mildly. "Jean has great feeling for you, even if she tried to ignore it for so long. It's better for her, better for her mother and me, for it to be forced out into the open. You spoke of feeling 'scattered.' I think Jean has felt that way, without knowing why. The strong bond between you two for all those years was broken so suddenly that in effect it's never been broken. Do you follow me?"

"Ours is broken," she said bluntly. "At least for her. I think of her as Roz, but she's Jean now, and she'd like to be a stranger to me. She doesn't want to be haunted by her own ghost."

"You're very eloquent," He put his glasses back on. "But there are things Mrs. Deverell and I would like to discuss with you. I wish you'd reconsider. Take it one day at a time. You can be driven all the way back to Limerock whenever you want, but we'd like it very much if you'd give us some time."

"I can't understand why!" she exclaimed, goaded out of her labored calm.

"We were all upset by your fall, whether it was an accident or not. We'd like to try to make it up to you."

"But I wasn't hurt," she argued. "I've had worse bruises. There's nothing to be made up to me."

She made herself walk past him, shoulders stiff and head up. In the doorway she said formally, "But thank you very much."

"Jule, I would like you to have dinner with us tonight."

She wilted then, not that he could see it, but knowing that any more opposition would be the blind, senseless obstinacy of a child who's taken a stand and can't give in.

"All right," she said. "I'll be there."

"Thank you."

When she started up the stairs, leaving the music behind, she knew that he was still sitting on the corner of the desk, one hand cradling his elbow, the other holding his pipe, his leg swinging slightly.

37

EVERYONE SEEMED to think it natural that she wanted to go to bed early after dinner, when she'd had very little to say. She was asleep before Roz came, and dreaming; this time there *was* someone or something on the path, something shifting, coiling, changing shape in the windy shadows. She was trying to see, determined not to call out lest she should arouse it to attack. She awoke with a shock of happiness when the bathroom light snapped on. She blinked in the sudden blinding glare, and cherished it. Roz closed the door but the blessed light shone around the edges. Jule started to fall asleep again, blissful. *Wait till I tell it all to Billy B. . . .*

She awoke to daylight. A draped figure stood over her, she shouted in terror, and Roz hissed, *"Stop that!"* She was trying to put a small tray on the stand, nearly knocking the lamp off. "Go to the bathroom, wash your hands, whatever you have to do," she ordered. "Just get waked up. We have to talk."

"No, we don't," said Jule, "as long as—"

"As long as you get your money. Hurry up. I had to get up early in time to fix this before Martie and Rodina arrived." She held out a robe. "Here. It's chilly."

Jule went obediently to the bathroom. Was Roz going to usher her out of the house at the crack of dawn? The western sky over the woods was pale and clear, and the first sunshine was red on the tips of the tallest spruces over there.

Roz poured coffee into flowered mugs. She'd also brought thick slices of Martie's bread, lavishly buttered. They sat crosslegged on Jule's bed and ate and drank. "Remember eating like this on cold days up at the big house?" Roz asked. "Nothing tasted any better, even if we did have cheap margarine and instant coffee."

"No." Roz must think it was safe to be sentimental now that Jule was leaving. At this moment she was the same Roz Jule had known for eighteen years, as if she had never known herself to be anything else.

"Are you all right this morning?" she said suddenly. "Those bruises are a nasty color."

"I'm in better shape than I look."

"I didn't push you, if that's what you think. I didn't chase you silently out of the house thinking, Here's my chance to get rid of old Jule."

"Never crossed my mind," said Jule.

"Of course, when Mother told me you'd had an accident, I did think, nastily, What's she done *now*?"

"Sure that I'd do anything to get attention," Jule agreed. "Do you think I could ride to Bangor with Nick this morning?"

"Don't go," said Roz. Her eyes were full of tears. "I know I've been horrible, but that doesn't mean I don't love you underneath. I *want* you to go, damn it! But when I think I might never see you again I go all hollow inside."

Instinctively Jule put out a hand, but Roz shook her head blindly at it. "I know, I know! If I feel that way now, what about the past four years? When I came here I thought it was going to be Instant Paradise for our Roz who'd always been so damned sure of herself and what she was going to do. I knew my parents loved me and I should love them, but it didn't happen like turning on a light. And there were the others,

Nick, Fran, Piers, even the servants. I was the foreigner! I didn't know the language, and people could talk secrets in front of me and I could only suspect, I wouldn't *know*."

She wiped her eyes childishly on the sleeve of her robe. "I became some sort of in-between critter, neither Jean Deverell nor old Roz. If I ever paid for running out on you, it was then. Believe it or not there were times when I'd long for you just to rescue me. To make me something real that I could recognize."

"But not a word in those four years, Roz. Why?" She rubbed to ease the ache in her throat. Even when they were children Roz's tears had always affected her. "And why have you been trying so hard to get rid of me now?"

"That's part of the craziness! I know I'm Jean now, and I love my parents, and I know the language or most of it, though I doubt I'll ever *think* in it." She gave Jule a watery grin. "But between you and me there's something else, why I was afraid to get in touch with you. It always intervened, just in time. . . . Listen, Jule, I no longer feel threatened when the other three are around. But *you* threaten me, and you always have. It goes back to the time when Jondy told us the story."

"I can't understand you Deverells," Jule said, trying to be light. "They keep coming out with cryptic statements like that last beaut of yours."

"No, listen." She leaned forward till her face was close to Jule's, her eyes glossed with fresh tears.

"I said right away, '*I'm* the one, I always knew it!' But you looked at me as if to say, 'Why shouldn't it be *me*?' You didn't say it, you just looked it. And I've never forgotten it. Now, with you in the house, and the way they behave toward you, I'm threatened." Her laugh was almost a sob. "Isn't it insane? Just you sitting there while *she* plays the piano, and you driving into town with *him*. Even you helping Fran with the lunch.

And the way Piers and Nick are with you. Even Dave—well, never mind. Anyway, it doesn't take much to set me off. I know it's crazy, but I can't help it."

"Of course it's crazy," said Jule severely. "What's bothering you really is your conscience. The way you ran out on me. If I can face it, why can't you? It's over and done with." She handed Roz another slice of bread and butter. "Eat this, and think of all the breakfasts we've had together in our lives. I can remember almost back to high-chair days, can't you?" She wanted to tremble. "You're who you are, and nobody can change it. They're all being nice to me because they're sorry for this nice unassuming little thing with the embarrassing parents. But I don't want pity any more than you want to be burdened by the past, and that's what I brought with me. It's what I *am*. So when Nick leaves for Bangor I'll be with him."

Roz put down her slice of bread. "Jule, I asked you not to go. You didn't bring the ghosts, you just made them visible. But mixed up with all that is remembering how I missed you. There were nights when I'd go back to the Benedict house with you, or walk along the road to Nowhere. Days, I wouldn't mention you, I didn't want to take any attention off myself. When they'd ask about the other girl, I'd say you wanted to be left alone and have a life where nobody knew about your connection with Mummie and Jondy."

"That still goes, Roz," Jule said. "I'm not hanging around like Lazarus for crumbs from the rich man's table. I may not have much to be proud of in my parents, but I can have all the pride I want in myself."

"You've grown on your own," Roz said. "You're articulate, you can be fiery, you're in charge of yourself. I'm a little in awe of you. But Jule, *please* stay a little longer. I'll be good, I won't throw any fits."

"You mean you'll be good if I stay in my room, and just

be there for you to talk to when you need to knock on wood or something?"

Roz's face flamed, her chin went up. "Don't be so Jule the Mule!"

This insult straight out of their childhood broke the mood. They both began to laugh.

38

ROZ WENT BACK TO BED. Jule dressed in her jeans, sneakers, and sweater; someone had thoughtfully put them through the washer and dryer.

She went down the front stairs and out the front door. The grass was bediamonded, the mild air scented with green things and warm wet earth. There was a great deal of bird activity, and new migrants had come in the storm.

She set off down the driveway, not quite briskly because there was still a painful spot on one knee.

She heard Birnam Water before she reached it. It poured out of the wooded hillside to the west in a fast tea-brown current. When she stood on the bridge, it crashed out from under her feet and cascaded in white rapids around and over the boulders in its path. Some forty feet below the bridge it leveled off in long chains of bubbles and streaks of foam into a pool, which drained into a tranquil flow toward an alder swamp. Old forest loomed beyond the alders, and she imagined the water's silent progress glimmering through the sunspeckled dark, and the birds and animals who drank from it.

She left the bridge reluctantly and stopped at the old orchard turnoff. She was considering following it when Nick's car came down from the house. He stopped and invited her in, and then looked at her in silence long enough to make her nervous, though she wouldn't show it. Then his mouth tilted up at one corner, in duet with his eyebrow.

"I wonder just how long you could hold that poker face. What are you thinking, Jule?"

"Wondering what *you* were thinking."

"This is getting us nowhere. I'm glad you're staying, I hope you're here next weekend, and when you do get ready to go, will you let me drive you back to Limerock?"

Old Nick is more like it, Roz said. As if he guessed her uneasiness he said, "It would be with Fran's blessing, and with her company too, I hope."

"I'd like that, because I like Fran. Thank you."

"Dignity incarnate," he said. He held her chin lightly. " 'And they, that lovely face who view, why should they ask if truth be there?' "

"It's not lovely," she said composedly. "But truth is there. At least I try for truth. Anything else is so hard to live with."

He laughed and let her go, and she got out of the car. "Goodbye Nick."

"But only until next weekend."

At the house, family breakfast was finishing in the dining room. Mr. Deverell and Piers had gone out to build the railing. Roz was on her way to spend a morning with Dave, and had binoculars slung around her neck. "See you later, love," she cried to Jule.

She was gone, out through the kitchen, calling something to Martie and Rodina on the way.

"Was she always like this?" Mrs. Deverell was indulgently amused.

"Whatever Roz does she does with her whole being," Jule said. "She was the one who would always—" She almost said *Fight back.* Nobody urged her to finish the statement. Francesca said, "I'm glad you're staying, Jule. Jean told us she'd persuaded you." She took a fresh cup of coffee with her to the library.

"Will you drive to town with me, Jule?" Mrs. Deverell asked.

"I'd love to," said Jule. She'd probably be struck dumb the whole time. "I should change first."

"You're fine as you are. It's only errands."

They went first to a greenhouse on the other side of Tremaine, and the station wagon was loaded with flats of flower and vegetable seedlings. Then Mrs. Deverell selected a pot of pink tulips.

"That's going to the cemetery," she told Jule, once they were on the road again. "This is the errand Jean always refuses. I can't blame her. But even after I knew the baby was a stranger, I couldn't neglect her."

There was no answer Jule could make and one was not expected.

"In all the years Jean was lost, I had a recurring dream," Mrs. Deverell went on. "I suppose this happens to everyone who has lost a child. In the dream I was always looking and weeping for my baby, and always, after such tearing grief, I would find her again. She grew, this dream child, with the years. At first she was as I last saw her, a little baby, but as she grew older her face was never distinct. But there would always be light behind her, so that she came to me outlined by radiance, and I always knew who it was, and just as the grief in the first part of the dream was always terrible, the intense happiness never grew less."

Jule said huskily, "I know what dreams can do to a life. Some of them make you afraid to go to sleep. And some of them just make the days worse, so you wish you could go on sleeping and dreaming."

The woman nodded. "But I learned to cope with them by

myself; spiritualism was no help. They became a fact of life. Scott had dreams too, but for a long time he kept them secret. Once we could talk about them, it was easier for us both. Then when this beautiful, incandescent girl returned to us my dreams should have ended."

It took Jule an instant to catch this, she'd been so caught up in the other words. "Should have?" she repeated. "Didn't they?"

"No. I don't know why I'm telling you this, Jule." She half laughed. "It must be because you're the perfect listener. I think whatever is said to you drops into a deep well. . . . It would disturb my husband if I told him the dreams still went on."

"Maybe you're addicted," Jule suggested bravely. "The dreams kept you going for a long time, and now you don't need them any more but they're still a part of you."

"I wonder if that could be possible. Anyway, it's very strange. Not upsetting, because when I wake up I know I'm going to see my glorious child. But still they come, the tearing pain and then the rapture, and I don't really think I need the pain, after all those years of it."

"One of these nights maybe you'll think that in the dream and wake yourself up. I remember once being stuck in a real terror, and saying, Well, I can always wake up. So I did."

Now the laughter was free and wholehearted. "Oh, Jule, I did the right thing telling you! You make everything sound so simple!"

Jule was quite overcome by pleasure.

The cemetery behind the white and steepled church was surrounded on three sides by woods and birdsong. A little stone of polished pink granite had been set beside those of Mr. Deverell's parents. It read "Baby Girl" and the date of burial. Crocuses—purple, white and yellow—bloomed densely in the new grass. Jule thought suddenly of the kittens. She turned away, feeling in her jeans for a handkerchief.

"Yes, poor little baby," Mrs. Deverell said.

In the afternoon Roz went with her mother to make a call on the other side of Tremaine. Jule borrowed Fran's bicycle and rode out to the main road and back, bringing the mail with her. Francesca was ready for a break, and they went down to see the new railing.

It was a sturdy, rustic construction that didn't look out of place. The men were widening the path with axes and machete. Coney, the hired man, was introduced; he had a bony pockmarked face, some of his teeth were missing, and his narrow dark eyes, set deep in wrinkles, had a coaly gleam. He shook Jule's hand hard.

"Pleased to meet you," he said. "Only it seems I already know you."

"In your dreams, Coney, in your dreams," Piers said. "The first time I saw her I thought the same thing."

Mr. Deverell, slashing away blackberry canes with a machete, said to Jule, "Piers really uses that ancient line, 'Haven't I seen you somewhere before?' "

"He didn't use it on me that day."

"Because I never gave him the chance," said Francesca. "I think it's time he got a new approach or he'll be over the hill."

They had a family evening, with Piers home for a change, and Dave came up to play chess with Mr. Deverell. Mrs. Deverell played the piano for the others to sing, and Roz, carried on by the music, pulled Jule into the group. They exchanged secret glances, symbols of a lifetime of complicity; Roz's arm around her waist told her that she remembered how they'd put their whole hearts into harmonizing with Jondy down in the fish house.

When the singers' throats were dry, everyone went out to the kitchen. They sat around the table with beer, coffee, tea, or chocolate, and Roz in a state of high euphoria—singing had always done it to her—told them they were having a mug-up, and that when anyone was terribly hungry, they needed soul-and-body lashings. She didn't mention Mummie, but stayed on the ways and hows of their island existence. Occasionally she spoke of Jondy but without self-consciousness. With a reckless eye on her fascinated audience, she dwelt on the technique of stuffing corned herring into baitbags, and gutting fish; recognizing spruce gum and chewing it to the right consistency; the delights of rose hips and hearts of fern; boiling periwinkles or mussels in a can over a fire in the rocks; frying mushrooms in the can's cover.

"I don't know why you've been keeping all this wonderful stuff a secret," Piers said.

"I'll tell you one thing," Roz said proudly. "Jule and I could survive anywhere on an ocean shore."

Her parents said nothing; their faces told it all. They could not take their eyes off her.

39

FOR THE NEXT FEW DAYS Roz was attentive to
Jule by fits and starts, showing off her driving skill by taking
her around the countryside and to lunch in far places. At
home they hiked to parts of the property Jule hadn't yet seen.
Then she would suddenly be missing; usually she'd gone to
the marsh, and Jule on her own never went there at those
times, though the area had a great attraction for her. One day
Roz went to Waterville with her father, who had old associations at the college there.

Jule entertained herself. She read by the fire when it was
raw and damp out, went bird-watching with Francesca, drove
on errands with Piers. She did not consciously seek out Mrs.
Deverell, but was sometimes sought out by her, particularly if
Roz had vanished again, as if she wanted to show her gratitude for Jule's generosity in remaining there. She and her
husband gave Jule full credit for the way Roz had begun to
open up about the past. Jule, aware that she remained not out
of generosity, tried not to bask in a mellow ambience that
would end forever when she went back to Limerock. They'd
think kindly of her, no doubt, but she would never again hear
her name spoken by those voices.

When Roz and her father came back from Waterville in a
rainy afternoon, only Jule and Mrs. Deverell were at home,
having tea by the living room fire, with Joey in anxious at-
tendance. Roz was affectionate and charming. She said "Dad"

and "Mother" often, and called Jule "Love" or "Darling." Jule was wary the rest of the day and went to bed early. She was not surprised, only depressed, when Roz followed her upstairs. She wished that for once Roz wouldn't be so predictable.

Still, her arrival was amicable; perhaps Jule had misjudged her. She brought a tray holding a tall flowered pot and two matching mugs. She was extraordinarily beautiful in the lamp-light; a rich bloom had come upon her, like the dusting of gold spilled from the heart of the rugosa roses on the island.

"Dear Francesca made some hot chocolate. If we're both dead in the morning we'll know why. I think she knows all the ways. She's likely president of the local coven."

"You'll probably succeed her. Let me pour, I don't trust you not to splash."

"Neat as a cat, our Jule." Roz took her mug to the foot of the bed. "Well, here goes. I feel as if I should make a farewell speech. Like Socrates and the hemlock." She tasted, and considered. "Damned clever. I can't taste anything but chocolate."

"It's probably one of those invisible poisons that disappear in the body. The inquest won't show a thing."

Wearing a foamy brown mustache, Roz said abruptly, "Look, Jule, I'm a selfish beast, but you always knew that."

"I never did," said Jule. "You were more aggressive, but it was always share and share alike when we were comrades in adversity. Until you flitted with the funds, so to speak. . . . You'd better wipe that off before it dries on. I think I should tell you that a mustache does nothing for you."

Roz drank more, with an air of gulping down brandy for courage. "Anyway," she said rapidly, "I've come to realize that I've been especially *awful*, and you should have the whole sixteen hundred dollars because I've got plenty now." Another drink. "And I've been so selfish in expecting you to hang around here."

Jule sipped her chocolate and watched Roz over the rim of the mug. Roz was uncomfortable. She got up and walked back and forth, knelt on the window seat and peered down at the marsh, walked again.

"Anyway, I just had to come to this decision, much as I hated to. It's unfair to you to tie you down here, begging you to stay where you can't possibly feel at home. So I'm releasing you from your promise to stay. You can leave tomorrow if you'd like. I know Piers would drive you to Bangor in time to get the early morning bus for Limerock." She talked to the walls as she paced. Even Roz couldn't carry this off with a straight face. "You could leave quietly, with no embarrassing farewells, and write Mother and Dad a nice letter after you get home."

Jule didn't move or change expression. One way to shut Mummie out; one way to throw Roz off balance. A half-minute of silence was intolerable to her. She seemed to go off in all directions at once, whirling toward Jule, hands flying.

"And besides the sixteen hundred, we ought to be able to do something about all that money in the bank. If you just had the right lawyer! Nick's brilliant, and besides, Dad knows a lot of important people. *Judges!*"

"Roz, if I can't prove I'm entitled to it, the Supreme Court can't give me that money."

Roz wasn't to be stopped. "Then I'll ask Dad to give you a good sum outright. How about five thousand dollars?"

Jule stared at her. Roz said frantically, "*Ten* thousand! He can chop it off my inheritance, so it'll be from me. I'll talk to him tonight. Right now!" She started for the door.

"No," said Jule without raising her voice. Roz went motionless, then turned and came back, looking innocently bewildered.

"Why, Jule?"

"The Deverells don't owe me a thing, and you're not buying me off, Roz. You don't want to share with me out of love."

Roz, wordless for once, turned to leave the room. Jule called softly after her, "Roz, nothing can ever take away the good times we had together, and the bad times too, when we were all we had. I'll never forget them."

Roz looked back. Her eyes glittered with tears. She laughed shakily. "Comrades in adversity, right?"

"Right!"

Roz left. Jule lay back, depressed by her small victory, and wished she could go away right now.

40

THE NEXT DAY Roz surprised her mother by offering to drive her to a luncheon meeting for one of her good causes. Mr. Deverell and Fran were busy in the library, Piers went to Bangor to the dentist; he said he saved this for Maine rather than New York, where he lived and worked, because Bangor was more homey. "Maine always meant so much to me when I was a kid that even a dental appointment shares in the overall charm," he said. Jule refused an invitation to drive in with him. It was a fair day after a cold wet one and she wanted to spend it here, where her time was running short.

She took Joey and went down to the marsh. Dave was a tiny figure, far off to the west below the ridge of woods. The tide was up enough to float the boats, and she pulled in the skiff. The instant she was aboard and fitting the oars into the oarlocks, she felt wonderfully alive and wholly natural. Joey, sitting on the stern seat, was a bonus.

The day was open-and-shut, great clouds billowed from south to north, and the wind that carried them was sea-scented but caressingly mild. Between the clouds there were ponds of blue and the creek changed colors as the sky did. She rowed downstream and around the bend until she could no longer see the house, then she rested her oars and sighed with pleasure.

She had to row again or be carried back, but she enjoyed the contest, and the music of the ripples breaking against the bow. Joey watched the banks for anything that moved. When she knew she should start back she hated to, and the tide took her too fast; she needed the oars only to steer.

I'm a fool and a coward for not wanting to go back to the island, she thought. She wondered if Billy B. had collected his mail yet and read her postcard; for a dazzling moment she imagined herself arriving along with it.

Piers had a date that evening and left before dinner. Dave joined them for the meal, but he had night work to do, and told Roz she'd be more a hindrance than a help. She turned her attention to her father and demanded a chess game. Jule wasn't interested in television and couldn't put her mind on reading across the hearth rug from Mrs. Deverell, knowing that Roz would be aware of the most casual remark passed between them.

But she was too restless to go to bed. She went to the library and asked Fran if she could borrow her bicycle for a moonlight ride.

"Of course! Any time!" Francesca was trying to decipher old script through an illuminated magnifying glass.

The moonlight came and went as the sun had done all day, and between the periods of illumination there was no real dark, but transparent dusk as if everything were seen through shaded glass. The orchard road enticed her; deer might be cropping the short grass there or nibbling the tips of branches. But her first destination was Birnam Water. She coasted down to it and halfway across the bridge. Here she dismounted and leaned the bicycle against the railing.

As if she'd come on stage, the clouds suddenly left the moon and the whole scene was flooded with white light. The water surged out from below her, and exploded in diamonds of light; the white birches and pale trunks of poplars formed a ghostly company crowding the banks.

She stood there transfixed for a long time, hearing and

seeing nothing but the water. Then clouds swept over the moon, and below her the froth and foam showed vividly white but now ungemmed on ink-black water. Going back to the house after this would be terrible; she'd suffocate. She decided to go on up to the main road. Riding through the dark avenue of spruces, then under the maples and past the stone walls and pastures, wouldn't be as spectacular as this, but it would be another new experience, and she could stop on the bridge again on the way back.

She began to walk the bicycle across the bridge, intending to mount it by the mailbox. The monster came roaring down from the spruces with no lights, and the noise was masked by the tumult of the water below. She experienced for an instant a ghastly astonishment, then knew that the monster was a car, and she had nowhere to go.

She dodged backward toward the rail, still holding the handlebars as if the bicycle could be a shield between her and the monster. She pressed against the railing, the bike crumpled away from her, she was lifted up and hurled through space, hands futilely grabbing, while in her head there growled and snarled the image of a dragon.

She was crying out, or thinking that she cried out. Then there was water in her nose, throat, and eyes, water dragging at her with a persistent, mindless force. She was deaf and blind and choking, but still grabbing.

OUT.

She woke, making little angry cries as she struggled against the pull of the water and tried to hold on to exposed roots and haul herself toward the steep bank. She was some little distance below the bridge. Her hands were so cold they had no strength, her legs were stone, she couldn't move them. Spray splashed over her and she began coughing and choking again. A new force dragged at her, and she struggled fiercely.

"For God's sake, girl, stop fighting me!" it blasted in her ears. "I'm trying to get you out and up this bank!"

"All right, all right," she tried to answer. She tried to help him, realizing with a faint thrill like a tiny spark of fire that her legs hadn't yet turned completely to stone. She was drawn roughly up the bank among the trees. Another voice was swearing softly and reaching for her legs with hands that gripped like iron.

On the grass of the orchard road she was wrapped in a blanket. The world had stopped whirling and the lopsided moon stood still in the sky. She knew that the man who stood over her, who had been saying *Jesus Christ* over and over, was Coney. Shivering in a blanket, she was held against another man's chest, and she saw the moonlight on his face at the same time he recognized hers.

"*Jule?*"

"Billy B." She thought her brain had been knocked awry. "Am I *dead?*"

He hugged her. "No, you are not. Can you move your legs? Your arms?"

"Let me go and I'll try." He loosened his grip slightly; everything hurt but was movable. She was soaked and cold.

"Jesus, she ought to be dead," said Coney. "That was the goddamnedest thing; I heard it over the racket of the water. He must have hit that bike at a pretty good clip. Thank God you yelled, girl. Brought me up all standing. You don't look big enough to have a yell in you like that."

"But where did you come from, Billy B.?" she asked.

"Where did I come from, baby dear? I met him—*it*—on the way out. No lights, and he nearly took me head on and threw me over a stone wall. Then I drove along thinking these Deverells are mighty impetuous people, and found this bicycle hung from the broken railing out over the water, and there *you* were. Thank God you were draped over a rock with your face out of water."

"I can't believe it," she said faintly. "You saved my life."

"Don't forget, this man heard you scream. He was on his way to you."

"Coney, thank you," she said. "This is Bill Benedict. Coney what?"

"Just Coney'll do." They shook hands over her head. "If he hadn't stopped to bash you I'd have got him when he reached this side."

"I'm sorry," she said between chattering teeth. "Who is it?"

"I dunno, but Nick told me someone's been parking nights lately in the orchard road, prob'ly to keep an eye on the comings and goings. Nick found where the car'd been, and somebody's filtertips where they'd stood around smoking. He cleaned 'em all up but never said anything to the family about it, so as not to get them worried, maybe for nothing. He didn't want Mr. Deverell or Piers coming out here on their own to investigate and maybe getting tunked by some young hellion."

"Well, somebody got tunked all right," said Bill. "Come on, Coney, let's get her up to the house and warmed up."

"I'm plenty warm now," she muttered, in protest at being moved. Once he let go of her she would freeze and never warm up again.

The two men hoisted her to her feet. She was hurt but mobile, if not exactly under her own power.

"This is worse than when I fell off the path," she said between gasps.

"When was that?" Bill was half carrying her.

"Oh, a few days ago. The date's hazy. *I* am."

"You may have a concussion. You were knocked out, and I thought you were drowned."

"Like Ophelia but not so pretty. Is this your blanket?"

"Yes. Would you like it for your hope chest?" He put her into the front seat, and Coney got in behind.

The confusion in the house was brief; Deverells didn't flap. Coney went at once to the kitchen to telephone the police, and give Rodina and Martie the story. Bill gave the family an admirably short description of the event, and Jule was hustled up to bed. "Can you carry her upstairs, Mr. Benedict?" Mrs. Deverell asked.

"I'll do it," her husband said.

"I can walk," Jule protested, wavering. "Oh Fran—your bike—"

Fran put a hand on her shoulder. "Don't worry. You're worth more than all the bikes in the world." Suddenly Jule realized that she might have died when she couldn't hold on any longer. That was why they were all looking at her like that. I could be dead *now*, she thought in horror, and struggled painfully not to break down.

"I'm accident prone, I think," she mumbled, wobbling toward the stairs.

"I'm calling Dr. Matheson," Mr. Deverell said.

Jule made it to her room with Bill giving her a lift at each step. Roz was sent ahead to turn on the electric blanket.

"Don't go away yet," Jule said to Bill. "Away from the house, I mean."

"I have no intention of it. I got your card and I came here to see how you and Roz were making it after all this time."

"Beautifully," said Mrs. Deverell, "and we'd be happy to have you stay as long as you'd like. We can't thank you enough for coming along when you did. Even with Coney there."

Roz, white around the mouth and uncharacteristically silent, steered her into the bathroom and began stripping off her wet clothes. Jule yelped when Roz began to rub her down.

"For heaven's sake, let me dry *naturally*," she gasped. Roz wrapped her wet head in a blue towel turban, and fetched pajamas. It was all done without a word from her until she ordered Jule to get into bed.

Jule obeyed, collapsing with a groan into the warmth. "It's not like you to be so quiet, Roz."

"I was stunned, that's all. You being carried in like Ophelia, and by Billy B.! Of all people! It was like a hallucination. I'd never thought he could be so *macho*. The way he's matured! He's better than handsome. He could be a secret agent, or a soldier of fortune—do they still have them?" Her color was coming back with her natural bossiness. "Now you lie there and keep absolutely still."

"I don't want to keep absolutely still. If I'd died, I'd be absolutely still right now and forever. I have to keep convincing myself I didn't die. Where are you going?"

"For my hair dryer. Unless you want to sit there with your head done up like a maharaja."

"Remember how we went around being Kim, and whoever thought of it first in the morning got the part for the day? It was queer your saying Ophelia just now, because that's what I said when Billy B. said he thought I was drowned. Roz, wherever I go, however we're separated for the rest of our lives—"

Roz was looking strangely at her, and she thought, Is this how you feel when you're drunk? "There'll still be Us," she went on. "Each of us will be a new person, but nothing can destroy the *Us*."

"I hope this isn't your new person, because nobody's ever going to be able to shut you up."

"No, but listen, isn't it strange? If I should ever go back to the island even as a very old lady—though if this last week's a sample of my adult life I'll never make old bones—I'll still be able to see the Us. 'We were as twinn'd lambs that did frisk i' the sun.' And we'll still be there, for always."

"Stop that!" Roz exclaimed. She almost ran out of the room. Mrs. Deverell brought in the doctor. He assured Jule that she had no broken ribs, and no sign of a concussion. He gave her something for pain and to settle her down.

While Roz dried her hair, Mrs. Deverell left to make a hot milk drink for them, and Mr. Deverell brought up a state trooper to hear whatever details Jule could give. There were none, except that the car had no lights.

After the trooper left, Francesca brought Bill up. "Nick called a few minutes ago," she said, "and I told him the news. He sends you his love. And Piers is home. He was scared out of his wits by finding police cars at the bridge and my bicycle hanging on the broken railing. He's really shaken up by what happened to you, and now the police have impounded his car for close examination in case he was the person who hit you."

"That's ridiculous!" said Jule indignantly.

"They're simply doing a thorough job," Bill told her. "They want to look at mine too."

She wanted to beam drunkenly at him, between uncontrollable yawns, but Mrs. Deverell arose and sent everyone out. She kissed Roz, who murmured in a subdued voice, "Good night, Mother." Then she kissed Jule's cheek, and Jule lay down with the memory of that touch upon her, and turned her face away from the lamp.

41

THE PAINKILLER couldn't prevent her dreams.
They were tortuously involved, and not always frightening,
except that she thought she would never get out of this surreal
world. She awoke with a jolt when the first morning light
slapped her face like a cold wet towel; Roz had forgotten to
draw the curtains. She gazed at the sky with unbelievable
pleasure. It was too early to tell what sort of day it would be,
but she was awake in it, and safe.

I could be dead, she kept thinking. I'm alive but I could be
dead. Gallows humor struggled through; this was hardly positive thinking, was it? How about *I'm alive!* And Billy B. is in
this *house!*

She needed to go to the bathroom, and braced herself for
the effort of getting out of bed, but by the time she was on
her feet she knew she could make it. Her head was light, but
that would be from the sedative. The mirror showed her a
meager face with a black and blue lump almost filling the
forehead; she was lucky that she didn't have two black eyes
as well. Her hair was feathery and flyaway from the dryer.
She was glad to get back into bed.

She went to sleep again, this time with no dreams. When
she woke up the day was well advanced, cool and sunny with
a dry, brilliant, northwest aspect. She knew exactly how it
would look on the island on such a day; Billy B. had brought
the island to her. She was watching the crows rising and fall-

ing against the clouds when Roz came in. She was dressed for out-of-doors, and her heavy sweater gave off a cold breath.

"I've been giving Billy B. the grand tour. The parents think he's super, you can tell. Even Fran and Piers are impressed." She started to bounce onto the bed, but restrained herself in time. "Oh, and Nick called bright and early. I got to the phone before dear Francesca, and we had a nice long conversation while Fran tried to pretend she didn't care. First he asked about you," she added hastily, "and he said he'd be out with flowers for you today, except that he can't leave Bangor."

"Do you suppose you could get me some breakfast?" Jule asked. "Some oatmeal, or something?"

"I forgot!" said Roz merrily. "I was supposed to ask you what you wanted." She left, whistling. She had become eighteen again overnight. Because of Billy B.?

Visitors came and went all morning, everyone but Bill, and she supposed jealously that Roz was keeping him occupied. She told Francesca that she was going to pay for the bicycle. Fran didn't argue the point.

"I hope you're not humoring me," said Jule.

"I wouldn't insult you that way. But when the police find out who did it, he'll have to pay."

Mr. Deverell came in, and stood for a time without speaking by the windows toward the marsh. His ruggedly handsome head was like a piece of sculpture against the light. She thought he had come in out of duty and couldn't think of much to say, so she tried to make a joke.

"I'd better get out of here before the third time, because that never fails."

"You aren't going anywhere today, Jule, or for quite a few days," he said abruptly, and left the room. A few minutes later Mrs. Deverell let Joey in.

"He's been dying of curiosity about you," she said. "All this steady traffic in and out of your room." Joey settled on the foot of the bed. Bill arrived next and Joey arose bristling, then gave doggy grins through his whiskers.

"Well, Jule, how are you? Apart from the aches and pains, I mean." Bill pulled up a chair and tried to accommodate his length to it. His gray eyes were familiar and yet strange; it was as if years had intervened since she'd last seen him.

"I'm fine," she said banally. She saw things about him she'd never noticed before, or couldn't remember. An old scar in one eyebrow, for instance.

"Did you get what you came for?" he asked.

"I'll have a check to take back, if you mean money. Otherwise—well, you know Roz. She loves me one minute, and I'm a nuisance the next. I guess I'm the same way about her," she said honestly. "The sooner we go our separate ways, the better. Anyway, I've got to leave before this place does me in. It's rejecting me," she said with a grin. "It knows I'm not the True Princess."

"Mmm," he said, then added with some amusement, "The police asked me how I happened to arrive at just that moment. I couldn't tell them we have mysterious but unbreakable psychic ties." He stood up. "You look beat, so I'm going to leave you now." Joey arose too. Jule pushed up from her pillows.

"Where are you going?" she asked anxiously. "You're not leaving me here yet, are you? You won't go without telling me?"

"I won't go without *taking* you. I'm waiting till you're on your feet, and then I'm driving you back to Limerock."

"Oh, Billy B.!" she said joyously, and he looked pained.

"I thought we'd abolished that."

She chuckled, and he tipped down his glasses and gave her a long severe stare. "Behave yourself," he said solemnly. Joey left with him, and Jule fell back in a light-headed haze of happiness. She could stand it now if Roz appropriated him for the rest of the day. To drive away from here with him was all she asked. For *now*, she added, being a realist.

Roz brought a lunch tray for them both. Jule wondered who had suggested it, but Roz seemed happy enough to be alone with her. She'd been with Dave, who sent Jule his good wishes. Then she said, "Billy B. says he's taking you home when you're ready."

"It's Bill now," said Jule. "Billy B. makes him feel like a chum of Christopher Robin."

Roz smiled and said wistfully, "I've seen the time when I'd have done anything to go somewhere alone with him. I used to say he wasn't romantic, but I really thought he had banked fires." She burlesqued a sigh. "And now you're going to drive away with him."

"All the way back to Limerock," said Jule, "and look what *you've* got. Piers, Nick, Dave, and a pair of loving parents."

"I'm glad you left out Cousin Francesca. She's probably taking Lucretia Borgia lessons so she can get me one of these days."

"Francesca was very nice to me about her bike," Jule said, "but I'm still going to pay for it."

"Why bother? What's a bike to her when she and Piers could inherit a fortune?"

"Roz, are you serious?" Jule asked sternly.

"Nope! She's never liked me, but who could blame her? And she'd like me even less if she—well I think she's resigned to my existence. . . . I'll try not to eat my heart out about Billy B. I mean Bill. How did he know you were here?"

"I sent him a postcard," said Jule. It seemed a year ago.

42

JULE GOT UP Thursday afternoon and had dinner with the family that night. They welcomed her, and Piers made a joke about her ability to bounce, but there was an undercurrent of strain. By now the police knew about the burgled cars and stolen tools, and Coney's reason for being in the orchard road that night.

A stranger at the table would never have suspected the tension. Martie Foster had made an elaborate chocolate mousse in Jule's honor. For Jule the fact that Bill was at the table was celebration enough.

Roz took him over as soon as Dave left; she had regressed five years in twenty-four hours. She gave no one else a chance at him, but Jule didn't mind. They were leaving together, weren't they? Bidding the True Princess adieu, the Happy Commoners go out into the Great World.

She went early to bed and slept well. The vision of the lightless car didn't return that night.

Nick arrived late on Friday. It was a windy, showery afternoon, and everyone had gathered for tea in the living room. He had brought Jule flowers, as he had promised: a spring arrangement, moistly fragrant and utterly luxurious. A simple "Thank you" was inadequate, Jule thought, but she could manage nothing more. It had been easier thanking Martie for the mousse.

Roz was charming about it. "Nick's never sent *me* flowers." The look she gave him should have glimmered amorously over a fan. Jule took her flowers upstairs with her that night.

Saturday was brilliant, with warm winds full of more returning birds. Jule wished she and Bill were leaving right now, but she had set Sunday as the day for telling the Deverells, and Monday morning was the time of departure. Besides, she still had some lame muscles that began to suffer if she didn't rest at regular intervals. Two days should make quite a difference.

Roz was up early and singing, off to spend the morning tramping devotedly and volubly in Dave's footsteps. He was going home later to see his parents for over Sunday, and until he left he wouldn't have a moment to himself, except for the necessary private purposes, if Roz could manage it.

At lunch there was the usual discussion of afternoon plans. Roz and Piers were going to play tennis, Francesca and Nick were going to drive somewhere to look at an old diary whose owner wouldn't let it out of the house. Mr. Deverell was taking Bill on a long hike around the borders of the property. Jule expected to spend the afternoon on her own until teatime, and she didn't mind. But as they were all leaving the table, Mrs. Deverell touched Jule's arm.

"Jule, would you like to see some photographs of your parents?" she asked.

Torn between manners and the truth, Jule couldn't compromise. "I don't think so. If you don't mind."

"I don't mind. It's just that they were kept along with other pictures because for so long we had no reason to want to destroy them. Now I'm going to burn them, but I thought—" Color flared in harsh blotches on her high cheekbones. "Oh, I don't know what I'm trying to do! You have to admit it's not an ordinary situation. You should have the chance if you want it."

"I don't want." She tried to soften it with a nervous little grin.

"Would you come up to my room for a talk just the same?"

In half an hour the house was cleared, and Jule knocked on the door of the master bedroom.

Though it faced east and north, it seemed sunny because of the pale yellow walls and honey-colored woodwork and floors. By the windows looking over the front lawns, there was a grouping of comfortable chairs around a low table. Feeling apprehensive now, and appallingly shy, Jule sat on the edge of a turquoise blue cushion wondering what to do with her chilly hands. She folded them and immediately squeezed till the knuckles whitened. The books on the table were leather-bound photograph albums. She turned her head sharply away, and didn't know where to look.

"I mounted all these pictures when I was in bed," said Mrs. Deverell. "Waiting for Jean to be born, and afterward when I was waiting to be strong enough to take care of her myself. But we needn't be concerned with them. Let's put them out of sight, shall we?"

Jule helped her carry them to the chest under one of the northern windows.

"There," Mrs. Deverell said. "Forget them. Now make yourself comfortable. I'm sure you still have many lame places. Put your feet up on that hassock." She took up her work, a crib afghan she was making for a private child-welfare organization. "For years I've been knitting for unknown babies," she said, "because I couldn't knit for my own. I can't count how many sweaters and vests I've knit for Jean in the last four years, trying to make up for lost time."

She had to be the one who made the yellow sweater and bonnet for the baby. What had she thought, seeing them again? Down on the tennis court Roz was racing after a ball, brandishing her racket like a fly swatter, and Piers was laughing at her.

"I thought you should have some knowledge of your mother as she was before it struck her, the aberration, the madness, whatever you want to call it," Mrs. Deverell's quiet voice went on. "You should know something about your background. Since you are the girl you are, I can speak to you—I think—of her. It will be as good for me as for you. Are you willing?"

How could she not be? She would do anything for this woman. If Mrs. Deverell could make herself speak of Beatrice, Jule could make herself listen.

"The names Rosalind and Juliet," Mrs. Deverell said, "are because she loved Shakespeare, and she wanted to be an actress. She wouldn't have been good as either of those girls, but as Lady Macbeth and some of the other wicked or tragic women.... Yes... well, Jule, this is what she told me about herself, and it was the truth, because after we thought she was dead, her sister came to see us, and she corroborated the story. She was a nice woman, the sister."

"I've met her children," Jule said flatly. "My cousins, I suppose, but their lawyer says no. If I can't prove I'm Beatrice's child, he may be right. I won't mind."

"*I* believe she was your mother, Jule," Mrs. Deverell said. She sounded admirably dispassionate. "She was born in a small town in western Massachusetts, in a family in which many of the children died young or at birth, so that only she and her sister grew up. They were *good* people, Jule. Nothing to be ashamed of. The wealthy family of the town, the mill owners, saw to it that the most deserving young people were educated or taught a trade. The sister married young. Beatrice went through the local academy and seems to have been talked into becoming a baby nurse." Now that she was well into her story, Mrs. Deverell had the objective clarity of a skilled raconteur. "I thought myself, when I heard about those stagestruck dreams of hers, and heard her read, that she'd seen the nanny idea as a chance to get to Boston and theatres. She had the sense to take advantage of the training; she graduated with a top ranking, and was placed in a good situation. But in her time off she haunted the theatres, and was finally taken on by a struggling repertory company. You look incredulous. You can't imagine her as a slim, fiery young woman."

"I know she was slim once. There was one old picture. . . . But fiery?" Jule mused on that. "Maybe." We were scorched and seared often enough, she thought.

"She left her good position at once, without notice. When the company folded up there she was, high and dry. She knew the school wouldn't help her, she'd tarnished its reputation. She was too proud to work as a waitress or a salesgirl, and she wouldn't go home, where her benefactors would be making their royal disapproval known to one and all. Through an employment agency she got work as a nanny again, but there was always something wrong—there was never anything as good as that first place, where she'd gone with the blessings and approval of the school."

Mrs. Deverell seemed to be talking about someone else. Never Mummie, solid lard-white flesh in a rocking chair. *Loving Shakespeare?*

"We lived just outside Boston in the winters then, and came to Maine in April. I'd had Jean late—I was thirty-six—and there'd been severe complications before and after the birth. We had a nurse, but she'd made it clear that she wouldn't leave her young man to go to what she considered absolute wilderness. A friend of mine undertook to find someone, and happened to arrive at this particular employment agency the day that Beatrice came in from a position. Her references were good, the family just didn't need her any more. The agency played her up as a graduate of a highly regarded school, and Beatrice was candid to my friend about the reason the school itself wouldn't recommend her. This was impressive, and besides, she was eager to get out of the state." She held up the afghan and murmured, "It's almost done. I made a yellow one for Jean before she was born."

"Was Mum—was Beatrice as good a nurse as you hoped?"

"We thought she was a prize, a gem beyond price. She was not only willing to come here, but she wasn't one of those iron-willed 'my baby, my nursery' nannies. All I had to do was to get my strength back, and cuddle and play with my baby when she was brought to me. Beatrice did the physical part and left the rest to me. I didn't know what she did with her time off except that she always went to Bangor, either by bus or driven by John."

She fell silent, watching the rosy wool slipping along the needles. It had been some time since Jule had felt the punch in her stomach, but Jondy's name did it. She tried not to double over with it.

"Scott and I used to joke about them," Mrs. Deverell said. "She was quite magnificent, really, in her carriage and manner, and he was such a slim-jim, and so boyish. Peter Pan, we called him. He seemed to get older all at once after Beatrice and the baby vanished. In the winter, when the other baby—" She frowned at her work and Jule wondered if she had trouble seeing it through tears. "He wept at the funeral—great choking, tearing sobs."

"I think that was for you," Jule volunteered. "When he told us about it, how you suffered for so long, we could tell it was still on his conscience. But not enough, and not soon enough."

"Perhaps you're right. You know him better than we did."

The long face was austerely calm. "It seems that we never knew him at all." She got up and walked about the room, straight and thin, her hands in her skirt pockets. Can't she face me any more? Jule wondered. Does she wish I'd leave her now? She put her hands on either side of the chair, ready to stand up, but Mrs. Deverell returned, saying, "When John first came to us, even though he'd been in the army so he was really not a youngster, I used to worry about him not having enough fun, and smoking too much, and not drinking enough milk."

"Jondy always looked like a boy," Jule said, subsiding into her chair as Mrs. Deverell sat down again and picked up her work. The tennis players were having a conference across the net. Suddenly Roz threw up her head in a familiar gesture and strode away from the net, and poised herself for action. Piers served, Roz leaped for the ball, and made Piers scramble for it.

"There was a Shakespeare club in Tremaine in those days. It no longer exists, and it was feeble then. The few younger members had been hauled into it, as I had, by some elderly relative. I loved seeing Shakespeare done even by a high school cast, but I didn't love sitting around with a group of women reading all the parts and skipping the earthier bits." She smiled. "You have no idea—! However, Scott's great-aunt, who was one of Tremaine's grand old ladies, got me into it. I had a good excuse for several months after Jean was born, but finally I felt I was up to having them here and getting it over with, and I asked Beatrice if she'd like to sit in on it. They were reading *Macbeth* that night, and some of us were having a hard time keeping our faces straight. Boys might have done the female parts in Will's day, but women were certainly never intended to play those bloody warriors. . . . The woman who was to read Lady Macbeth was overcome with hay fever, and just to liven things up I suggested that Beatrice do it."

She put down her knitting and folded her strong hands on the work. "I don't suppose that she was great, but she was good. She was too big for the room, too full-blooded for the rest of the cast, who must have heard and seen for themselves their own silliness. *Indecent!* one of them called it in a fierce whisper. She was applauded by the rebels, including myself, and from that moment on the club was on its way to dusty death."

The tennis session was over; Roz was quitting while she was ahead. The players left the court arm in arm, swinging their rackets.

"Can you believe all this, Jule?" Mrs. Deverell asked.

"Yes, I can," she said honestly. Beatrice had become real to her at last. Beatrice inside Mummie. Beatrice despising them all and managing to look contemptuous on her deathbed.

"A month later she was gone," said Mrs. Deverell without emotion. "Murdered, we believed. I grieved for her, you know. I was fond of her. I sympathized with her ambition and her frustrations. So much for my talents as a judge of character."

43

THERE WAS A SUBDUED RAP at the door, and she called, "Come in, Scott." Joey ran in ahead of him, his coat giving off the fresh scent and coolness of late afternoon in the woods. He went to Mrs. Deverell and then to Jule who, to cover her shakiness, picked him up and hugged him.

"Have you two had a good talk?" Mr. Deverell asked.

The question seemed to call for more than Jule could answer. She put her face down to Joey's rough head and left the issue to Mrs. Deverell, who said, "I've talked. Jule's been a patient listener."

"Jule and I will have a talk soon," he said, and she felt him watching her. "But not now."

Not ever, if I can manage it, she thought. How could there be anything more except the horrible part? Her stomach reacted in warning of danger. Why did they want to tell her about it? To punish her, perhaps, for being who she was. The facade was just too impeccable to be true.

She put the dog down. "Thank you," she said to Mrs. Deverell, and went out. The hall was full of afternoon light from the landing window, and Roz and Nick were just coming up over the top step; she heard the murmur of their voices before they saw her. Nick caught sight of her first. "Hello, Jule, my jewel," he called to her.

"And what have *you* been doing?" Roz asked. It was meant to sound light, but Roz's eyes gave the lie to that.

"Talking about my mother and father," said Jule bluntly. "Mrs. Deverell thought I should know something about my background."

"Thieves and murderers, were they?"

Jule walked past her into her own room. She was shaking so hard she was frightened. Bill had to be downstairs somewhere, but she didn't think she had the strength to go to him. If she met someone else on the way she wouldn't be able for once to hide behind her face, and she couldn't tolerate the exposure. She sat tightly on the window seat, knees hugged to her breast and chin digging hard into them, blind to the glories of the sunlit marsh below, while she waited for Roz to finish showering and changing. She wished there were a way to lock her door into the bathroom. If Roz should come in, she didn't know what she would do, and again her own reactions badly frightened her.

She heard Roz out in the hall, blithely calling, "Hello, Dad and Mother!" For my benefit, Jule thought. She uncurled her aching body. If she couldn't reach Bill right now, she could do *something*; not be ever again in the same room with Roz, for instance. She washed her hot face in cold water and brushed her hair. She still had many sore spots, but that pain was a relief, something one could live with because it would go away. *It would go away.* What was that? Some phrase had hit her and made an indelible mark.

Touch it; the marble eyelids are not wet: if it could weep, it could arise and go.

Then the first line. *I tell you, hopeless grief is passionless.* And it would not go.

Someone tapped on the door, and sensation returned, like agony into a finger she'd thought frozen to death. *"Bill?"*

"Sorry." It was Nick. "Come on down, Juliet."

"I have a bad headache."

"A cup of tea will do wonders. I heard what she said.

ELISABETH OGILVIE

She's got a wicked tongue, but she's probably sorry already."

What do you bet? Jule silently asked the door. I spent the afternoon with her mother, and she can't forgive that in a hurry. But why should she think she's banished me, damn it?

When she came into the hall he pulled her arm through his and took her hand, palm to palm and fingers laced. "Isn't this cozy?"

She smiled; she had to get her face right, and she might as well start now. The only person she saw or wanted to see when she first entered the living room, was Bill, a very tall and angular silhouette against the sun-filled window over the marsh. She would have gone directly to him without looking at anyone else, but Roz was holding onto his arm and talking, half laughing. To Jule it was alarmingly unintelligible, as if she'd gone deaf or had lost the faculty of comprehension, yet she could hear Francesca telling Mrs. Deverell about the priceless diary. Piers was inspecting the teacakes.

"Do you suppose Martie can make *madeleines?*" he asked.

"I think Martie can do anything," his aunt said. "Why don't you ask her?" She looked past him at Nick and Jule. "What a handsome couple!"

"Aren't we though?" Nick said. "We're thinking of becoming a dance team and going on the road. We go for the flamenco stuff, all the stamping and castanets, and so forth. You might not believe it, but my partner's a dynamo."

Nonsense helped, and so did the cup of tea. Let Roz monopolize Bill now, it was her last chance. She excused herself in a little while, saying she wanted to rest before dinner. Then she was afraid Mr. Deverell might follow her out to the hall and ask about their talk, but he didn't.

Over and over she examined the new facets of Mummie, this voraciously ambitious young woman who had become a mass of flesh in a rocking chair. The manner in which she had been able to attain such power over them all was a riddle which could take all of Jule's life to solve. If she didn't put it behind her now she would be as mad as her mother was.

For dinner she put on the dress she'd bought for herself, not the one Roz had given her. She felt feverish but calm. No one could make her do anything, those days were behind her along with the riddle of Mummie. She did not have to talk to anyone, and she would say so. There'd be no mighty back-hander to punish her, no Jondy with puckered face and swimming eyes.

When they were taking their seats Bill said to her in a low voice, "I've missed you today."

"I've missed *you*. Do they have any plans for you tomorrow?"

"Nothing hard and fast. Piers mentioned going down the creek."

"Could we leave?"

"Of course." He didn't ask her what was wrong.

"But let's not tell anyone tonight," she said. "Let me tell them in the morning."

"No private conversations at the dinner table," Roz called. "Unless you're willing to tell everybody what they're about. It's a new house rule."

"We can't tell," said Bill. "We just swore a vow to the death."

"Of whom?" asked Piers. "Anyone we know? Should we drink a farewell toast?"

"Piers is a late bloomer," said his sister. "We hope that someday his humor will get above prep-school level."

In the evening Bill asked Mrs. Deverell to play, but trying to listen to music in a room where other people talked, even in low voices, was not the way Jule wanted to hear it on her last night in this house. She moved out of the room by de-grees, unnoticed, and sat on the stairs, where she could listen without distractions, ready to escape to her room if Mr. Deverell should approach her. He'd been setting up a chess game with Nick, so he shouldn't come soon. She shut her eyes and leaned her head against the bannister and let the music flow around her.

She was disturbed by a movement close by, and resentfully opened blurred eyes: Dave was just coming from the dining room; he always entered the house by the back door. "Sorry," he whispered. "Beautiful, isn't it?"

He dropped onto the step below her, put his head in his hands, and instantly gave himself over to the music. He was so absorbed that she wasn't self-conscious about her own response, so she tried to let herself go with it again. She had almost succeeded when she knew that Roz was there, she could smell her cologne, but she tried to keep her out.

"Hello, you two." Roz's voice was as brittle as windowpane ice on a puddle when you shattered it with your boot. Dave gave her a blank look and she said with forced laughter, "Darling, I *adore* that beard! Don't ever shave it off, please!"

Jule arose and went upstairs. She got into her pajamas and packed the rest of her clothes, except the blazer and tartan skirt and a fresh blouse to wear tomorrow. When she got into bed even the electric blanket didn't warm her up. She'd been trying to get away from Mummie ever since she'd left the Deverells' room, but now she'd been cornered. Not by Mummie, but by a tall black-haired young woman who had never heard of Jule, who had demanded so much of life that when she met someone who understood that hunger she would have killed to grab what she could, and she'd done so, as far as she knew, when she stole the child.

Two babies given into the hands of a woman obsessed with envy and rage: the fact made a mystery of Jondy. Was he actually stupid? A simpleton? She shuddered at her own parentage. She wanted none of the money in the bank, it was as repulsive to her as if it had been scraped up out of a pool of blood and filth.

She had some of the sedative tablets left, but if she took one she might dream and not be able to wake herself up. She knew exactly what Hamlet meant.

She hadn't heard Roz in the hall or in her room, but all at once she came through the bathroom, lights flaring on around her. Jule slid deep under her covers, squeezing her eyes shut.

"I know you're not asleep," said Roz, "but if you are you can just wake up and listen to me." She gave Jule's shoulder a rough shake. "It'll be the last time as far as I'm concerned."

Jule bounced over in bed and sat up. *"Good!* Just keep your voice down, or I'll open the door into the hall so your parents can hear their glorious child in action."

"You little *bitch,"* Roz whispered venomously. "You can't stand it, can you? You're so jealous that it's eating you like maggots. You'd do anything to undermine me. Oh, I know you, *I know you!"* Her breath shook in her throat. "Trying to take over my parents because yours are so disgusting. Trying to take over Dave, the two of you so damn soulful out there on the stairs. Trying to take over Nick, while you're swearing you *like* dear Francesca."

She loomed over Jule as if to do murder. "You have these accidents. God knows how you manage them, but then everyone fusses over you and you sit there looking up at them with those big eyes, poor little lost bird, they all want to comfort you, and all the time you're scheming away in that hard head of yours—" She almost choked on her own fury.

Jule said softly, "You sound just like Mummie, except that she didn't *ever* run out of breath."

Roz slapped her. Her head sang with shock, her eyes felt knocked out of focus for an instant, but she repeated, "Just like Mummie." Roz's hand flashed up again, then she thought better of it. She had her checkbook in the other hand and she ripped out a check and thrust it at Jule.

"There's the damn money, every cent of it. It ought to go far, especially if you can get your poison pussycat claws into poor old Billy B. He's always had a weakness for you, and now he thinks he's your knight on a white horse. Better make the most of it while you're young. You'll turn out to be one of those ghastly little old women everybody runs away from. Right now you're so damn smug, but you just wait!"

Jule hadn't moved while the tirade washed over her as Birnam Water had done, except that this tirade was pure acid, hissing and fizzing, and she'd be surprised to find she had any flesh on her bones afterward. She can't always have hated me, she thought in astonishment, she *can't* have!

She hadn't touched the check, and Roz dropped it on the bed. "Good night and good riddance. I want to see you out of here tomorrow or I'll make you so miserable you'll wish that woman had aborted you."

Jule couldn't speak. She pointed to the open dressing case and the boxes from the dress shop beside it. Roz whipped her head around and stared as if at an apparition.

"You'll never be bothered with me again, Roz," Jule said to her back. "But I want to tell you something. I envied you once because I didn't want to be the one who belonged to Mummie and Jondy. But I don't envy you now. You're the one who has to live with your rotten, suspicious nature, not me, thank God." She licked her dry lips. It was terrible to be saying these things to Roz, in spite of everything Roz had said to her. "You turn my stomach, Roz. You really do. You'd better start trying to deserve someone like the Deverells."

She picked up the check and put it on her stand, under her book, while Roz, unmoving, watched with eyes strained wide. "Thank you for the check. It'll be a help to me. Good night." She lay down and turned her face to the wall.

There was no sound or movement from Roz, and she could feel her heartbeat throbbing through her head and echoing back from the pillow. She wanted Roz to be gone before she fell apart completely in some spectacular way, with noises she'd have to suffocate in the blankets.

"Don't turn your back on me!" Roz snapped.

With her ignominious collapse about to begin, Jule rolled helplessly over, and in the instant before she broke she saw Roz's red and crumpling face. She knelt on the bed and tried to embrace Jule, who met her halfway. They cried a long time in each other's arms.

44

IT CAME TO AN END, with Roz alternately sobbing and laughing while she blundered around looking for tissues. "What a pair of messes," she muttered.

"Speak for yourself." Thoroughly winded, they lay side by side in an exhausted peace.

"I was abominable," Roz said to the ceiling.

"I suppose I do seem smug sometimes," Jule said, "but I'm not, really. I'm just frozen with not knowing what to do or say next."

"You could have fooled me. That last speech of yours—"

"My *only* speech. When you'd run out of invective."

"Ah, one of those fancy Osprey Island words. Jule, are you really going tomorrow?"

"Yes, and don't ask me to stay, or you'll hate yourself in the morning."

Roz prodded her in the ribs, and Jule recoiled. "*Ouch!* You know you will. You don't want bits and pieces of Osprey Island cluttering up your life."

"But I want to know everything you do and where you go," Roz said jealously. "I'll always want to know, Jule, and I've got a right. You can't say I haven't." They could have been in their room on the island, or up at the Benedict house. Roz doubled up a pillow behind her head, and ran her hands lazily through her thick hair like a gesture of love; it was something she had done since she was six or so.

"What are going to do, Jule? You aren't going to be a glorified house cleaner forever, I know that. You can do anything you set out to do. You've got the brains and the will. I'll be bragging about you one day, Jule. While I—" she stretched and pointed a toe elegantly at the ceiling.

"If you can ever bring yourself to leave the nest, you'll probably go into modeling. Then you'll be on the covers of all the shiny magazines. The respectable ones, that is."

"I suppose it's possible," said Roz complacently. "I photograph well. I love wearing clothes and showing off."

"Now who's smug? Well, it's your right."

Roz said absently, "Dave would never make it in a cigarette ad, would he?" She got up from the bed, turned off lights, and went to the windows overlooking the marsh. "I like him but I don't think I'm in love. I just feel awfully good when I'm with him. *Safe.* Look at it out there," she went on in a hushed voice. "Come here, Jule. Look at the creek. It's a ribbon of silver. Remember all the nights we looked out but we couldn't go? Well, we can go now, so let's! We don't have to stand here remembering poetry, we can *be* poetry. Get dressed, Jule. Let's go rowing right now, and nobody'll know but us."

She was Our Roz again, elated and irresistible. "Dave?" Jule questioned.

"He went off on his motorbike after the music. He'll be gone until tomorrow night, and everybody else was thinking about bed when I came up—it's after midnight." She was shedding her dress and it floated out behind her like ectoplasm as she ran to her room to change into jeans.

Out in the hall she went ahead of Jule as if she couldn't have held back to a decorous tiptoe, but she made no sound, she went like a spirit past closed doors that gleamed blindly in the moonlight from the landing window. Jule stopped to struggle with a zipper, and when she looked up Roz had disappeared, and she heard the patter and tap of Joey's nails in the sitting room.

"Oh, *damn* the zipper," she whispered, and hurried on past. As she reached the sitting room she thought she heard a door click open behind her, but she didn't look back. Remember what happened to Lot's wife, she thought, wanting to erupt in a geyser of giggles.

"Stay , stay," she whispered to Joey, who went dejectedly to his basket. Roz was already down the stairs, and when Jule reached the foot and shut the door behind her it almost blew out of her hand and slammed in the draft from the open outer door across the kitchen. She ran toward the rectangle of porch-shadowed moonlight, and heard Roz singing to herself around the corner. Jule came upon her dancing across the lawn to her own music. She looked back to see where Jule was, gestured *Come on, hurry!* and slipped into the woods. Her light jacket glimmered for an instant among dark shapes, and then vanished.

Illogically panicked, Jule sprinted to catch up, and found Roz waiting to pounce. They rocked in each other's arms, hugging hard, trying to stifle their laughter.

"Come on, let's go," Roz gasped. "I feel so wonderful, I could get up and walk along the new railing and never lose my balance. I couldn't *possibly* fall, I'd float like a gull feather."

"Don't try it!" said Jule, grabbing at the back of Roz's jacket.

"Don't worry!" the exuberant voice came back to her. "Oh, Jule, it's really happened, we're free! I think it just hit me, the way we talked tonight. Nobody can take it away from us, we can believe in it at last!"

She was right, Jule thought. This was what they were celebrating, and alone, which was the way it should be.

Down on the marsh the tough grass was crisping with frost. The creek looked like the finest, clearest, mirror glass, and the white skiff and dory seemed powdered with diamond dust above their flawless reflections.

The girls whispered so as not to break the spell of their own immortality. "It's colder than I thought," Roz said. "I'm going over to Dave's tent and snatch a sweater. You want something more?"

"No, I'm fine. I'll haul in the skiff, or do you want the dory?"

"Let's take the dory, in memory of ours. Listen, I'll have to probably dig a bit around in Dave's stuff, and it's hard enough to get into that tent when it's zipped up tighter than a drum. But we've got all night." She ran off toward the knoll where the tent was camouflaged by black streaks and splotches of shadow from the surrounding trees.

Jule knelt and untied the half-hitches around the stake, and saw jewels falling from the ropes as she lifted them clear of the water. The dory moved with obedient grace toward the bank, and the perfect glass shivered without breaking. "You darling," she whispered to the dory as she untied the painter from the loop.

She heard steps on the frosty turf behind her, and she turned her head to look at Roz and speak, but she never made it. She was seized by the throat and shaken back and forth like Joey's rag rabbit in Joey's mouth. She pinched and dug at hands that offered no surface to be pinched and dug, she tried to kick behind her, to reach behind her to pull and twist, but her hands were losing strength as her brain lost blood; her head was filled with roaring, her lungs were going to explode, colors burst behind her eyes, and then blackness began to move in.

"*No, no, no, I won't!*" she screamed inside her head. She

went heavily limp, so abruptly that she slithered out of the killing grip and pitched forward; a cold wet scent came up to her, her head was hanging over the edge of the bank, almost touching the water. She didn't see, but she knew. Then she felt the hands reaching for her, and she knew enough to hang like a wet rag or Joey's rabbit as one arm went around her shoulders and the other under her knees. She was lifted; she held her breath and let her head loll as if from a broken neck. Next would be the icy plunge to finish what had been begun, if by chance she wasn't already dead.

But I won't die! she screamed at Mummie's huge white face. Outside her head there was another scream. Roz's voice echoed up to the sky and back again. "You bastard, you killed my sister!"

A violent jolt hurled Jule out of the encircling arms. She went overboard and under, her mouth, nose, and ears were flooded with salt water, and the cold struck like death through her clothes, but it was not death; she had never been more alive. Instinctively refusing to breath water, she reached out blindly and felt the dory move lightly away from her. One of her frantic toes touched bottom, so it wasn't over her head here. She had to have air; she could only hope she'd come up behind the dory.

But the freed dory was not there. Shaking her head, spitting, trying to clear her nose and ears, she came up against the taut lines of the skiff. She held onto them while the water tried to lift and carry her away like the dory. She saw in the moonlight a monstrous scene, not to be believed by her blurred and smarting eyes.

An octopus writhed there on the bank, like a scene from some underwater delirium. Blinking madly, she saw the shapes begin to change as sounds began to penetrate her hearing. She saw Roz fall free of the tentacles, onto her hands and knees, and then start to stand up, turning toward the attacker as she rose. He was as distinct in the moonlight as if it had been high noon.

Roz said clearly, "Nick, why Jule?"

He struck her and she grunted and fell back in silence. He knelt on one knee beside her. There was an interval in which Jule thought he could look out and see her dark head against the luminous water, but he was concentrating horribly on Roz. Holding to the ropes, Jule worked cautiously toward the shore against the water's weight and opposition. She saw Roz's face as blank and peaceful as a statue's as her head rested on his thigh. There was a pause, then a narrow flash of reflected light in the shadow of his body, and then he dropped Roz, stood up, and ran away from the creek back toward the woods and the path. He hadn't looked toward the skiff.

Jule pulled herself up by the haul-off stake and over the bank. "He's gone, Roz," she whispered, but Roz didn't move. The blood was spurting out from her throat, just under the left side of her jaw. The moonlight was so bright that the blood showed red, not black.

Jule had never seen so much blood in her life. She could not take her eyes off the small scarlet fountain, and she did not know where to press, where to squeeze, to stop it. Nothing worked. Her hands were covered with blood, slippery with it. Finally she sat cross-legged with Roz in her arms, staring without belief into the calm marble face while Roz's blood pumped away in a warm stream over Jule's arms and into the sponge of the marsh.

45

THEY WERE LIKE THAT when the people from the house found them. In her waking dream she saw the figures coming onto the marsh; she recognized Piers's hair, white with moonlight, and Bill's lanky height. Nick, nimble and eager, was running ahead of the others. Then all at once he stopped, and Jule knew what had stopped him. He hadn't expected to see *her*. Sitting there holding Roz, she must have appeared to him like a figure risen up from the grave.

He bolted in the direction of Dave's camp, and a voice came up out of her throat, terrible in its strength which she hadn't expected; she thought it had all gone out of her with Roz's blood.

"Nick killed her!"

Piers veered sharply after Nick. Bill ran for the first time in Jule's experience, straight to her. He took Roz gently from her arms and laid her down. The unreality of the scene was a sort of insulation for Jule, but when he lifted her to her feet and tried to embrace her, all in silence, she backed off in protest. "I'm covered with blood. I'm *standing* in it! I have to wash it off right now, in the creek. I *have* to!"

"All right," he agreed reasonably. "Into the creek with you."

She slid off the bank, shutting her eyes so she wouldn't see the water stain. Her teeth chattered and she set her jaw against that, welcoming the pain.

"It will all go out to sea with the tide," Bill said above her. He helped her out, and put Dave's heavy cardigan around her.

"The dory's going," Jule said. "I was supposed to go too, I think." She went to kneel by Roz. The face was ageless, dignified, remote. *Touch it; the marble eyelids are not wet.*

"Don't, Jule," he said urgently, trying to take her away.

"She saved me. He never had a chance to see me come up. And I saw him kill her. I couldn't get to them in time." She squirmed around to look up into his face. "Can't we go away now? Just drive off?"

"You know we can't, Jule," he said sorrowfully. His eyes were glistening. "They have to know."

"I wish they didn't. I wish they never had to wake up and know she's gone again." She leaned against his chest, not weeping. *If it could weep, it could arise and go.*

Piers had run Nick down and knocked him out, and lashed the limp body to a tree by the tent. He came to the creek bank and looked down at Roz, then went away and threw up. When he returned to them, wiping his mouth with a handkerchief, Bill said, "Piers, your sister is going to have a rough time of it."

"I know," he said thickly, "I'll be there for her. But oh God, what about *them*? Jule, are you all right? That's a stupid question . . . *Jean*," he whispered. "I can't believe it."

"You'd better get a blanket from the tent," Bill suggested, and Piers went off at an eager, stumbling run. When he came back he was crying. "I'm sorry," he kept apologizing as he laid the blanket over Roz and tucked it carefully around her as if to keep her warm. "But who's going to tell them? Oh, Christ, it's so damned unfair!"

Bill went to collect Nick from the tree. He seemed dazed, and the bruise of Piers's blow was darkening along his jaw. He didn't look at the blanket on the ground, but stared off across the marsh toward the distant trees. This rumpled, silent man driven along with his hands tied behind him was hardly anyone she knew. She wanted to cry to him, as Roz had, *Why, Nick?* But she couldn't look at him long enough to make him recognizable.

"Come on, Jule," Bill said to her. "We'll go to the house."

"I can't leave her alone here," she protested.

"We should leave this one with her," said Piers harshly. "Tie him down beside her and cover them both with the same blanket. He wanted her once, let him have her now."

"Never mind now, Piers." Bill's manner gentled him. "You help Jule and I'll see to him."

"It's you she wants," said Piers. "You can trust me not to break his neck, though it would spare the rest of us a lot of grief." Nick stood mute, his hair mussed for once. "Get going," said Piers.

Jule still held back, but Bill's arm propelled her forward. "Nothing can hurt her now. Nothing will disturb her."

Once on the way up to the house Nick stumbled, and Piers caught and steadied him, roughly. When they passed the ravine Piers said, "I ought to toss you down there and then come after you and bash your head in with a rock."

It occurred to Jule, whose brain seemed to be operating in a special sphere of preternatural lucidity, that such an ending might have been planned for her, but the unexpected presence of Joey and Dave so close by had spoiled it. Those stealthy stirrings above her that night—animal or Nick? She'd probably never know.

The accident on the bridge—no, an intentional assault, proved by the missing lights. But Nick had called from Bangor right afterwards, so it couldn't have been his car. But what if he'd called from somewhere else, much closer to Tremaine?

"Why, Nick?" she shouted suddenly, startling them all.

Nick, driven ahead, didn't answer. Bill tightened his hand on hers. "Sh . . . sh . . ."

"Don't shush me," she said in a bright clear voice. "I know why he killed Roz. She saw him try to kill *me*. That has to be it, don't you see? But why *me*?"

There was no answer.

At the house Joey scratched and whined at the foot of the back stairs until someone opened the door to quiet him. He was prepared to be convivial, but found strange scents that raised his hackles and sent him under the big coal range, to look out with brilliant suspicious eyes. Piers pushed Nick into a chair and refastened his wrists behind it.

"You'll stop the circulation, Piers," Bill said mildly.

Piers spoke from colorless lips. "Maybe he'll get gangrene and both arms will drop off at the shoulders."

"Now, Jule, listen to me." Bill put his arm around her. "You've got to help out here. Go upstairs and strip off those wet clothes, take a hot shower, dress again. Then Francesca and the Deverells have to be waked up. I'm going to call the police now."

She looked tearlessly into his face. "I'm always being dragged in wet, like Ophelia. I would have been Ophelia tonight, if Roz hadn't stopped him. He couldn't have known she was there too, he must have heard something and when he opened his door he saw just me crossing the hall. I *heard* the door click open. That's the way I've figured it, Bill, and I want to tell the police about it while my mind's this clear. Because later—"

"I know, honeybunch." He kissed the top of her head. "Go get dry and warm now."

"You idiotic girl." Nick's voice issued incongruously from the bruised and white-faced man tied to the chair. "You didn't see who attacked you. It was some drug peddler who was expecting a shipment up the creek. We all know someone's been around the place, but you two fools had to go out wandering on your own, and you—"

Keeping her eyes fixed on Bill's face, she said, "Roz called him by name, then he knocked her down and cut her throat. I saw him do it."

"He came and roused us up, saying he'd found Roz dead," Bill said. "He didn't expect to find a live witness."

Nick didn't speak. Piers, leaning against the sink, stared at him without moving. Bill gave Jule a little shove toward the back stairs, and took the telephone from the wall.

On the stairs Jule met Francesca. She was in a warm blue dressing gown, and her fair hair was soft and loose around her face. "Good heavens, what's going on?" she said in good-humored surprise. "You're wet again, Jule! What *have* you been doing?"

Jule's crystalline thought processes stopped. In the silence they heard Bill's voice in the kitchen. "I'm calling to report a death."

The resemblance between Piers and Francesca became very strong. Her face went waxy and gaunt. "Piers?" she whispered. "Nick?" Jule shook her head to both.

"Not Jean? Oh, dear God. How will they—how *can* they—?"

She looked back as if through the walls she could see Scott and Caroline Deverell sleeping while this waited for them. Then she ran down the rest of the way, and Jule ran up, not wanting to be listening when Francesca went into the kitchen and saw what awaited her.

She concentrated on obeying Bill's orders. Hot shower, and don't look at Roz's toothbrush or her scattered clothes where she'd changed to go rowing in the moonlight, her hairbrush, her cologne. Jule dressed in the clothes she'd left out for traveling. Ten days ago she'd arrived in that outfit. She sat on the edge of her bed for a little while, hands folded in her tartan lap. She wished she had someone to pray to besides Bill, someone who could wipe out ten days and leave her back in Limerock, writing appointments in the Clean Sweep date book.

When she came out of her room, Francesca was knocking on her uncle's door.

46

THEY MOVED THROUGH THE DAYS in painstaking balance like high-wire walkers, watching each other for signs of a fatal wobble that could topple them all. Jule was moved into Piers's room so she would be close to someone if she had bad dreams in the night; Francesca said with a wraith of her usual smile, "It works both ways, Jule. If you hear anything from me, come in and wake me up."

Piers took the other twin bed in the guest room with Bill. In the county jail Nick had regained his poise, at least a mad version of it. He was very chipper, admitting to nothing but a shameful panic when he led the others back to where he had found Roz's body, and had discovered this ghostly figure sitting there. He swore that he hadn't known Jule had also been attacked and left for dead.

He still admitted nothing when they found his bloody gloves and clothes stuffed in a trash bag in the trunk of his car. He'd changed them before going up to rouse Piers and Bill. The clasp knife was with the clothes, and there were the tools from the workshop, and the missing articles from his and Piers's glove compartments. He must have enjoyed balancing on the fine-honed edge of peril as he drove back and forth with this earlier evidence in his car. Someone less in love with his own intelligence and nerve would have gotten rid of these items in the first quarry he passed on his way out of Tremaine.

The man who'd repaired the dents and scratches on one fender of Nick's car the day after the bridge incident came forward with the information. The police were advertising for anyone who might have seen this car parked by a public telephone, or outside a store where there was one, anywhere between Tremaine and Bangor; possibly off the main route. But with everything else they had, the telephone evidence wasn't essential.

When the compulsory autopsy was done, the public learned that Jean Deverell had bled to death after the left carotid artery was slashed.

The Deverells were inhumanly self-controlled. When he first found out about Nick, Scott Deverell said simply, "I'm glad his parents aren't living." He said nothing more, at least in Jule's hearing.

She herself had not cried yet, and the funeral seemed to have nothing to do with Roz. She was afraid of this quiet in herself; she was afraid that when it broke she would disintegrate into tiny, unrecoverable fragments, and she wanted to get away before that happened, and stay away until the trial.

But they had asked her not to go yet. Mr. Deverell's brother and his wife had come, and Jule thought that should be enough, but Mrs. Deverell, her eyes set in dark hollows, repeated the request, and Jule could refuse her nothing, even to save herself.

Rodina, weeping, had cleaned Roz's room and put away her clothes. Martie Foster cooked like a mad genius, trying to tempt people to eat. Dave, who had nearly broken down at the funeral, stayed on the marsh. Jule wanted to see him but couldn't make herself go down there, and he wouldn't come to the house. Piers also stayed away a good deal after his parents came, though she suspected he was driving alone most of the time. Francesca puzzled her.

She mentioned it when she and Bill took Joey for a walk out to the old orchard the day after the funeral. "If I loved a man as much as Fran seemed to love Nick," she said, "I'd be out of my head by now. But she keeps at her work."

"It's her salvation. Besides, sometimes you know something about a person without admitting it to yourself until the time comes when you can't escape facing it." He shrugged. "Of course, intuition's no help when the thing finally comes true. It doesn't make the shock any less. She may never speak of it to anyone. They're all very private people, to use a cliché I'm tired of. You're a private person, too, Jule. You could be throwing yourself around in screaming hysteria."

"It would be a relief to scream, but I can't here. It's their tragedy, and I'm the catalyst."

"My God, Jule, if *that's* what you're carrying around with you," he said heatedly, "you need to hear something I wasn't going to tell you. Things can't get much worse, can they? So just listen." He pulled her down beside him on a fallen tree and held her there with his arms around her. "Piers told me this. It was on his mind, and I wasn't one of the family, so I was a safe listener. A few years ago he found out by accident that Roz and Nick were having an affair. He just walked into the facts by a fluke and backed out before they ever knew. Roz was innocent and vulnerable, and swept off her feet by all that attention. Apparently now that Fran wasn't one of the chief heirs Nick made a play for the principal one. Piers was furious for both Roz and his sister. But he thinks it didn't last long, and that Roz broke it off. Nick went through a gloomy irascible period, but Roz was very light-hearted at the same time."

"She kept telling me she didn't want to be possessed," Jule said. She was surprised not to be surprised, until she remembered Roz's hints and threats about "Old Nick." She must have resented Fran because she felt guilty. "If he assumed too much, she'd be frightened off."

"Anyway, he must have given Fran some satisfactory excuse for his rotten mood. Piers didn't know if Fran had sensed that something was going on, but he was glad he'd never told her. She was happy, and it certainly didn't seem to have hurt Roz any, while Nick seemed to be more in love with Fran than ever. They began talking marriage, as soon as Fran got her doctorate. She'd like to teach at Orono, did you know that?"

"No, I didn't," she said numbly.

"But lately Roz had been needling Nick. She thought she was safe enough—that nobody else but Nick knew what she was talking about. She didn't realize how sensitive Piers was, any more than she realized that kind of needling could be lethal. Piers didn't know either, he was just afraid that Fran would pick up signals as Roz got more reckless. So he tried to get her to cool it, but she flew off the handle, wanted to know what he was accusing her of and so forth. So he gave up, and hoped for the best. Who'd expect murder? Another man in Nick's position might have called her bluff and made her feel like a fool for running to Fran."

"I wonder why he didn't," Jule said. "He could be very convincing. He convinced me that he thought the world of me."

"Maybe he wasn't sure enough of Fran," Bill said thoughtfully. "He might have doubted his ability to make her believe that Roz was lying to cause trouble. Even if she didn't give him up, he might lose some of her esteem. Nick *had* to be well thought of, Piers said. He could never be indifferent to the opinions of others."

"But to kill!" she protested. "Just to keep a good opinion intact—"

"*And* a chance at the money! He wasn't getting Roz, and

he might lose Fran as well, if she chose to believe Roz."

"Why did he try three times to kill *me*?"

"Maybe as camouflage for the real target. Two girls are wiped out when they surprise a drug-crazed intruder." Abruptly he stood her up. "Come on, let's walk." He whistled to Joey.

"But I want to talk about it some more," she protested.

"There's no more."

"I think there's something that you don't want to say. You stopped too fast."

"What could there be?" he asked blandly.

"Everything's hanging over me like an avalanche about to happen," she said. "I'll be buried under it, but I can't run even when I still have the chance."

"You won't be buried, Jule." He took her in his arms again. "You'll dig yourself out, and I'll help."

"Oh, Bill, I owe you so much," she said. "I can't expect you to hang around rescuing me all the time."

"Thank you again for promoting me from Billy B. You sounded like a woman just then." He was trying to make her smile, so she did, a little.

Tea was still served every afternoon, but Mrs. and Mr. Deverell stayed in their room or walked outside, and Francesca or her mother poured. Mr. Deverell's brother resembled him in the blue eyes and the shape of his head, but he was overweight, and florid. He was kind to Jule, in a gentle, embarrassed way, and obviously relieved by Bill's objective presence. His wife ignored Jule, who didn't resent it. She knew the woman wanted to spend more time with Francesca than her daughter would grant, and was made irritable by her anxiety.

Two days after the funeral the Stuart Deverells left, and the next afternoon Roz's parents were in the living room at four o'clock. Piers was back too; it was a roomful of Deverells, the same open, kindly people whom Jule had first met, but life seemed to have flowed out of them as Roz's life had flowed into the marsh grass beside the creek. Roz had filled this place. Without her, the silence had frightful echoes; even the terrier heard them and was subdued.

Jule was so grateful for Bill that she wished she could have held his hand openly, as Roz dared to do. Roz dared anything. She had been daring to the death.

"Well, Jule," Mr. Deverell said all at once, "you and I have not yet had our talk."

"I thought—" She broke off.

"That it was cancelled? No, only postponed. Shall we go into the library?"

She looked around at the others. Francesca was unsurprised, but why should anything now touch her with wonder, after what she'd been through? Piers was lighting a cigarette. Bill's lean face was as noncommittal as ever; too much so, she thought vaguely. She looked last at Mrs. Deverell, who nodded encouragingly.

"Take your cup with you, dear. Let me put more hot tea in it."

She went, concentrating on keeping the rose-sprigged cup steady in its saucer. Mr. Deverell awaited her in the library doorway and stood aside to let her pass, as courtly as he had been on the first day. She was glad to set her cup down on the desk, her wrists had gone so weak. He shut the door into the hall.

She couldn't bear this any longer. "I shouldn't have come to this place!" she cried out. "I'm to blame for what happened, I *have* to be! It was me he was trying to kill all the time, and I don't know why, but it's the truth. Is he *insane*? Is he so loyal to you that he hates me because of them?"

He was shaking his head slowly all the time. When she finished on that anguished question, he said, "Sit down, Jule, please, and drink some that of hot tea."

She obeyed, holding the cup in both hands. He sat down across the desk from her and took up a silver-framed photograph. He waited until she had put down her cup, and then he handed it across the desk to her.

It showed a young girl with thick dark hair done up on her head. Her white dress was in a style of the early 1900s. She held a small bouquet and was posed against a background of distant groves and dim columns. She looked out of the past with solemn eyes, the full young mouth tucked firmly secretive, and she had Jule's face.

"It's my mother," he said, "when she graduated from Milton Academy. She was eighteen. Jule, there's no way to be subtle about this. When I saw you on the stairs that day, I saw my mother as a young girl. Do you realize what I am saying?"

The picture was too heavy to hold, it had the weight of the world. She put it down, carefully.

"You are my child, Jule. For all the years that my child Jean was gone, dead to us, I thought another child of mine had been murdered too, still in its mother's body. Then when Jean came, and mentioned the other girl, I still believed that my child had been miscarried or died young, or had not even existed. It could have been a lie in the first place, considering what the woman was capable of. But she existed and she didn't die. And she's here now."

"Does Mrs. Deverell know?" She was more deeply ashamed now than she had ever been of Jondy and Mummie; more a part of their evil.

"She's known about Beatrice for a long time, but we've been through too much hell together for recriminations. Losing Jean blotted out everything else for her. By the time she was able to come to terms with that, after a long and dangerous road, my crime was unimportant to her. I was the one who had the dreams about my other lost child, and she pitied me for that. She has never reproached me for setting the whole obscene mess in motion."

Jule sank back in her chair wishing it were a shell into which she might curl like a periwinkle.

"This confession is almost as hard as the first one," he said, "especially when you look at me with my mother's eyes." He picked up a pipe, fingered it, then put it down again. "Years ago I was very much like Piers, but by the time Piers is thirty-five he'll be quite a man. I wasn't. This is in danger of sounding like the memoirs of a Victorian rake, so I'll shorten it by saying my wife had a good deal to put up with, which made her childbearing difficulties all the worse. But I did *not* know your mother before she took the position here. All that took place afterward, and I have no apologies or excuses, because it's too late for that."

She started to speak, but he said sternly, "Don't interrupt. When your mother told me she was pregnant, I wanted to be sure. I insisted on seeing a doctor's report for myself. She talked marriage, but I didn't; I wasn't in love, and I don't think she was. I promised that she and the child would be well provided for, the child's future would be assured. If there *was* a child. She told me she'd made an appointment with a good man in Bangor, but before she could keep it she and my six-month-old daughter were supposedly abducted when John had them out for a drive. He'd left them in a side road we'd all driven over many times, and walked up a short lane to a farmhouse to get some vegetables my wife had ordered. When he came back, with the farmer wheeling a load of produce, Beatrice and the baby were gone and the note left."

He put his fingers inside his shirt collar as if it were choking him. "Evidently he'd left her and the baby in a safe hiding place before he ever went to the farm. But he appeared so shocked he fooled us completely. He was as much of an actor as she was, or else he was genuinely shaken up by the enormity of his act."

"I think he was," she stammered. "But he thought it was *his* baby they were getting the money for, he always thought it." This baby seemed not to have been herself, any more than this man could be her father.

He went on as if he didn't hear. "Francesca, Piers, and Nick all know that photograph. Jean too. It's been on my desk until recently. But Francesca was the only one who really looked at it. She'd find herself gazing into the girl's eyes when she'd stop to think what to write next. So the first sight of you was a shock. She didn't know anything about my past, of course, but the resemblance hit her between the eyes; you had the exact expression." He smiled faintly. "You have it now, you know. . . . She prepared me by saying the girl at the motel looked a good deal like my mother. Believe me, Jule," he appealed to her, "we wanted to meet you anyway for the reasons Francesca gave you. And then I saw both my daughters coming down the stairs to me that day."

Her voice rasped in her dry throat, out past dry lips. "Did Piers and Nick—"

"Not at first, and they weren't told. Piers said you looked familiar, you reminded him of some girl he'd known. Then all at once it hit Nick, after he left here that day. He came out from Bangor the next day to see Francesca about it, meeting her at the public library."

I saw them, she thought. I believed they were having a lovers' talk. It was beginning then.

"Francesca was satisfied that you didn't know anything about it. I put the photograph out of sight to keep anyone else, mainly you and Jean, from making a connection before I had a chance to collect myself. My wife and I decided you must be told."

She started to stand, but he waved her back. "After Francesca told me that Nick had put two and two together, I told him I would be changing my will and providing for you as my other child. He was very warm and sympathetic. But if he had his own plans, they were now seriously threatened." He stood up and faced her across the desk. "I am proud to claim you as my daughter, but you have a right to say whether or not you want to be named as such in my will. You'll be in it, regardless."

She felt powerless to move or speak; the avalanche had fallen.

"It's too soon for you make decisions, Jule. You take all the time you need. Shall we go back?"

"Could I stay here for a while?"

"Certainly. I think I'll take Joey for a run." He left quickly, and she heard him whistle to the dog, then the front door softly closing. She wished Bill would come to her, but she knew he wouldn't. This was a worse solitude than when she'd waited alone with Mummie. *No worst, there is none.* She knew the poem. Did poets exist to give you words like daggers when you needed them least?

So they were really sisters. She wondered if Jondy had known and blotted it out of his mind, or if he really believed she was his. It didn't do to wonder what Mummie had thought of her, or what Mummie had thought of *anything*.

The specific knowledge of sisterhood could not make any difference in all those hours, days, years, with Roz. How could she go on and make a life, knowing that Roz was not alive *somewhere*, even if they never met? They'd been so innocently happy that night, running out in the moonlight. It had been a reprise of their whole life together, their schemes and conspiracies, their aid and comfort to each other in time of war.

If you bleed to death, how can you tell anybody anything?

ELISABETH OGILVIE

Roz, at fourteen, trying to sit up with a bloody nose; and now she *had* bled to death.

A cry broke from Jule, and she crammed it back with both hands, she huddled herself together and wept until she felt as if there were nothing left of her, and still she couldn't stop.

It began to wear down, finally, and she realized that someone was in the room with her. But she was beyond shame, she hoped that if she kept her head down and shut them out they would go away again. But she could hardly breathe, and finally had to lift her swollen, smeared, red face, and gulp air. A lavender-scented handkerchief was put into her hand.

"She called me her sister," she said, working for the breath to say it. "She didn't know, she *couldn't* know, but she said, 'You bastard, you killed my sister.' It was because in spite of everything she still thought of me as her sister."

"Yes," said Mrs. Deverell. She brought a chair up close to Jule's. She had aged, but her voice was still strong and vital. "It's too soon to ask you to consider this your home, dear. But it would give us—"

She couldn't bring herself to say the word *pleasure*, after the second and final loss of her child. "You belong here, Jule, if you choose, and we hope you do. When this is all over, even if you go away you'll need a home base, and this could be it, unless you absolutely cannot stand the sight of us."

"It should be the other way around. How can you be so *good*?"

She smiled sadly. "Oh, Jule, you make me sound impossible. I'm not good. I'm very human."

"I have a cat, Hodge. He selected me," Jule said, without expecting to. "That sounds ridiculous."

"No, it doesn't. You could bring him, you know. Joey likes cats better than he likes dogs. He adored Rodina's cat, who died of old age in the winter. . . . Just don't forget us."

"I couldn't ever do that, and that's a promise."

Mrs. Deverell arose. She lightly touched Jule's head. "I'll try to find your father now, but I'll send Bill to you, shall I?"

"Oh, please." Jule thought she was going to overflow again, but pride pulled her up before Bill came. She refused to be a sodden sponge which anyone would want to deposit somewhere to drip rather than clasp it to his breast. She was standing up when Bill came in. She knew her eyes were still red, and probably her nose too, but she couldn't help that.

She held the picture out to him. "That's my grandmother."

He took it, studied it, and nodded, omniscient as always.

"All that surprises me is the strength of the resemblance. I suspected something. Nick had to have a very good reason for wanting to get rid of you. What are you going to do about it?"

"I don't know yet." She set her mouth to keep it from trembling. She didn't really want to cry any more, but she felt all broken apart. "Remember what I told you about the avalanche?"

"Yes, and I remember what I told *you*." He folded her comfortably into his arms. "Does this help any? . . . Look, when Piers and Francesca have to go, this house will be horribly empty in a way it never was except just after the baby went. I don't think they're the kind who'd smother you. But it would be someone young, someone of their own."

"Someone of *his* own."

"For her, that's better than nothing, after all she's been through. You could help her, Jule."

"Oh, I want to!" she cried passionately. "Believe me, I want to! But how can I even *think* yet? If you only knew what my head feels like!"

"We'll go away," he said. "Back to the island, because the sooner you do that, the better." He nodded assurance at her. "And then you'll decide."

"Bill," she said on a long sigh and let her head fall tiredly against his chest for a moment before she braced back. "I haven't any right to hang onto you like a leech. How am I ever going to thank you for all you've done and been for us?" Her voice cracked on the last word. *Nothing can destroy the Us.*

"I'll let you know," said Bill, "all in good time. I'll be giving it a lot of thought while I'm waiting."

"For what?"

"You'll see."